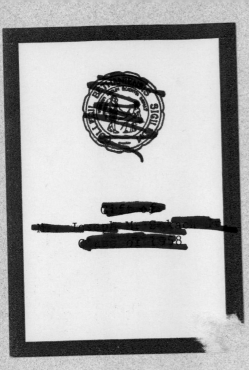

Leopards and Lilies

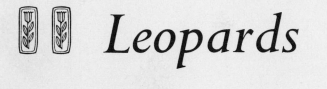

Leopards
and Lilies

BY ALFRED DUGGAN

Weybright and Talley

NEW YORK

Published in the United States by
WEYBRIGHT AND TALLEY, INC.
3 East 54th Street,
New York, New York 10022

Library of Congress Catalog Card No. 68–12874

PRINTED IN THE UNITED STATES OF AMERICA

Contents

1: Stogursey 1

2: Plympton 21

3: Farewell to Plympton 48

4: The King's Court 58

5: The Coronation 82

6: A Case of Conscience 111

7: The Tournament at Lincoln 139

8: Christmas at Northampton 170

9: Law and Order 181

10: Public Opinion 198

11: Choosing Sides 216

12: The Toils of the Law 232

13: Downfall 249

14: Desertion 262

Epilogue 279

Leopards and Lilies

1: *Stogursey*

FOR MORE than ten years, ever since the King returned in defeat from Normandy, England had
been restless; order never quite broke down, but
in castles and walled towns there had been gatherings of
armed men, blustering and exaggerating their strength to
overawe their opponents, then dispersing to meet again at
some other stronghold of faction. Now at last the crisis had
come and passed; in May the Exchequer closed and the
judges ceased to sit, an official acknowledgment that the
country was at war; then in June the King met his enemies
in a meadow between Windsor and London, granted all
their demands, and to everyone's surprise appeared to be
keeping the engagements he had sealed. Knights might ride
home to see their harvests reaped.

Even the King's Chamberlain, the lord Warin fitz-
Gerold, could spare a few days for family affairs; on the

29th of June 1215 he rode up to his principal manor, at Stogursey in Somerset, in time for dinner. He brought only a small escort to guard his clerks, servants, and baggage; for all the land westward from Windsor to Land's End adhered to the King, and an eminent courtier might ride through it in peace.

The lord Warin was about fifty years old; he was tall and dark, with the hooked nose and firm chin of a Norman warrior. But it was twelve years since he had ridden to battle, in the foredoomed retreat through Normandy, and he was growing fat. His hackney was a weightcarrier, slow and comfortable; last night he had lain at Taunton, less than twenty miles away, and he had taken four hours for the journey. He had sent a sergeant in advance to give warning of his arrival, and the household should be ready for him, with a good dinner roasting in the kitchen.

Stogursey was not a castle; all the buildings were of wood, or wattle-and-daub, and only the hall contained an upper story. But even an open manor needs a boundary of some kind, to keep out unauthorized cadgers; the buildings were grouped around three courts and the whole enclosed by a tall palisade. As the horses clattered to a halt in the dusty street both leaves of the gate were dragged back, and the four sergeants who preserved order on the manor flourished their spears in quite a creditable salute. Within the first courtyard stood a little knot of well-dressed men and women, the administrators of the fief waiting to welcome their lord; while in the background servants, male and female, cheered as they were bid. It was very well done, as though they were under good control and yet pleased to see him; the lord Warin, as a Chamberlain, had a high standard in these things, yet he was satisfied.

As he dismounted grooms ran to his horse, and he had

hardly touched the ground before a girl was kneeling at his feet to unbuckle his spurs. With a vague gesture of benevolence he patted her supple back, because it is always pleasant to be waited on by pretty girls; then he remembered that this was home, where he ought to set a good example; and that this was the principal business that had brought him.

"Let me see your face, my dear," he mumbled. "Yes, in two years you have grown up, but surely you are little Margaret, my daughter."

"Welcome to your manor of Stogursey, my lord," Margaret answered formally. "Dinner awaits you, and your chamber is prepared." Then in a more confidential tone she went on with a rush: "I wanted to stand in the gateway and hand you the key on a silver tray, as ladies welcome their lords in the poems. But Father Laurence wouldn't let me. He says the palisade has no key, and anyway it is absurd to pretend Stogursey is a castle. But I ought to practice these things, for one day I shall be a real chatelaine. At least I am the first to greet you, as is proper; for in your absence I rule here."

"If this were a castle you would rule it, child. Let me see, you must be all of thirteen, quite old enough to defend your home against enemies. But since Stogursey is an open manor I hope you take the advice of your elders about the sowing and harvesting of the demesne. In fact, I have come here chiefly to see if Father Laurence has gathered any silver, and now I must talk to him about all sorts of dull money matters. But you shall sit beside me at dinner, and then we shall discuss your future. I have important news for you."

Margaret threw to a nearby groom the long ornamental spurs, the insignia of knighthood, which were too precious

[3]

to be worn among the soiled rushes of the hall. Father Laurence, the steward who was also rector of the parish and of several other parishes on the Lincolnshire and Kentish fiefs of fitzGerold, came forward with his arms full of parchments and tallies. No one moved to go into the hall, for the sun was shining. Everyone above the class that must strip for manual labor habitually wore a great many layers of clothing; on a fine day it was more pleasant to do business in the open.

After a few moments Margaret realized that there was no part for her in the discussion. It was unlikely that she would be dismissed while most of the household were hanging about, for the lord Warin was too sensible to think he could hide his financial affairs from his servants. But it might happen, and if it did her pride would be injured. She strode purposefully away to the mews, as though she had urgent business with her hawks. She had long ago discovered that a girl who did not eavesdrop learned more of what was going on than one who had to be told to run away and play.

The lord Warin looked with pride and affection after that erect and slender back. He was proud of her, though of course she should have been a boy; it was most unfair that his wife should have died giving birth to another daughter, leaving him with two girls and no son to succeed him; the House of fitzGerold had been noble for two hundred years (well, for three generations anyway); it would cease when he died. On the other hand a magnate whose daughters would inherit as co-heiresses was very much courted by other magnates with unmarried sons. Because he had no son he was father-in-law to a Nevill, and would shortly, when Margaret had carried out the plan he had devised for her, be father-in-law to his most important

[4]

neighbor in the west; that was only because the girl would bring Stogursey to her husband. He put the matter aside while he turned to discuss finance with his steward; but he looked forward to telling little Margaret the good news at dinner.

When the horn blew for handwashing he was in a very good temper. During the last two years, when there had been no entertaining at the manor, Father Laurence had saved a chestful of silver pennies; by his own reckoning there was more than £60, though it was prudent to leave a large margin for error when counting nearly 15,000 little coins. Say he took £30 with him when he rejoined the King; that was a month's pay for 20 knights or 30 crossbowmen or 50 mounted sergeants. The King would not really accept his defeat by the Archbishop and the northern rebels, for all that he was quiet at the moment. In a few weeks serious fighting would start, probably as soon as the Pope annulled that ridiculous Charter, as of course he must. The lord Warin was unswervingly loyal, partly because his father had been Chamberlain to old King Henry and he had been brought up in loyalty, partly because he was pretty certain that the other side had already divided his lands among themselves and would not accept him if he tried to join them; but if he had money he could bargain for a considerable reward in escheated rebel land before he hired his mercenaries. And in the meantime, until the war began, he had some very pleasant news to discuss with his unmarried daughter.

When he entered the hall Margaret sat alone on the dais. It would have been more respectful if she had waited to be told where to sit, but of course she was within her rights; with a flash of insight, for he was an intelligent man, he realized that a motherless girl of thirteen must con-

[5]

tinually fight for her proper position against the middle class elders who really ran the establishment. His first impulse had been to summon Father Laurence and Madam Alice, the housekeeper, to share the high table; but it would give his daughter great pleasure to sit alone beside him, the two fitzGerolds above all the underlings; the mind of a competent Chamberlain is constantly occupied with precedence.

Father Laurence said grace and all sat down. When a dish was placed between them the lord Warin ladled minced spiced beef on to his daughter's manchet with the elegant flourish of a courteous knight. She blushed with delight and made to serve her father, seeking to take the spoon from his hand. "No, my dear," he said, "you are a damsel, not a child. Good knights serve the ladies first."

As she sat decorously straight he looked her up and down; he had promised her future father-in-law that she was strong and healthy and fitted for childbearing, though when he had last seen her she was a little round-shouldered rat of eleven; it was a relief to see that he had spoken the truth. She had long hands and feet, which meant that she would grow tall; her waist was small, but her figure showed maturity; her coloring was dark, but then her mother had been dark also; that was a defect, for nowadays the jongleurs sang only of ladies fairer than snow; but with powder, and a day of rigorous fasting before important occasions, any lady could make herself pale enough to pass. The curved fitz-Gerold nose was not too big, and even the determined chin looked only amusingly cheeky on such a young face. Later she would become bad-tempered and masterful, for already there were faint lines on her forehead and by the corners of her mouth; but then she would be safely married. Her hair, hanging behind her in the two plaits of maidenhood, was

[6]

long and black, with auburn gleams where it caught the
light. Her eyebrows were thick and bushy, but that went
with abundant hair and was easily remedied. Her big brown
eyes were full of expression, and at the moment that expression was a mixture of maidenly confusion and delight
at her father's courtesy. He remembered that when she was
taking off his spurs he had thought her a pretty girl. Now
that he looked at leisure the impression vanished; her face
showed too much character, and rather selfish character at
that. But an heiress might be very much uglier and yet
make a good marriage; if her father-in-law tried to return
her as physically unworthy he would put himself utterly in
the wrong.

The next dish was only a sheep roasted whole, for oxen
would not be fattened for the table until after harvest. The
lord Warin had no squire to carve for him, since normally
he dined at the King's table; he himself carved for his
daughter's manchet and his own. He saw with approval
that she ate daintily, touching the food with two fingers
only and wiping her mouth free of grease before she drank
from her cup; she would not shame him in any company.
When the third dish was set before him, wild duck stewed
in honey, he was no longer hungry; he opened the serious
conversation which was the chief object of his visit.

"My dear, please listen carefully. By Michaelmas England will be at war, and I have decided to remove my valuables from Stogursey. I shall send them to Corfe, to be kept
with the King's treasure. I have friends among the staff of
the Wardrobe; with any luck the King won't know of it
and I shall get back my property when the war is won. But
this hall will be unfit for a lady to dwell in; I shall leave
only a common bailiff to keep the villeins at their work.
Now I could bring you to court, and I know that is what

[7]

London
ENGLAND

English Channel

Bruges
Calais
FLANDERS
Boulogne

Amiens

Rouen
Caen VEXIN
NORMANDY
Mont St. Falaise
Michel

Rheims

CHAMPAGNE

Paris

BLOIS

Rennes MAINE

Sens

Atlantic Ocean

BRITTANY Le Mans

Orleans

Nantes Angers
ANJOU TOURAINE
Tours
Blois

BURGUNDY

Bourges
Nevers

BERRY

POITOU

BOURBON

Poitiers

LA
MARCHE

Clermont

Limoges
LIMOUSIN
AQUITAINE
PERIGORD
Bordeaux

AUVERGNE

QUERCY

AGENAIS

TOULOUSE

GASCONY

Toulouse

BEARN

NAVARRE

ARAGON ROUSSILLON

The EMPIRE of The HOUSE of ANJOU
1154 A.D.

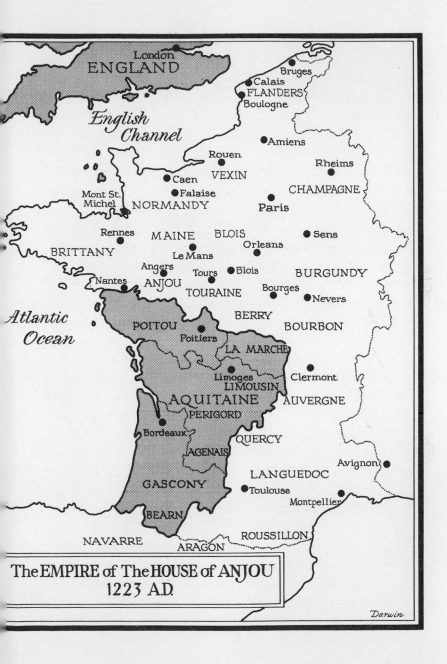

The EMPIRE of The HOUSE of ANJOU
1223 A.D.

you would like. But there are serious objections. The King will be riding every day, as always when he wages war; in winter you would find that most unpleasant. But the real reason is that the court is no place for a young girl. The King has a roving eye, and I should be in an awkward and undignified position if he took you so blatantly that I could not pretend ignorance. Honor would force me to change sides, but I think the rebels will lose in the end, and anyway they don't want me."

As Margaret bridled, glancing down at her young breasts, he continued: "I see you rather like the idea of being a royal leman, and I don't blame you; I suppose every young girl dreams that one day she will be another Fair Rosamund, living in luxurious shame. The jongleurs never sing of anything else, and they make it sound very attractive. But that was in the days of the Old King, who had the manners of a gentleman. I'm afraid King John behaves very differently. He would take you for the inside of a week and then tire of you. Really, the things that go on when the King feels lonely! I look the other way, and keep his Chamber as orderly as I can; but it is no place for my daughter. So, since you must leave here and you cannot go to court, I have decided you ought to get married. It is a little soon, but you look ready for it. I suppose I can count on your consent?"

He looked anxiously at this daughter whom he hardly knew. The Church insisted that at a wedding the bride should express her free consent, and most priests would refuse to marry a girl who shouted that she was unwilling. Of course there were ways of overcoming disobedience; but it took time, and he wanted everything arranged by nightfall. The war might begin any day. He was relieved when Margaret blushed and sighed. "Of course, father," she said in just the right tone of mingled shyness and obedience, "I shall do whatever you desire. I had looked for another year of maidenhood, but I am old enough to make a wife."

The lord Warin, a Chamberlain and the son of a Chamberlain, had very good manners, and expected good manners from his family. But this seemed too easy. A daughter must marry the man chosen by her father, but she ought at least to show some interest in the identity of her husband. It was disappointing to see his vital and important proposition taken as a matter of course. He spoke rather crossly: "Are you willing to be just 'a wife'? Won't you bother to ask who is to be your husband?"

"I expect you to choose my husband," she answered with dignity. "I did not look for marriage so soon, but you have given a reason for your haste. That was courteous, since you need not give reasons to a daughter who must obey you. I am sure you have chosen wisely, and that at the proper time you will tell me more."

Warin was stung out of his self-possession. He would make this impassive girl sit up and take an interest in her own future. "I have contracted with Count William de Redvers. You will marry his only son Baldwin. After dinner Father Laurence will hear your oath of betrothal in the parish church, and in a few weeks you must leave for Plympton."

That produced as much excitement as anyone could wish.

"Plympton castle and Carisbrooke castle!" she exclaimed, the words tumbling over one another. "I shall be a Redvers, and one day a Countess! Let me take your treasure with me to Plympton, so that they respect me as a great lady! It will be safer with me than with your friends in the Wardrobe. What about dresses and jewels? I have

[11]

nothing here. Did you bring any with you? I know of a clever tailor in Taunton. Perhaps I can stop there on the way. You must give me a whole barrel of silver. After all, though war is coming we are still at peace. The tenants of Redvers will expect a rich Countess. Oh, and who is this Baldwin? You say he is the son of Count William, but I've never heard of him. Has he been married before, and is he a brave warrior?"

"I thought we might come to him in the end," the lord Warin answered dryly. "Redvers is a noble line, and Plympton a fine castle; but your husband is also of some importance. Naturally you have never heard of him; he is just fourteen, and not yet knighted. He is Count William's only child, and the old boy never sent him off to another household to learn courtesy because he is always in very poor health. He has passed all his life at Plympton, and I shouldn't be surprised if he is a bit of a mollycoddle. You see, the Redvers descent must continue, and Count William was terrified that if his only son wasn't properly looked after he might catch a cold and die. But when you have produced a healthy son his father will not be so anxious. Do your duty quickly if you want a gay life while you are young enough to enjoy it."

"I can do my duty if he is man enough to do his," Margaret answered, preening herself. "I'm sorry he is a boy, and not apparently a very warlike boy. I see that I shan't be a Countess just yet. How old is Count William, and is he in good health?"

"A very reasonable question. I shall tell you what I know about the family, for such inquiries would sound tactless after you have reached Plympton. Count William is gray-haired and not very strong. I don't know how old, but beginning to fail. Redvers is not a sound stock; he succeeded his elder brother, who died in his bed. Or it may be that their castle is unhealthy; the Count has only this one son, and his lady died bearing him. They obviously don't expect the boy to make old bones; that's why they are in such a hurry to find him a wife as soon as he can get a son in his turn. It is not a warlike stock either; Count William will display the King's banner, but I shall be very surprised if he leads out his tenants to join us on campaign. Hard riding in the rain would not suit his rheumatism. He wants an alliance with some loyal lord who is always near the King's person. That's why he approached me in the first place. We didn't set it down in the marriage contract, because it might make John suspect my fidelity; but one term of the agreement is that I shall do my best to avert the King's wrath if Redvers stays at home. When he is summoned he will answer that he dare not leave his lands, beset by rebels; and I shall try to persuade the King that he is telling the truth."

"You say Baldwin is the only son? Is there any danger that his father might marry again?"

"He very nearly married you. What he wanted most of all was the friendship of fitzGerold the Chamberlain, and he thought the best way to get it would be to marry my daughter. It was I who reminded him that his son is old enough to take his place. Like any other old gentleman, he had been rather taken with the idea of marrying a virgin of thirteen; but, again like any other old gentleman, he shrank from the upset of all his comfortable habits that such a marriage would entail. He was undecided, until I pointed out that everyone spends more time out of bed than in it. I hope all this suits your wishes. If you marry Count William you become a Countess at once; but in a few years you would be merely a dowager, not even mother of the heir;

[13]

while if you marry young Baldwin you must wait, but eventually you will reign in Plympton."

"Of course you are right, dear father. I prefer a young husband, even though he is not yet a knight. After I have married him I shall persuade him to be courteous and brave. Would you say he is greater than Joan's husband? Remember, Joan married a Nevill, though of the junior line."

"Very much greater. That is as it should be, since two years ago, when Joan married, the King's party was losing ground, while now the rebels have overreached themselves with that fantastic Charter. Hugh de Nevill holds three castles, and Redvers holds only two; but Plympton and Carisbrooke are fiefs, while Oxford and Hertford and Colchester can be taken away at the King's pleasure, and Hugh as sheriff must render account at the Exchequer. When peace comes and the King wears his crown at Pentecost in the old fashion you will sit in a higher place than your elder sister. In fact," the lord Warin continued in a musing voice, "it's the best marriage that has ever come to a fitz-Gerold. Great families used to despise us ministers; they said we were only royal servants while they held their lands by right. But in the Old King's day his servants began to increase in power with their master. I am the last of the fitzGerolds, but I am certainly the greatest; I dare say a Blundeville or a Braoze will be proud to marry my granddaughter. Of course, that's only if we win the war; but I expect we shall." His voice sank to a murmur as he counted the strength of the opposing forces. All over England lords muttered thus to themselves as they picked the side they would support.

Margaret drained the cup she shared with her father. She had no definite plan of campaign, but even at thirteen

[14]

years old instinct told her that when she took the oath of betrothal that afternoon her cheeks should be glowing and her eyes sparkling. Her thoughts could not be suppressed, and she spoke uninvited.

"Tell me again my husband's name and titles, so that I get them right when I repeat them before Father Laurence."

That introduced a long disquisition on Count William's lands and castles. His fiefs lay in two great blocks, one in the southwest and the other in the Isle of Wight; he was known indifferently as Count of Devon or Count of Wight; his peasants sometimes called him Earl of Devon, after the Saxon functionary who had once ruled the shire; but in these days the King ruled every shire, and courtiers and officials made a point of referring to magnates by their names; he was Count William de Redvers, and Margaret would one day be Countess de Redvers. Margaret objected that the Count of Chester was hardly ever called Count Ranulf; but the answer was that this exception proved the point, for Count Ranulf reigned in his Palatinate, while only the King reigned in Devon.

At the end of the meal the betrothal was publicly announced to the household, and there were extra drinks all around. In the afternoon everyone walked down to the parish church; it had no vicar, for Father Laurence lived at the hall, and on most Sundays and holidays he found time to say a Mass for his parishioners. He now unlocked the south door, and this unusual proceeding brought in all those villagers who were not at work in the fields; when all were within, the priest, standing on the altar steps, made a little speech, to remind his flock that betrothal was not marriage, and that to anticipate the genuine sacrament was mortal sin. (Of course no lady would dream of doing anything of the kind, but it could not be too often explained to the incontinent peasants.) Then the lady Margaret fitz-Gerold came forward, and in the presence of witnesses who could testify that she was in fact the daughter of the lord Warin took oath that she would wed the lord Baldwin de Redvers, only son of Count William, and that she held herself bound to wed no other unless he released her from this promise. When the congregation dispersed Margaret wisely told herself that these important occasions always seemed rather flat while they were actually happening.

At least she was allowed a holiday for the afternoon, instead of going back to the new surcoat she was embroidering for her father; it was a big piece of work, which had frightened and bored her by its size, and she was glad to think that now it need never be finished. But a betrothal should have been the occasion for several days of feasting; nowadays it was even fashionable for the young man to appear in person, so that the maiden might refuse him if she found him physically repugnant. This had been a hurried, hole-and-corner affair, and no one had been warned in time to buy betrothal presents for her. Like so many other disagreeable things, it was all because the country hovered on the brink of war; but civil war had been threatening for as long as a thirteen-year-old could remember, and she was getting very tired of that excuse for every unpleasant lack of ceremony. She wandered into the little herb garden behind the hall; it held a few rosebushes as well, and it would be appropriate if she made herself a chaplet of flowers to wear at supper; no one else would bother to do anything special for her, even on this, one of the most important days of her life.

The world was very unfair to her. She ought to have a beautiful mother, and a dashing elder brother whose gal-

[16]

lant friends would play with her in the real rose-garden which should surround her father's castle. But here she was, a neglected orphan, living in a mere palisaded manor. Someone was very much to blame, though it was difficult to name the culprit.

Yet the sun shone on the heather-covered Quantocks, dinner had been very much better than the usual everyday fare she ate in her father's absence, and although that father had hurried her into wasting what might have been the excuse for a very enjoyable party he had found her a good husband. Margaret sat down on a turf-covered bench, and when she discovered that her bad temper had evaporated she was too sensible to call it back.

The real point was that quite soon she would be the first lady of a great castle; Count William was a widower, and there would be no one above her on the female side of the household, even though her husband was still only the heir. Like every other great man, Count William must ride out to hunt or to oversee his land for most of the daylight hours; then the castellan would come to her for the watchword, and consult her before admitting armed strangers or closing the gates against them. All day she would have great responsibilities, in addition to the care of the kitchen, the stores, and all the peaceful side of daily life, which would be hers even when her husband was present. Her husband . . . that was another subject to be considered.

Country-bred, she had known the facts of sexual life since she had been big enough to wander into the cow-house. But she had never been attracted to a man. This was because the only men she had seen were villeins, or middle aged clerks and sergeants. Even though some of the blue-eyed shepherd boys were handsome muscular creatures, to a fitzGerold they were hardly human beings. She knew that

[17]

her most precious possession was her reputation, and pride of birth had helped her to keep it unspotted. Everyone seemed to be agreed that wedlock was a very pleasant experience . . . though a maiden ought to show reluctance when led to the marriage bed. Her sister Joan had been very eager to marry Hugh Nevill; but then she had seen him at her betrothal party; and he was a fine figure of a man, if a tough, battle-scarred body was what you fancied. The wedding had been postponed time and again while they waited for the Interdict to be lifted; but as soon as the churches reopened, two years ago, Joan had ridden to Oxford faster than her baggage could follow. On the other hand, she had not seen her sister since the marriage, and it might have been a disappointment after all.

However, Hugh Nevill, the competent sheriff and rising professional soldier, could hardly be compared with a delicate boy of fourteen. What was fun with him might be a laborious and irksome duty with young Baldwin. And old women said childbearing was very unpleasant, particularly for a wife who was not fully grown; though perhaps old women exaggerated the troubles they had surmounted, as warriors boasted of their hardships on campaign. After all, everyone in Stogursey had been born of a woman, and a very large proportion had been born of fourteen-year-old girls; that was why Father Laurence had preached yet again on his favorite topic.

No, she could cope with her husband, Margaret decided. When the village children played together she had observed that girls often dominated boys of the same age, as though in childhood the female mind was more mature than the male. But to dominate her husband would not give her command of Plympton castle, for he was still subject to his father; Count William would be the greatest influence on her future happiness, and she must get on the right side of him. First impressions would be important; probably he was a very busy man, but he must be there to welcome her as she arrived; she should show him from the start that he had chosen for his son a sensible wife, a wife who could be left to live her own life in peace.

She shut her eyes, trying to summon up a mental picture of the Redvers family. What were they like? She knew that they were well-born, better born even than the fitzGerolds. But they were quiet and retiring, prone to ill health, and reluctant to take part in politics; she had not even been sure, until her father told her, whether they supported the King or the northern rebels. Count William would presumably admire a daughter-in-law who displayed formal, rather old-fashioned manners, who paid her husband due deference in public but shouldered her responsibilities behind the scenes, who dressed simply and did not waste money on pet monkeys and sugar; though he would not mind if she bought jewels, for good jewelery could easily be turned back into silver. Before she could behave properly Margaret must first make a picture in her mind of what was expected from her; the picture was always very vivid, and once she had composed it the appropriate behavior came quite easily.

Unfortunately, when she tried to visualize the rest of the household at Plympton the result was a blank. But common sense told her that they would all hate her on sight, as she herself would hate her stepmother if her father married again. The right line to take was to keep the servants working very hard, with a careful eye on waste; though, of course, the head cook must be allowed his reasonable perquisites. Probably her only friends would be her own ladies. She must be careful in her choice of them. She

[19]

began to run over in her mind those tenants of fitzGerold who had in their households superflous ladies. They should be of gentle birth, but not so well-born as to be rivals of their mistress; Madam Alice would just qualify, and she would be useful to look after linen and clothing. Margaret's mind luxuriated in this lordly distribution of patronage.

Ladies were brought up to marry in adolescence, and generally speaking they were married to strangers. Margaret was not surprised at being contracted to a youth she had never seen. The rules of behavior between husband and wife had been laid down in great detail, and if they were observed it was not too difficult for mere acquaintances to live in close intimacy. Latterly she had planned her life at Stogursey with forethought, to make sure that a motherless and neglected orphan received the outward deference due to her birth. She would plan with equal care for Plympton. She faced the unknown with equanimity.

2: *Plympton*

BY Michaelmas it was known all over England that the Pope had annulled the rebels' Charter, as he was bound to do; for a promise extorted by fear cannot bind. The King was mustering his forces in Kent; there he interposed between the rebels in London and the reinforcements they expected from their allies in France. While there was still a chance of papal mediation no one was anxious to strike the first blow; but the war was on the point of breaking out, and soon there would be little time for weddings. On the 1st of October the lord Warin fitzGerold brought his daughter to Plympton.

It was a journey of more than seventy miles, and they were two nights on the road; for this was the sort of thing a Chamberlain liked to plan in careful detail, and he wished their horses to look fresh on arrival. He had taken trouble to compose a dignified procession. First rode a score of

Italian crossbowmen, the most valuable and expensive mercenaries that any lord could hire; on their surcoats they bore the Angevin Leopard, to prove their employer's loyalty. Behind them rode the lord Warin himself, clothed in an embroidered cotte which reached to his ankles, and over it a hooded surcoat lined with otter fur; he carried no weapons, for swords at a wedding are omens of strife; but behind him two pages bore his crested helm and emblazoned shield. Then came a curtained litter slung between two stout mules; the curtains were gay with the impaled arms of Redvers and fitzGerold, but the bride could not be seen. After that rode three ladies on hackneys, then women of lesser rank on ponies, and a train of pack mules laden with the chests of the dowry. Last of all was another clump of mounted sergeants; but these were local Somerset men whose pay was little more than half that of the Italian mercenaries.

At mid-morning they reached the outer ditch of Plympton castle, and a page blew on a trumpet. The drawbridge was immediately lowered, while banners broke from every tower. Count William, in the long robes of peace, met them at the outer gate; his sumptuous furs made him the most imposing figure in the procession; however, he was the only Count present, and Warin the Chamberlain thought it proper that he himself should be outshone. In silence the Count led them through a second gate to the inner bailey, and there, below the motte, they at last encountered the crowd of spectators. A ragged and unskilled band of trumpets and cymbals made a cheerful noise, the crowd hurrahed, and at the door of the chapel the bride at last emerged from her litter.

Since the procession started that morning Margaret had been sitting in darkness. She had not even peeped

[22]

through the curtains, partly because she did not want to spoil her first proper view of her new home, partly because a bride made a more pleasing picture of maidenly confusion if she allowed herself to be dazzled by a sudden burst of daylight. For most of the last month she had kept herself in the dark, to be sure of a pale complexion; now the warmth of the sun made her blush all down her neck in a most becoming manner, while the dazzle of light brought genuine tears to her eyes. As her foot peeped timidly from beneath her cotte to feel for the threshold (for at first she could see very little) the crowd cheered harder than ever at sight of such an appealing and frail-looking maiden.

Only the gentry entered the small chapel; the doors remained open, to fulfill the demand of canon law that the ceremony should be public; but a nobleman of breeding did not wish the lower orders to gaze too curiously on the face of his bride, and weddings were normally as private as the Church could permit. Margaret swayed forward a few steps on her father's arm, and then suddenly felt herself alone. She suppressed a smile of genuine pleasure; thanks to the darkness of the litter and the sudden flash of sun as she entered the chapel she was giving a most convincing performance of the shy virgin reluctantly consenting to be handed over to a fierce male. Certainly her father could plan a ceremony.

Someone at her side helped her to kneel on a cushion; as he knelt beside her she looked for the first time at the youth who in ten minutes would be her husband. Oh, well, he was heir to Count William and the fiefs of Redvers; with that in his favor he would just do.

The young lord Baldwin de Redvers was not prepossessing. He would have been tall for fourteen if only he had held himself straight, but his head poked forward; kneeling

[23]

he made it worse by sticking out his behind as well. His long sandy hair was curled to fall on his shoulders; that would be all right in a page, but at his age he should have cut it short for comfort under the helm. The curls were obviously the result of hot irons, and the hair itself was very fine and scanty; at thirty he would be bald. His face was made up of a long pointed nose and a runaway chin under a wet mouth; its skin was as pale as a girl's, but his large hands were red and he held them very awkwardly. He was evidently suffering agonies of shyness and hating every minute of the short and business-like ceremony. Count William had dispensed with the Nuptial Mass, which Margaret considered wise; young Baldwin looked the kind of boy who would be sick if he was asked to do anything important without a good breakfast inside him.

Now the priest was asking her the vital question. She might answer No, and then the whole power of the Church, the mighty power which had defeated the King himself in the long struggle over the See of Canterbury, would be put forth to save her from this marriage. There would be a devastating quarrel between fitzGerold and Redvers, and her father would punish her very severely; but unless she gave her free consent, in this holy place where to threaten her would be sacrilege, the wedding would be stopped at once.

The thought of refusal did just enter her mind, but only because it would be enormous fun to cause such a disturbance; as some years ago she had only just overcome the temptation to loose the village bull during a Rogation procession at Stogursey. Then she gave her consent in a clear and confident voice, putting out her hand for the ring. Her eyes were now accustomed to the gloom, and she permitted herself a cheerful smile. That was in accordance with etiquette; a maid should be nervous of marriage, but she was now a wife and should rejoice in her new condition. The person of her husband was not important, she reflected, and she might improve him as he grew older; what mattered was her new status.

Some women had ugly or repulsive husbands, as some women had birthdays during the Twelve Days of Christmas, never enjoying a proper celebration for themselves; it was a piece of bad luck, which could not be altered. But a wife, even the wife of a nasty little boy, had a very much better time than the most beautiful and sought-after maiden. Above all, a married lady could experiment with the dangerous inclinations of love. A maiden was supposed to be cold as ice; any gentleman of ordinary politeness who sat by her at table, or chatted with her in a hall, was expected to fill his conversation with extravagant expressions of adoration; but if he met with the slightest return of his conventional affection he would be dismayed, and the bystanders would be shocked, that a well-bred damsel should be so ignorant of the rules of polite society. A wife was different. By common consent she could not be in love with her husband, since he took by right what all women desired to yield as a favor; but she had been awakened to the possibilities of love, and public opinion would be pleased if she took some knight as her official cavalier, to serve her in public and wear her colors in battle. Whether his extremely public devotion was ever rewarded in private hardly mattered, except to her husband; possibly the cavalier himself enjoyed the ardors of the chase without any strong desire to capture his quarry; but a formal attachment was one of the recognized diversions permitted to the lady of a great castle. As Margaret de Redvers she was going to lead a most amusing social life; if that silly young Baldwin had been a little less gawky she would have felt quite grateful that his father's offer of his hand in marriage had brought all this about.

When the short service was ended she walked on her husband's arm to the feast in the great hall. Now she had leisure to inspect it Plympton seemed a very fine castle. At dinner the food was adequate and the wine plentiful and very good indeed, as it should be since they lay so near the ports where Gascon wine-ships came to harbor. She sat, of course, in the place of honor, between her husband and Count William; the lord Warin was several places away, too far for her to talk to him. Young Baldwin was both nervous and bored; he ate very little, and began by drinking heavily as though to shut away reality; but almost at once the wine made him sleepy, and then he slouched in silence at her side. Count William had cumbrous old-fashioned manners; he told a few dull stories concerning the trophies on the wall, and seemed glad when entertainers stepped into the cleared space in the middle of the room and conversation could cease. First a jongleur sang about some minor skirmish of the First Crusade. The queer foreign place-names meant nothing to Margaret, and since he had begun in the middle of what was evidently a long epic she could not tell whether all this was supposed to be happening before the liberation of Jerusalem or afterward; but once or twice she caught the name of Redvers, and understood that the extract had been chosen because it mentioned her husband's ancestors. Then a team of dancers took the floor, and they were really amusing to watch. There was a bear on his hind legs, wearing a skullcap and pallium to represent the leader of the rebels, the Archbishop of Canterbury. There was a chubby young girl who danced most of the time on her hands; she wore a very full

[26]

skirt which seemed about to reveal everything until at the critical moment she bent her legs backward and you were disappointed. There was the usual muscular young man, playing the flute as he danced; and two rather full-blown women who banged on cymbals but were disinclined to bend their joints. When the young man finally compelled the bear-Archbishop to eat his Charter the whole hall dissolved in laughter.

Margaret would have liked more of these dancers, but when they retired and three harpers bowed before the high table the spectators became alert for what was evidently the chief amusement of the feast. One harper began to sing a very ordinary French love song; the second suddenly took him up and completed the line in English; presently the third joined in, singing in another language which Margaret recognized as Cornwelsh, though she could not understand it. The French song was a decorous affair, the usual pleading of a lover who does not really expect his lady to yield; but the English additions were closely concerned with what might happen later in the evening; the Cornwelsh was probably even more outspoken, to judge by the giggles of its hearers. Margaret found herself blushing, which annoyed her; presently she must go to bed with her husband, but that was the chief purpose of marriage, and there was nothing funny about it. Rationalizing her annoyance, she suddenly discovered that the whole affair showed very bad taste; bawdy songs were an essential part of a wedding-feast, but it was uncouth of these westcountry provincials to expect their guests to know English and Cornwelsh. Unfortunately she had already betrayed her comprehension of the English words, though any lady who looked after her own horses would hear those very words continually in the

[27]

stable; now she looked down her nose and absently crumbled the bread of her manchet.

"I am sorry, madam, if this song displeases you," Count. William whispered. "We are proud of it here, for it is very difficult to rhyme in three languages at once. Those harpers spent many years perfecting it, and we hear it at every wedding-feast. You may console yourself by remembering that next time you hear it another maiden will be blushing, while you look on as a wife."

"The words do not disturb me, lord Count, since I cannot understand them," Margaret answered firmly. "I speak French and Romance, and enough Latin to read my Missal. But at Stogursey it was not necessary to learn the tongues of the villeins, since our baliff spoke good French."

"Of course our baliff here speaks good French, madam. But perhaps there is too much English spoken in the castle for civility and good manners. Since we seldom leave Plympton my sergeants marry local women, which means that they pick up the dialect by the fireside. And farther west even the gentry speak Cornwelsh. You will find a knowledge of that tongue useful."

"I obey you, my lord, as I obey my husband. But I did not think that one day I would be asked to converse with my equals in any tongue except French."

Count William sighed, turning back to the harpers. An alliance with fitzGerold was a sound move, while politics were in their present disturbed condition; but he had been right to marry this lady to young Baldwin, not to himself.

At last even this long afternoon drew to a close, and it was time for the happy couple to retire. As her ladies escorted her up the steep winding stair to the marriage chamber Margaret displayed the conventional reluctance.

[28]

Count William had been very generous to his heir. No one could expect the lord of the castle to give up his own chamber at the end of the hall, the only really private room in the building; but he had caused a large curtained marriage-bed to be erected in the uppermost room under the roof of the lookout tower. That was out of the way, and no one need enter it except the sentry on his way to his post; if they drew the curtains they could not be seen, and only two or three sergeants and the castellan who inspected them would be in a position to overhear. Margaret had feared that they might be expected to sleep in the bower, while her ladies listened and giggled; she was encouraged by this evidence of her father-in-law's consideration.

Presently the gentlemen escorted young Baldwin up the same stair. Margaret, naked inside the curtains, dared not put out her head; but she recognized her father's voice and called to bid him good-bye. She owed him gratitude for this splended marriage, and she might not see him again for a long time. As a matter of fact she never saw him again.

Next morning she was a properly wedded wife, and, what was equally important, she had established a complete ascendancy over her husband. Young Baldwin was timid, and remarkably clumsy; he must have been brought up very virtuously, one disadvantage of being reared at home instead of being taught manliness in a neighbor's castle. But perhaps it was all for the best.

At the end of a week she began to find her way about this new life. It was odd to be subject to such an ineffectual lord as young Baldwin. He appeared as anxious to leave her alone as she was to avoid him, though they continued to share the curtained bed in the tower chamber. But a thirteen-year-old wife cannot expect complete freedom. Although her husband was not truly her lord, everyone in the castle was under the command of Count William. He was the man who could make or mar her happiness, and she set herself to get on the right side of him.

Count William was an eccentric, whose desire for obscurity was so strong that it had made him famous. Counts were few in England, and most of them were taking very prominent parts in the civil war. The King, with his mercenaries and a few faithful English lords, had laid siege to the Archbishop of Canterbury's strong castle of Rochester; the Archbishop, the leader of the rebels, was in Rome to appeal against the annulment of his cherished Charter; his followers were gathered in London, waiting anxiously for the promised help from France and trying to pluck up their courage to take the field openly against their liege lord. It looked as though there must soon be a great battle, as famous and decisive as the great battle at Bouvines a year ago. Naturally both sides sent urgent messages to their supporters in the provinces, bidding them hasten in arms to the decisive seat of action. But Count William stayed at home. Plympton flew the Angevin Leopards beside the banner of Redvers, and the Count sent a few barrels of silver to the King's Wardrobe, though he kept more, for he was rich. He had summoned his tenants, as the King's writ ordered; but he had let it be known that he had received a rival writ from London. Therefore some of his knights joined one of the armies, royal or rebel, some stayed at home or found it convenient to go on pilgrimage beyond the sea; only a few came to Plympton, and they were ordered to remain in garrison. But the Count did not distrain on the lands of the defaulters, and his clerk wrote to the King explaining that the southwest was so disturbed that even a loyal magnate could do no more than hold his own castle in the King's interest.

Count William was quite frank with his daughter-in-law. "You see, my dear," he said as she sat beside him on the dais, during one of those long dull evenings when the sergeants of the garrison must be allowed to drink themselves into the mood for bed, "you see, I don't like leaving Plympton. Of course I would never hold it against the King, in the way my great ancestor held it against King Stephen. With King John you know where you are; what he demands from his vassals is money and plenty of it; luckily I can give him that since my fief is rich and I don't waste silver on journeying. He isn't always badgering his tenants-in-chief to visit his court and gape at him wearing his crown; the Old King, his father, could never have enough of that and a great nuisance it was. But that was in my brother's time. This king was bullied in childhood by those untamed devils, his brothers, and as a result he grew up ill at ease in the society of gentlemen. They say he even permits routiers to dine in his hall, though that may be an exaggeration. But your father, when I came to court to arrange your marriage, was forced to admit that the King's favorite companions are mercenary captains of dubious birth. He doesn't really want to see me, for all his writs of summons. My money is more use to him than my sword. The tenants know I'm not much of a warrior, and they would follow me without enthusiasm. The Chamberlain will always swear to my loyalty (that's why I brought you here, my dear) and with any luck that tiresome war will not move to these parts. Why should any army ride to an out-of-the-way corner like Plympton? I suppose if the rebels come here I must close the gates in the King's name. But they can only get here after taking Corfe, and if that falls the King will have lost the war and it will be time to negotiate. Perhaps I won't close my gates against anyone.

[31]

We can make up our minds when we have to, and not before. I hope you think I am acting wisely? Your husband is eager to ride to Rochester, but since he is not a knight no one would follow the dear boy, and Master Julian says campaigning in winter would be bad for his health. We shall stay here, warm and comfortable, until the spring. Then perhaps he can go and besiege some small castle, to get a first look at a gentle kind of war."

Count William was accustomed to doing all the talking while he sat at the high table; Margaret murmured polite agreement, and continued to think her own thoughts. Though the Count was lord of Plympton the whole life of the castle revolved around that sickly boy, her husband. On a crisp autumn day with the sun shining all the ladies and knights must go out to help him fly his hawks; he was fond of hawking, but always in trouble with the hooding of his birds, for he was nervous, and his snatching made the hawks nervous also; yesterday he had been bitten in the thumb, and there had been enough boiling of wine and brewing of salves to cure a gallant knight of a lance thrust in the shoulder. But today it was raining, and so no one might ride out; getting wet was bad for Baldwin's cough, but he fretted if others took exercise while he sat by the fire. The silly creature always did what he was told. Though really, Margaret thought, they might allow him to enjoy himself; with that cough he would not live long anyway, and if he had any sense he would make haste to get himself killed gallantly in battle, so that at least he would be remembered after he was dead.

Now the youth was asking whether he might go out later, to try the evening flight of duck at the river mouth; but Master Julian looked wisely at the narrow window and advised waiting for better weather. Master Julian spoke an extraordinary jargon of bad Latin and worse Romance; he had papers to prove he was a sub-deacon, and claimed to have studied medicine at Salerno; he wore the long gown of a Master of the University, but apparently the teachers of Salerno did not give their pupils written certificates of proficiency. Margaret suspected that he had never been near the place, for surely any school in the Norman kingdom of Sicily would teach in French, the language of gentlemen? By his own account, all the eminent patients he had treated before he came to Plympton were dead, and could give no references; but Margaret was the only member of the household who thought that a reflection on his skill, and when he gave orders concerned with young Baldwin's health Count William always enforced them. There would be no hawking that afternoon.

It was unfortunate, for Margaret preferred hawking above any other amusement. She rode well, but she did not enjoy fighting an unruly horse, and she was disappointed to find that stag hunting meant sitting for hours through the bucking and rearing of an over-fresh hunter who could hear the belling of the lymners and wanted to start galloping; if the horse got away with her the harborers scowled, and took their precious lymners off the line of the quarry to shelter them from the hoofs. Of course, if all went well there was a gallop eventually, but by then she would be too tired to enjoy it; and Count William, who saw her as a fragile vessel containing the seed that promised continuance to the House of Redvers, grew very angry if she risked a fall. Until her marriage she had never gone stag hunting, for Stogursey lay in the royal forest of Quantock, where only the King and his court might hunt. It was a great disappointment to find that what by common report was the supreme diversion of great lords was not after all very amusing to a slight and easily tired lady.

But hawking was a fascinating pursuit. For one thing it was the custom to ride a quiet hackney; it might be necessary to scramble through streams and marshes, but as a rule there was no frenzied galloping. There was also an element of competition; out hunting the Count's short-tempered chief huntsman was in command, and you had to keep back until he let you go; but every sportsman flew hawks of his own training, and it was most satisfactory to bring down your own to her lure while your husband's, perched in a tall tree, displayed every intention of staying out all night. Margaret was deft with her fingers, and her movements were never abrupt. She carried her favorite hawk everywhere she went, so that it should grow used to the noise and bustle of humanity; in hall it perched on her chair of state, and she took it hooded on her wrist to Mass; though that was specifically forbidden by canon law, and the chaplain didn't like it.

Besides hawking, there were many other occupations for the lady of a great honor. Some of them were really duties, but to Margaret these were enjoyable as well. She spent hours hanging about the stables watching the horses fed and cleaned and physicked; that was really in the man's sphere, but the bitter smell of ammonia set young Baldwin to coughing, and Count William was bored by it. He had been heard to express the extraordinary opinion that one destrier was really very like another; to Margaret, as to most ladies and gentlemen of good birth, horses were more individual than the most eccentric human characters. Then there was the spring of drinking water to be inspected daily; it lay in the inner bailey, under the keep, so that if both baileys were lost and the garrison made a last stand they would be in no danger of thirst. But unfortunately the kitchen had been placed near by, to save trouble for the lazy scullions; they threw about garbage indiscriminately, and it was important to taste the water every morning to make sure that it was sweet. Luckily Master Julian fussed over that subject, and since the kitchen staff feared his enchantments they tried to please him. At Stogursey there had been a well instead of a spring, and that was a much greater nuisance; if it was not watched continually the villeins dropped into it superfluous puppies or even unexplained babies. Besides the stable and the spring, the storerooms must be visited daily; otherwise the cook saved himself trouble by taking meat from the cask nearest the door; then the casks at the back would lie undisturbed for years, and if ever the castle was besieged the emergency reserve would be found putrid. Apart from laziness, cooks always wanted to use the freshest provisions so that their dinners would taste well; but a castle without six months' stores might as well be unwalled, and it was essential to consume it in due order.

When she had finished these daily inspections it was Margaret's duty to spend most of the winter daylight sewing with her ladies in the bower. Count William bought his cloth from traveling chapmen, and the common serge of the lower classes was woven in the township; but the ladies of the household were expected to do all the sewing and embroidering. In the bower there were nine ladies: Madam Alice and the two young daughters of fitzGerold tenants who had come with her, and six wives or daughters of the castellan, constable, butler, and other functionaries of Plympton who ranked as gently born. This was the most boring part of Margaret's life; she could embroider neatly, but it did not amuse her; and the conversation of the ladies was inexpressibly tedious. They never talked about anything except the doings of their children or the progress of a futile love affair. Love affairs were the normal pastime of every housebound lady, but at Plympton there was no scope for adventure. Count William disliked the new custom, recently introduced from Provence, by which every lady chose a knight to serve her with extravagant public professions of devotion. As a rule there was no harm in it; a castle was so crowded that a gallant was unlikely to corner his mistress in solitude, and some of them didn't try to very hard. But the Count could not grasp that the sighings and handclaspings and wearing of favors were all part of a formal time wasting game. He had been brought up in the old-fashioned atmosphere where a husband took a whip to his wife and a sword to her suitor. He let it be known that the utmost decorum must prevail in the presence of the young wife of his son; his knights, who mostly kept peasant concubines in the township, were quick to obey his wishes; and Margaret's attendants must make the most of accidental encounters on the stairs or unpremeditated jostling when a gust of wind extinguished the torches on the wall. Of course that did not stop them weaving fantasies and choosing hypothetical partners; but to Margaret it seemed an unrewarding amusement, unworthy of a married woman nearly fourteen years of age. She chose no knight to serve her; that sort of thing could wait until she visited the King's court.

But presently she understood that Count William never left home, which was perhaps the most eccentric part of his eccentric behavior. His fiefs lay in two blocks, about Carisbrooke and Plympton; and she had taken it for granted that he would spend half the year in the Isle of Wight, consuming the produce of his demesne. But she discovered that corn and cattle from Wight were sent by boat to Yealmpton, whence there was a road passable for wagons right up to the castle; the Count said that in Wight he had a castellan and bailiffs whom he trusted, and that he had told the King he dared not leave Devon; if he took the road at all he would be expected to join the army. Anyway, he added, as a young man he had followed the Old King to Aquitaine, and King Richard as far as Sicily. That was enough traveling for anyone, and if only the war stayed the other side of England he would never leave the stronghold of his ancestors.

He talked a good deal about his ancestors, and even more of the future of the House of Redvers, until Margaret understood exactly what he had in mind. Devon was out of the track of a campaign that sought to conquer all England; he would sit quietly at home, nominally loyal to the King, until both sides, exhausted, offered great rewards to a fresh ally. He already had the Third Penny of the County Court, though that was not granted to every count; presently the King, or the rebels, would offer him the right to nominate the sheriff and justiciar of the county; he might even get the pleas of the crown in his lands, as the Count of Chester and the Bishop of Durham already held them. Then he would be supreme from the Exe to the Tamar, as great as any man in England. And then? Why, then he would go on sitting still in Plympton, but no one could order him to ride away from it.

Margaret took it for granted that every magnate should strive to increase his power, even though he was perfectly loyal to the King. But it seemed extraordinary that this lazy old man, who was always fussing about his health, should run such risks for the sake of his grandchildren. For, of course, his policy was full of risk. Suppose the

[37]

King won the war, crushing the rebels completely? His was said to be the weaker side, and most people expected the struggle to end in a compromise; but King John was showing remarkable energy and courage. He had captured Rochester, and now he was making northward, leaving London to the east and obviously intending to cut off the rebels from their base beyond Humber. He might win outright, and then those who had not given him their aid when it was needed would lose as much as if they had been open enemies.

She said as much to Count William, during another of those dreary sittings in hall; but he had a reasonable answer, for his words were always reasonable. You felt that if he ever did anything it would be the right thing to do; but as, in fact, he did nothing it was impossible to be certain.

"My dear," he said, with a doleful sigh, "it's no good laying plans about what to do if the King is completely successful. In that case even his most loyal followers will be helpless against his power; every magnate will lose his liberty. On the other hand, if the rebels win the bad old days of King Stephen will come again, and a Redvers will be lost in that struggle of wolves and jackals. Whoever gets Cornwall and the Stannaries will gobble up Devon also. I must assume that things will fall out as I wish, with the King strong enough to make terms, but not so strong that he rules unfettered. In that case Redvers will flourish; if not, we shall disappear. Though perhaps one of my descendants will be a mighty warrior; it's about due, by the ordinary rules of chance."

"Perhaps the mighty warrior will be my son. I wonder how soon you can tell that kind of thing about an infant?"

"Place in his cradle a weapon of iron, madam, so that it is the first thing he grasps," put in Master Julian. "Mean-

[38]

while you should eat the flesh of wild boars and other brave beasts, and I shall search among the grocers of Exeter for an ointment made of the fat of lions. The infidels of Barbary ship that ointment in great quantities to Genoa and Amalfi, and some may be found in England, though we are a long way from the source of every precious and potent drug."

The castellan made a coarse remark, suggesting the substitutes the merchants of Exeter might use if there were no lion fat available; some laughed, but Count William frowned, for he took his prospective grandson very seriously. After only two months of marriage Margaret had been able to inform him that she was doing all that could be expected of her; the infant was due in the following July, and it was not yet Christmas, but Count William was already making plans for his grandson's education. He, and everyone else in the castle, took it for granted the child would be a boy; Margaret dared not think of the disappointment if it was not.

Nowadays she could sleep undisturbed, a precious luxury envied by other married ladies. Of course, she still shared the marriage bed, for if she lay alone envious tongues might whisper about the baby's parentage. But young Baldwin, who was always very tired by nightfall, kept to his own side of the mattress; he had asked her not to talk to him, and seemed to enjoy pretending she was not there. Poor young Baldwin! His existence was the only drawback to her pleasant life as lady in charge of a large castle, though she did not dislike him personally. He, on the other hand, disliked her, partly because, although they were about the same age, she was adult and he still had the mind of a child; partly because she was always there when he wanted to be alone. It was unlucky that he was the only son; if he could have been spared to follow his own bent he would have made a popular and incompetent abbot. But as heir of Redvers and leader of a great mesnie he was clumsy on a horse, shy with the knights who must one day follow his banner, and afraid of physical pain. He should have served God, for to the King he would be a very useless servant.

The real trouble, Margaret thought, was that Plympton seemed a little world of its own. She was supreme lady; but it was no fun occupying the best chair in hall, and exacting obedience from a large staff of servants, if she never met an equal whom she could impress. She would have liked to invite her sister for a visit, or better still to have visited Joan with a large train of knights and ladies; but Joan had met with misfortune, and now she was living in retirement at the other end of England. Hugh Nevill suddenly lost his shrievalties, apparently because the King suspected his loyalty. Everyone else knew he was faithful, but the King was notoriously suspicious of gentlemen of good birth, relying on jumped-up mercenary soldiers who owed everything to his favor; a Norman bastard of low origin called Falkes de Brealte had been appointed sheriff of Oxford and Hertford, and Colchester was in rebel hands; Hugh Nevill had withdrawn to the far north, where his numerous and powerful kin were doing quite well by raiding the Scots. Joan sent a letter to announce the change; she was not depressed, for Scotland was a good country to raid, and if it was too strongly defended no one would blame Hugh, after the treatment he had received from the King, if he changed sides and began to raid in England. But she could not come to Plympton until the war was ended.

Once a month her father sent her short and uninformative duty-letters; but he was riding with the King and could not get away to visit the west. Reading between the lines Margaret gathered that he was unhappy and fearful of the future, though he never told her more about the progress of the campaign than she could learn from any traveling merchant. King John had seized the line of the Trent, proposing to keep Christmas in Nottingham. In the field he was a better warrior than any rebel; but every time he captured a castle from his enemies some of his supporters went home; loyal knights who would charge fiercely to save him from captivity or exile relaxed their efforts when he seemed to be doing well. The lord Warin was very firm that his daughter should not come to court, and Count William told her that it might be very expensive indeed if a valuable hostage from the House of Redvers fell into the King's hands. The muddling indecisive war would go on for years, and meanwhile everyone was too busy for visiting.

But that Christmas the war seemed very far away. In the west there was no fighting, since the rebels had foolishly accepted help from Llywellyn and other Welsh chieftains, and that automatically brought the warlike Norman lords of the March to the King's side. In the same way the Cinque Ports adhered to the Archbishop, and therefore the unprivileged ports of the western Channel were loyal. Windsor and Reading blocked the valley of the Thames, while Winchester guarded the southern route from London. The whole of the ancient kingdom of Wessex obeyed the rightful King. The twelve days of Christmas, when no work was done and everyone settled down to eat and drink through the only vacation of the year, ought to be a very joyful occasion.

Yet Margaret was bored. She wished she had not informed Count William of her condition; so far there was nothing to show, and she might have kept it dark for another month or two. She was now excused the embraces of her husband, but her life was in many other ways confined. Master Julian had taken charge, and he was delighted to give orders to a noble lady, especially since she had been foolish enough to let him see that she considered him a charlatan. She was forbidden to ride, which meant no more hawking; she was even forbidden to get drunk, though during the holiday there was nothing else to do; jongleurs who amused a tipsy household seemed extraordinarily unpolished to one who had drunk only two cups of watered wine. Her bed had been moved into the bower, and two or three ladies were always within call; those who were married described with gusto the pains of childbirth, and the maidens sighed and made much of her as though they were dealing with an infant of six. The staid life of the old-fashioned castle continued without her; if she visited the stable someone came running with a stool and a pomander against the smells, and the head groom was afraid to settle down for an interesting chat about the mind and nervous system of the horse, lest he be beaten for overtiring his lady. The mews was her only refuge, until even that was barred to her; a peregrine which Baldwin was supposed to be training moved sideways off her glove, digging its talons into her forearm; the bird was hooded, but nervous handling had spoiled its temper even on the perch. The scratches did not bother her, but they bled through her sleeve until Count William noticed them; it was all she could do to save the hawk's life, and she was forbidden to visit it again. Master Julian had stuffed the old Count with stories of the sympathy between mother and unborn child, and he feared that if when her time came she was scarred his grandson might be born with a blemish.

[42]

The real trouble was the all-pervading Redvers inertia. While Count William ruled there would be no fighting, and so long as she was pregnant she might not oversee the household. In other castles there would have been love affairs or political intrigue to pass the time, but not in Plympton; the Count was too old-fashioned to approve of courteous love, and too damned cowardly, as Margaret said to Madam Alice in a flash of bad temper, to take advantage of this remunerative and exciting war in the east of England.

Madam Alice was the only friend with whom she could be frank; her maidens hoped to marry among the tenants of Redvers, and would gladly curry favor with the Count by passing on any of their mistress's indiscretions. But Madam Alice was a middle-aged widow, with no dowry and no hope of another husband. If Margaret did not want her she would be dismissed, homeless and penniless; on the other hand, the Count might dismiss her to punish Margaret if he was vexed with his daughter-in-law, so the old lady did all she could to make the bored young bride appear content.

"Never call any knight a coward, my lamb," she answered at once. "It's the one accusation that is never forgiven. If he heard it Count William might prove his courage by beating you. Try and make the best of things. You have plenty to eat, and a comfortable bed, and you can peer out of any window without being ready to dodge an arrow. That's a great deal, as you will learn when you are older. You must give them a male child; that's what women are for. When you've done that they will leave you in peace. You should be thankful that the war is far away; if you had to ride a forced march, or go on half-rations, you and poor young Baldwin might have to begin all over again.

[43]

At least you are the first lady in this castle; that was what you always wanted. And your husband is not the man to flaunt mistresses in your face."

"If he was I'd like him better. But no one would sleep with Baldwin unless she was paid for it."

"Quite so. But you have been very well paid. Do your duty and think of the future. No one can accuse me of ill-wishing if I say that you are likely to live longer than both your husband and the old Count. Then you will be Lady of Plympton, ruling until your son is of age."

"Suppose it's a girl?"

"Then you must try again. But it won't be. I gave a black pig to the Cornish wizard, and a big cheese to the hermit on the Tor; one will intercede with the Devil and the other with the Saints, and between them they must bring you good luck. Eat what Master Julian tells you, and especially pickled cucumbers, for their shape has a male influence. Then your first-born will be a son."

"He will be a mollycoddle like his father, all the same. Yet I shall have done what is expected of me, and they must leave me in peace. Perhaps they will even heed my advice, and make war on the rebels of Devon."

"Perhaps. But never ask the Count for more than he is willing to grant. Remember that from now until the summer you are in a delicate condition, and everyone will be nervous of thwarting you. Insist on anything that adds to your comfort, but don't interfere in the affairs of men."

Madam Alice was a useful ally. She knew what was due to a pregnant lady, but she knew also that men always attribute female advice to the whims of the feminine condition.

As spring advanced the war quickened. A large force of Frenchmen, more than two hundred knights, had sailed up the Thames to reinforce the rebels in London, and the King marched south to block their communications with the Cinque Ports. In May the lord Louis, son and heir to King Philip of France, landed at Sandwich; King John, fearing to be caught between two hostile armies, retreated westward from Kent. At Winchester he turned to bay, but now all the southeast was in rebel hands, save for the besieged castle of Dover. Waverers made haste to change sides, and even Count William fitzHenry, the King's bastard brother, hoisted the French banner over Salisbury castle; the Queen and her two little sons wandered uneasily between Corfe, Exeter and Devizes, for only in that southwestern district was she safe from capture. The fighting had crept nearer to Devon.

But still Count William did not call up his knights. Life went on peacefully in the castle of Plympton, and Margaret carried her swollen body from the hall to the bower and back again, her only chance of fresh air to sit with her ladies in a little garden under the walls of the keep. The Count gave orders that the roses should be carefully tended and the grass spread with cushions for her comfort; but even that evidence of his goodwill annoyed her, for in time of war ground under the walls should be leveled and swept bare. The flourishing rose-trees proved that her adopted family were not prepared to take part in the great struggle. Young Baldwin spent his days practicing with lance and shield, until by evening he was exhausted; he talked of joining the King at Winchester, but it was only talk; since he had never been knighted the tenants would not follow him, and when it came to the point he had no intention of defying the old Count's wishes. Margaret recalled, for it was the most famous story of her childhood, that at the age of fourteen Count Arthur of Brittany had besieged his grandmother, old Queen Eleanor, fighting stoutly in person until he was captured and later murdered by his uncle the King. But the race of Anjou were descended from the Devil; her husband came from a more pacific and earthly stock.

After eight months of married life she hardly knew her husband. From the start young Baldwin had taken it for granted that she would dislike him, because that was what most people did. He was at bottom a kindly youth, so he kept out of her way as much as possible. He had been very glad to be relieved of his marital duties, which made him feel shy and interfered with the plentiful rest which Master Julian considered good for him. He greeted his wife courteously when he met her, and saw to it that her authority was upheld in the household; but when he was not practicing with his weapons out of a sense of duty his pleasure was to glance at fine painted books, or to play the harp with the uncouth and short-tempered Cornwelsh minstrels. His French was absurdly old-fashioned, and he frequently let fall English or Cornwelsh words in a manner that betrayed too much knowledge of those plebeian tongues. He had so often been bitten by his hawks that he had grown tired of them, and really, when they did find themselves together, husband and wife had very little to say to one another.

Margaret did not identify herself with the family of Redvers. They were out of things, when so many exciting events were happening all over England; if old Count William wanted to wait and see what would come to him, and that seemed to be his policy, then she would watch also. If the Count had boldly chosen a side, gambling all he possessed on the chance of victory, Margaret would have been pleased to help him. Which side did not matter; evil things were said of King John, but there was no reason to suppose Louis of France would make a better ruler, and she had never met either of them. But if Plympton was neutral in the war she would be neutral with regard to the fortunes of Plympton. Madam Alice sometimes reminded her that the lord Warin, her father, was the King's Chamberlain; but the King had taken back his castles from Joan's husband, her brother-in-law; perhaps life would be more amusing if the courteous French knights governed England.

Meanwhile, it was very dull to be stuck in this dead end of the country, burdened with pregnancy; while other ladies defended castles, ransomed their captive husbands, or rode with the armies.

3: *Farewell to Plympton*

 ON THE 15th of July 1216, Margaret was safely delivered of a son. He was a large, pale, healthy baby, though he did not cry loud enough to content his grandfather, who wished the whole castle to be continually aware that another generation of Redvers had come into residence. Young Baldwin was delighted at this proof of his manhood; he visited his wife as soon as she was well enough to receive him, offering her the pick of the Plympton stable as a reward for her achievement. Margaret was feeling as though she would never ride again, but the gift pleased her. It showed that in future she would be allowed to lead her own life, though of course she must provide as many spare replacements for the heir as the family thought prudent. She lay back in the great bed, surveying the clean, pleasant bower and sniffing the herbs which burned to perfume the air; at the age of fourteen years and one month she had accomplished her duty; the rest of her life stretched before her, in which she was already mistress of a great castle and soon to be a mighty Countess. No one now would mind her going to court, when the war was ended and the court was gay.

The baby was baptized in the castle chapel, and named Baldwin after his father. He was known, naturally, as little Baldwin, since there was already a young Baldwin. During the short absence which made him a Christian Margaret fretted, and clutched fiercely when he was returned to her. It surprised her to discover that she loved him so earnestly. She was still indifferent to his father, and to everyone else at Plympton, and though Madam Alice had warned her that every mother is ridiculously attached to her first-born, she had found it hard to believe that the awkward encumbrance in her belly would be lovable when at last it emerged.

In the middle of August she left her bed and began to spend her days in the stable, since she was still too weak for riding. Little Baldwin came with her everywhere; he was swaddled tightly, that his limbs might grow strong, so it was easy for a waiting-lady to carry him. Margaret was determined that any son of hers must grow up a gallant knight, and privately she blamed much of her husband's lack of vigor on the too great care that had been taken of his health; a baby who would spend his adult life in the saddle should get to know horses as soon as possible. While she suckled him she talked to the head groom, or to one of the household knights, of famous feats of arms; first impressions are important, and he must be reared in an atmosphere of chivalry and courage.

That meant, regrettably, that he must be kept away from his father. But young Baldwin did not seem to care.

During the summer his destrier had slipped, galloping on wet grass; that had given him a nasty fall, and ever since he had been coughing worse than before, sometimes bringing up blood. He was content to sit for hours in a window of the hall, turning the pages of an illuminated psalter. He liked to be alone, and none were anxious to disturb his solitude. He seemed unnaturally weak and lazy, but Master Julian said it was only the damp humor of summer that had got into his body while he lay helpless under his fallen horse; the brisk cold of autumn would restore his vigor.

Then one morning, late in August, young Baldwin refused to get up. Margaret went back to sleep with the other ladies in the bower, and her husband was moved to the tower chamber, where he lay coughing all day. But his mind seemed to grow wakeful as his body weakened, and he liked Margaret to sit beside him and talk to him. He was full of plans about what he would do when he was Count, and chattered incessantly about his son's education. He had made up his mind to join the King's army as soon as he felt better, which would be in the winter; Master Julian had said it, and all Plympton believed Master Julian.

Since young Baldwin was so certain that the King had the right of it, Margaret naturally began to incline toward the rebels. Her father and her father-in-law were royalists, and what had they gained by it? Indeed her brother-in-law, through misguided loyalty, had lost his castles. It was universally admitted that the King was not a courteous gentleman. But the lord Louis of France was a gallant knight, and his followers gay young nobles; for new fashions from Provence, the center of courtesy, often reached Paris before they came to England. The rebels had driven King John from Winchester to Corfe, which proved they would win in the end; though most of them continued to live comfortably in London. In England it was a new idea that gentlemen should lodge together behind the walls of a town, though in Italy and Provence they had done it for years; traveling jongleurs related that London was now as gay as Naples. It would be a great pity if a new form of social life grew up in the southeast while the Lady Margaret de Redvers was prevented by the silly prejudice of her elders from taking her rightful place in it.

On the 1st of September the ladies in the bower began to stir half an hour before dawn; the days were already growing shorter, and all were eager to make the most of what summer remained. Margaret was in her shift, choosing by the light of a candle the cotte she would wear for the day's lounging in the sunshine, when there was a thunderous knocking on the bolted door. Some of her ladies were already dressed, and she sent Madam Alice to open while she wrapped herself in a cloak for decency. It might be a message from the stable, though it sounded too urgent for that; or it might be news that the war was coming to these parts, which would be nothing but a cause of interest and excitement to a lady who did not care which side would win.

As the door opened Count William burst in. He looked haggard and much older; his gray hair was tousled, and he wore only a fur cloak, fleece-lined slippers showing below bare legs. "Madam," he called as soon as he had recovered his breath, "you are a widow. When they came to rouse him the lord Baldwin was dead. His blankets are bloody, but we can find no wound; it seems that he bled from the mouth, and so died. The page who sleeps by his door heard nothing. I have ordered that the rogue be flogged, but there may have been nothing to hear. Master Julian has disappeared. He must have heard the news early, and climbed down into the castle ditch. When I catch him I shall hang him by his thumbs until he dies, and thus save others from his blunders. But my son is dead, and vengeance will not bring him back."

Margaret's thoughts were racing. The death of an intimate acquaintance is always a shock, for it emphasizes the brevity of life. But she felt no sorrow for the husband who had never been her friend; her only conscious desire was to end this painful scene and get properly dressed. Yet it would never do if the old Count saw she was indifferent. What was the most appropriate utterance for a young widow in the first shock of her sorrow? There were rules for correct behavior on every conceivable occasion, and she had learned them thoroughly in childhood; if only she could call them to mind at this moment.

"My lord," she said, with a slow, pained smile, blinking hard in the hope of summoning a tear, "all must die and face the Judgment. Young Baldwin was a good man, and a good Christian; we may be confident of his salvation. But even the best of kind husbands can be helped by the prayers of the living. Give me leave to dress myself in fitting mourning, and then I shall join you in the chapel. Have you informed the monks of Glastonbury? We are benefactors of their house; they owe us their prayers and a tomb near the high altar. Hark, the little orphan grieves for his father. Before I mourn I must comfort him."

Little Baldwin was, in fact, howling at the top of his lungs, upset, like any other baby, by a disturbance of routine. All the ladies were wailing, some with grief, others as an expression of good manners while they continued to comb their hair or searched for mourning cloaks. Before this concerted feminine sorrow the old Count quailed; he crossed himself and withdrew.

[52]

Later, as she sat beside her father-in-law in the chapel, listening to the first hasty requiem over the thin, young corpse, Margaret was chiefly aware that she had missed her breakfast, and that no preparations were being made for dinner. But there were more important matters to consider. She was completely in the hands of her father-in-law; what would he do with her? He might send her back to her father, or order her into a nunnery. Luckily the Church would not permit him to marry her to some other relative of the Redvers kin; though that would be the easiest way of keeping her dowry in the family. On one thing she had made up her mind; she would not willingly return to her lonely life at Stogursey. But they would never dare to send her there; the baby, now direct heir to his grandfather, must be guarded carefully. She would suffer a year of dull and monotonous mourning, and then she would probably be shut in some strong castle until little Baldwin was old enough to leave her. Oh, it was maddening to be a mere woman, while all the time her mind was as active and interested as any man's! Just because she bore a child she was debarred from arranging what would become of him, or even of herself. Well, first she must think of a good plan, and then she must persuade the old Count to carry it out. Luckily his manners were courteous, and he would not go out of his way to give orders to a lady, just to prove he was the stronger. But until she had eaten she could not even think of a plan. Poor Baldwin! He might have been much more tiresome than she was, and now he would never bother her again. Since she was stuck on her knees in this chapel she might as well say her prayers with her whole mind. "Eternal rest grant unto him, O Lord, and let perpetual light shine upon him." That perpetual light would suit the quiet and studious boy; he could look at his books forever and ever. . . .

By evening the local cooper had knocked together a temporary coffin, and the body was removed to the crypt of the chapel. Eventually it would be wrapped in lead and taken to Glastonbury for a ceremonious funeral. Meanwhile the mourners might relax to eat a scrambled and badly served supper. Margaret drank a good deal of ale; she was already tired and sleepy, but it was a wise precaution against the nightmare. She was annoyed when after the meal Count William summoned her to his solar. It was a compliment, of course; she had very seldom been there before and it proved that she now took her husband's place as second in precedence in the household; but what she wanted was bed.

The Count's first words, however, brought her completely awake. "Do you realize who you are now, little Margaret?" he began. "You are the Lady of Plympton, very nearly as important as if you were my daughter and heiress. Until little Baldwin comes of age you will represent him. I shall not be much longer on this earth. Master Julian warned me, and I think he told the truth; though he was mistaken about my son, and I should like to question him with red-hot pincers. By the way, he can't be found, and with this war raging round us we shall never catch up with him. Let us forget him, and return to the affairs of Redvers. When I die little Baldwin must inherit Plympton; in other words, for the next twenty years you will hold it. Or rather, your second husband, whoever he may be, will hold it for his stepson. And since it is held as a fief of the crown the King may make your marriage. You are at the mercy of King John, and his mercy is not tender to the great and noble. The best thing is to forestall him. Will you marry

[54]

one of my knights, tomorrow; or would you rather go into hiding?"

"Oh dear, I don't want another husband, if it can be avoided," said Margaret wearily. "I would like to live as a widow, devoting all my time to little Baldwin." It was true that she looked forward to the independence of widowhood; the second clause came almost without conscious thought, because she was so accustomed to saying the proper thing to old Count William.

"While I live you might remain a widow, under my protection. But as soon as your infant son holds land you must have a husband to guard it for him. It would be my duty to arrange that, even if the King neglected it."

Margaret suddenly saw her way clear before her. She had been pining for the delights of London, and she knew that she could convince her father-in-law of anything if she tried really hard.

"My lord," she said, with her most winning expression, "the King of England has my marriage, as overlord of the fief. But we are looking to the future, and it is possible that John fitzHenry will not be King much longer. If he marries me to one of his followers whose lands are escheated by Louis of France, Plympton may be lost at the same time. Remember the hermit of Pontefract who prophesied that John would lose his crown within the year; that was more than a year ago, and it hasn't happened yet; but he may have been mistaken only in the date. Windsor is hard pressed, and after its fall the rebels may sweep westward unhindered. You hold Plympton for King John, so you may be compelled to yield it. But if I went to London, taking my son with me, we would have a foot in each camp. The lord Louis might permit me to remain a widow, provided he holds little Baldwin as hostage for your loyalty. Even if

[55]

he marries me to one of his knights it will be a forced marriage in time of war, and when peace comes I can get it annulled for lack of my free consent. Let me ride to London, at once."

It was a startling and novel proposal. Count William must think it over for some time, to get accustomed to it; but the longer he thought the sounder it seemed. He was old-fashioned, and he had taken it for granted that if what you wanted was to keep what you already held, loyalty to the reigning King was the safest policy. No one had suffered for being loyal to the Old King, even when his rebellious sons chased him to his death through the woods of Maine. Rebellion was a game of double or quits which held no attraction for a wealthy magnate. But if Louis of France became King of England even his ancestral castle of Plympton might be escheated.

He could send a letter to King John, explaining that Margaret had fled secretly without his consent; the King would not believe him, but he would not attack the castle of an ostensibly loyal Count and so drive him into joining the rebel party. William de Redvers had always intended, one day, to make his weight felt by threatening to change sides. In sending his infant heir to London he was making a demonstration that should bring him valuable offers from the weaker, Angevin, cause.

Eventually he agreed to Margaret's proposal, for one reason because at that moment the expedition seemed safe and easy. The King lay at Corfe, and all the open country eastward had been abandoned to the rebels; Margaret and little Baldwin could travel to Glastonbury with the funeral cortege, and then slip over the Cotswolds into the Thames valley. Somewhere near Oxford they ought to get into

[56]

touch with French knights, and then they would be safe. It was decided that they should start, with the coffin, on the very next morning. Haste was essential, for it was rumored that the King might march east, and she must not encounter his army.

4: The King's Court

 ON THE 15th of September, when she had been a
widow for exactly a fortnight, Margaret was near-
ing that King's Court which had been the subject
of so many of her maiden dreams. But she had never
dreamed of such an arrival. She still rode her well-paced
hackney, but her hands lay empty on her lap and a grim-
looking mounted crossbowman led the beast. On the other
side rode Madam Alice, holding the baby very carefully; her
horse was also led by a mounted sergeant, which meant riding four abreast, an awkward scramble where bushes had en-
croached on the ancient road; there had been plenty of
room while they followed Ermine Street, but at Wimpole
they had turned off eastward, and the ordinary traffic to Cambridge and the Fens was not enough to keep the way wide
and clear. But though it made traveling awkward the Bra-
bançon ruffian in knightly mail who commanded the party

[58]

had soon learned that the lady would not follow quietly unless she could see her baby all the time.

King John had upset everyone's calculations by suddenly beginning to fight like an Angevin. As Margaret rode out from Glastonbury he was sweeping down the valley of the Thames like a whirlwind. As far as Reading she followed in the wake of his army, traveling by by-lanes and concealing that her destination was rebel London. Then she learned that the King had swerved to the northeast, though Windsor, still flying the Leopards of Anjou, closed the direct road to London and safety; Margaret also turned northward, following a rumor that the rebels had put a garrison into St. Albans. But that brought her into greater danger; the open country for twenty miles around London was infested by plundering bands of mercenaries. Two days ago, as her little party descended the slopes of Chiltern, a group of horsemen galloped around a hanger and ordered them to halt.

It might have been worse. These mounted crossbowmen were trained professional soldiers who obeyed the commands of their leader; no one was killed, though her escort suffered rough treatment before they were turned adrift in their shirts, their weapons, mail, and horses the legitimate prize of their captors. Her baggage and jewels went the same way, but when a soldier suggested that they should each in turn rape the young woman before giving her a suit of tar and feathers, the commander called them to attention and reminded them that they were fighting a civil war, in which public opinion must be respected. He inquired quite civilly whither the lady was bound, and Margaret realized, with a sudden shock of disgust, that so far these men had no reason to suppose she was a supporter of Louis of France; they were treating her as helpless travelers were always treated by troops in the field.

Madam Alice spoke up at once, explaining who they were and adding that they were on their way to seek the protection of the King; of course, that was the only thing to say, and it had saved them from further insult. But the commander, who introduced himself as Sir Reginald Croc, a knight bachelor of Brabant at present in the service of the lord Falkes de Brealte, told them firmly that his band would escort them to Cambridge, where the court lay at present. He added that it would be necessary to lead their horses, to protect them from the rebel and French mercenaries who roamed over Chiltern. It was a decently polite way of taking them captive, and later this Reginald assumed a courteous manner; he might really be a knight who had sunk in the social scale by mixing perpetually with mercenary ruffians.

There was nothing to do but make the best of it. For two days they rode together without incident, through a country of empty barns and deserted villages. Though the peasants had not been killed, they could be seen watching the horsemen from the edge of thick woods, and some of their children, too young to know better, even attempted to beg from these jingling, well-nourished travelers. Reginald explained that his troop had been sent to collect the harvest of Hertfordshire, a district considered loyal to the King; his soldiers, therefore, had done it no harm according to his lights. They had merely taken everything of value.

Now they were approaching Cambridge, their pace hindered by the herd of cattle they had swept up in their foraging; every beast bore a sack of grain on its back, and there were ox-wagons as well. But much corn had been burned in the stack, for lack of transport; as Reginald explained, that at least made certain that Louis of France would never get it.

Margaret saw she had been wrong to hope the war would come nearer to Plympton; that might have relieved her tedium, but soldiers conducted their affairs in a very wasteful and disorderly fashion.

She knew, as she sat slackly in the saddle, gazing toward the shimmer in the sky that marked the beginning of the Fens, that she ought to be much more worried and distressed than in fact she felt. She was the helpless captive of a band of scoundrels who could do with her as they would; they were taking her to King John, the lecher in whose hall no virtuous woman was safe, the cruel tyrant who had inflicted on Matilda de Braoze such a ghastly fate. If he commanded that she be shut up to die of hunger and thirst in a dungeon, like that unhappy lady, she would have no hope of rescue. There was no reason why he should shut her up; but he might very well treat her as a hostage, and torture her to make old Count William join his army.

But Margaret was always interested in meeting new specimens of the human race, and she found her companions so absorbing that there was no room in her mind for fear. She had never before encountered professional soldiers, though of course she had heard from the jongleurs that they were uncouth savages, beneath the attention of a lady of gentle birth. It was surprising to discover that they were craftsmen, following their intricate trade as carefully as any carpenter or wheelwright. Crossbows were complicated weapons, built up of numerous little bits of horn, sinew and wood; the sergeants at Plympton always kept theirs stacked in the middle of the guardroom, well away from any rain that might drive in through the window-slits. When these men had ridden through a shower they at once

[61]

dismounted, built fires, and took their bows to pieces to dry them; it was fascinating to see their blunt, scarred fingers fitting the little pieces together. The thorough inspection of every horse each morning, and the careful poring over any suspected sore back, appealed to her tidy mind; most of the sergeants owned more than one horse, the spares being ridden by young grooms, but every animal was looked after as carefully as if it was the only specimen of its race, just landed from the Ark of Noah. Scouts made good every coppice and fold in the ground before the main body, with its valuable convoy, was permitted to pass the scene of a possible ambush, which meant very slow marching; they made up for it by starting early and continuing late, so that in fact they got over a great deal of ground. But she felt that chivalrous knights, at least any of the knights she had met, would have chanced riding past unscouted cover for the sake of an early dinner.

They had not really treated her badly. At first there had been the terrible danger of rape, which was not only unpleasant in itself, but rendered any woman who had suffered it an outcast for life; a woman who lost her chastity lost her value as a potential wife, and no man would bother to support her. But after he had learned who she was Reginald Croc guarded her carefully. If she was unharmed she must carry the County of Devon to her next husband, and that meant he was bringing to the King a large and valuable fief.

Of course, this was only true while she was the mother of the infant heir; little Baldwin was also extremely valuable, and the soldiers took as much trouble over his welfare as did Madam Alice or herself. On this dangerous raid in the enemy's land they had brought no women, but most of them had concubines with the main army at Cambridge;

[62]

they knew roughly the sort of things women demanded for very young children, and there was never any difficulty about getting him plenty of milk, a warm place to sleep, and hot water for his bath. In fact, she consoled herself, no harm had really come to her, except the plundering of her baggage; and in a civil war that might happen to anybody.

She had suffered one other shock, though she had not been deeply affected. She had, of course, inquired whether her father was with the King, and had been annoyed to discover that these soldiers, who thought only of war, had never heard of the King's Chamberlain. At last Reginald Croc (she could not think of him as Sir Reginald, though she was careful to give him the title when she addressed him) had recalled that a lord Warin fitzSombody had been wounded outside Reading, and carried to the abbey to die. So she was fatherless, as well as widowed. During her childhood she had seldom seen her father, and after her marriage he had gone right out of her life; he was almost a stranger. She prayed for his soul, resolving to order Masses as soon as she got hold of some money; but what impressed her most deeply was not the loss of a parent, but the knowledge that half the lands of fitzGerold were now hers. Even while old Count William lived she was the rightful holder of a considerable barony.

She had never before seen a countryside like the flat East Anglian plain, and as she rode she gazed about with interest. Madam Alice must be shocked at her cheerfulness, but the soldiers liked it; Margaret seldom found it difficult to please public opinion, and the public opinion she now wished to please was that of King John's army.

Presently she saw, rising above the plain, a square pile of masonry; evidently an old-fashioned castle, all in one block, with no separate stone bailey. Before it lay a huddle of mean thatched roofs, and she was puzzled by a number of poles sticking above the horizon to the right. The sergeant beside her explained that Cambridge was chiefly a great bridge over a river which flowed into the Fen; the castle protected the bridge and the poles were the masts of ships anchored at the head of navigation. On the northern horizon billowing clouds of smoke climbed the sky. "Our captain, the lord Falkes de Brealte, set out to reap the harvest of Ely while we rode to Chiltern," said her conductor, with a chuckle. "It looks as though the monks were stingy."

As they drew nearer the bitter smell of burning thatch was carried on the wind, mixed with a sweet, sickly stench. Reginald remarked on it. "You never met that smell on Chiltern, madam," he said cheerfully. "The country was friendly and we had orders to do no harm. But a bishop and chapter who resist the lawful tallage of the King must expect to smell corpses after the captain of the King's crossbows has paid them a visit."

Margaret did not reply. She could not decide whether these men were deliberately trying to frighten her, or whether they were genuinely indifferent to the destruction and massacre of war. They were not fit companions for a lady, but that would soon be put right; whether or not the King was pleased to see her, he would not leave her in the company of hired soldiers.

At last, after crossing a great ditch, they entered the squalid and overcrowded village. Flaunting women pressed close to the horses, calling inquiries about plunder and abuse of the empty-handed; to judge by the crowd, every able-bodied soldier had a great many mouths to feed.

As they pushed through the throng Margaret tucked a

wisp of loose hair under her kerchief and smoothed her riding-cotte, whose ample skirts covered her legs to the ankle as she sat astride her horse; soon she might be in the presence of the King, and she wished to make a good impression. But now there was a pause; for the first time these trained efficient soldiers seemed uncertain what to do next; the plundered beasts were led aside to the walled courtyard of an inn, while Reginald remained halted in the roadway. Looking earnestly at Margaret as he spoke, as though half to himself: "You are really the widow of young Redvers, and that baby is heir to Plympton and Carisbrooke? It may be true. You are obviously a lady born, and that useless escort of yours spoke like Devon men. No young lady would say she was a widow if she had a husband to protect her. Now what shall I do with you?"

As Madam Alice glanced up with an expression of terror Margaret understood what was passing through his mind. "You are quite right, Sir Reginald," she said firmly. "If you marry me you will hold the Honor of Redvers as guardian of my son, and you are forgetting my share of the Honor of fitzGerold, if it's true that the lord Warin, my father, died in Reading. Your plan has only two drawbacks. Without my free consent the marriage will not be valid; any bishop would annul it as soon as he heard my appeal. And I would quickly be widowed for the second time. When the King learns that one of his mercenary captains has found a great County by the roadside, and stolen it for himself, he will order a suitable punishment. I believe he favors killing his enemies by starvation, to avert the pollution of bloodshed. You look as though you enjoy your food. Shall we ride on to the castle?"

Croc laughed, shrugging his shoulders. "Ride on, madam," he said cheerfully. "Such a prize tempted me, but

[65]

of course you are right. I might seize it, but I could not keep it."

Leaving the band to store their booty Reginald led the two ladies over the famous Bridge. There was a private discussion with the seedy knight who commanded the outer gate of the castle; Margaret could not overhear it, but in the end she was admitted to the bailey, assisted, quite politely, to dismount, and taken up a narrow stair to a little chamber under the roof of the keep. This chamber was contrived in the thickness of the wall, as in most old-fashioned castles; but it was lit by a narrow window, and contained a pitcher of water for washing, a truckle bed, and a garderobe. A clumsy peasant girl brought wine, good wheaten bread and rather rancid salt beef, before the door was bolted on the outside, best of all, little Baldwin and Madam Alice were shut in with her. Margaret was still a prisoner, but she understood that her present captor took some thought for her comfort.

After they had washed and eaten Margaret sat on the hutch at the bed end to feed little Baldwin. Alice gazed through the window toward devastated Ely, where as darkness gathered the glow of burning roofs pricked through the black smoke. They had heard the awkward servant stumbling down the stair, and for the first time since their capture they could talk in private without being overheard.

"Well, my lady," Alice said briskly, "the King has the marriage of the widow of a tenant-in-chief. Even if you had never left Plympton he could have sent down another husband. And since we are in the middle of a doubtful civil war he will find you some decent gentleman, so as not to offend Count William. Your virtue is unharmed, and you are very valuable. Things might be worse."

"Young Baldwin held no land, so I am not the widow

of a tenant-in-chief," Margaret answered. "Still, that's only a quibble. No King keeps the letter of the law unless it's in his favor. But I'm not quite so helpless as you think, my dear Alice. Remember what I said to Reginald Croc; unless I give my free consent my next marriage will be invalid."

"For the love of God, my lady, you will not defy the King in his own strong castle?" cried Alice in great agitation. "Remember how he treated Matilda de Braoze, and what he did to Count Arthur, his own nephew. If you won't do what they ask they have only to kill you; then little Baldwin is in the King's wardship until he grows up. That might be easier for them, anyway. Don't do anything to make them consider it."

"Do you take me for a fool? I never defy those who can hurt me. Why do you think I married young Baldwin in the first place? Of course I shall give my consent when the priest asks me. But while I am held prisoner it cannot be my *free* consent, can it? Plenty of marriages have been annulled because the bride was forced to say Yes when she meant No. If the lord Louis wins, which is what most people expect, he will help me to get free from a leader of the losing side; even if the King wins I can take refuge with any bishop, who will be bound in honor to protect me while the case is argued before the Curia. Don't you see, darling Alice? I have a choice that comes to very few women. I can take my next husband on trial, free to break the marriage if I dislike it."

"That's as may be," grumbled Alice, disappointed that her young mistress was not displaying the emotion proper to a tragic heroine of romance. "God has laid down good laws for His Church, but ladies who carry title to great Honors don't always get their full legal rights. And in the meantime you must submit to the embraces of the knight the King chooses for you. I hope he won't be too revolting."

"Oh, embraces, and that sort of thing? They don't bother me," said Margaret gaily, not because it was entirely true, but because once she was embarked on an argument she liked to win it. "A lusty old debauchee would make a change after the half-hearted fumblings of young Baldwin. But I hear footsteps on the stair. In a minute we shall know the worst."

While the door was unbolted, with great creakings and clangings as if to emphasize that she was indeed a captive, Margaret laid her son on the bed, nervously straightening her cotte. A blaze of torches filled the narow doorway, and she knew that the short, stout, dark-bearded man who entered first must be the King. She sank gracefully to her knees, and rose again without waiting for permission, as was the right of the widow of a magnate; a Chamberlain's daughter was familiar with the etiquette, even if she had never before visited the court.

King John, on the other hand, was notorious for his lack of manners; first he stared without speaking, then motioned to a page to hold his torch closer. At last he grunted, and called over his shoulder to someone outside the door: "All right, she is truly Warin fitzGerold's daughter. That's his forehead, and his sulky expression." Then he looked in her eyes, frowning. "Well, my girl," he said, "you are an unprotected widow, seeking help from your liege lord; or at least that is what we shall put down in the records, though it's my private opinion you were on your way to London when Croc and his cutthroats caught you. You must have a husband to guard your infant son, and you've come to the right place to find one. I shall send him up in an hour of so, when I have chosen the lucky man.

[68]

You look him over, and then give your formal consent. Tomorrow you can be married by my chaplain, in my presence. That's honor enough to content the kin of Redvers. You shall celebrate your wedding-feast in my hall; but until you are safely tied to your new master you must remain in this elegant chamber. I'll send you more wine, and some facepaint. Your husband will be marrying Plympton and Carisbrooke, but you will live easier if he admires your appearance also. So do what you can to look pleasant, and remember to smile. Good night."

As the door closed Margaret broke into sobs of injured pride. It was humiliating to be inspected in this casual way, and then dismissed from the royal consideration. If the King had ordered her to share his bed, as he did to many unprotected ladies, that would have been very distressing, but not so contemptuous.

Presently the serving-maid unbarred the door, to bring in a jack of wine and a tray of little pots. Margaret observed that the sullen girl was herself extravagantly and incompetently painted; she must be the current royal concubine. It was a common reproach that the King preferred low company, and was uneasy in the presence of the gentry; for once that was a good thing, if it saved the honor of fitzGerold.

It was now the turn of Madam Alice to be brisk and cheerful. "Then it's marriage," she said with relief, "not rape, or even imprisonment. Louis would have found you a husband if you had got into London, so you are really no worse off. They call the King cruel, but he seems only very busy and rather offhand in his manner. At your age you can do without paint. Just drink a cup of wine to make your cheeks glow, and then I shall comb your hair. What we

[69]

really need is clean linen, but that is a thing men never think of."

The boisterous din of the King's men came up from two floors below them; there would be great scope for indelicate jokes, and the chosen husband would probably drink deeply to bolster his courage for an awkward interview; for the next hour or so nothing would happen.

After putting little Baldwin to sleep Margaret sat down on the hutch to recover her composure. This was really just as exciting as arrival at Plympton in a bridal litter; a new life was about to begin, and as widow of Redvers she was now more important than at her first marriage; the King must in ordinary common sense choose a very great lord to receive such a very great dowry. The wine was excellent, better than she was used to at Plympton. This was not the ending she had planned for her journey, but it would do.

Then the bolts were withdrawn again, and with keen intensity she watched the opening door; in a moment she would see for the first time the man who would probably share the rest of her life (though there was always that chance of annulment in the background). First a page entered, bearing several horn lanterns, for the little chamber was now nearly dark. When he had arranged the lights about the room he stood stiffly by the door, announcing in a formal voice: "The lord Falkes de Brealte, castellan and sheriff, waits on the lady Margaret fitzGerold de Redvers."

The man who hustled in with quick eager strides was short, but he was also thin and straight and in the prime of life; he was dressed in a magnificent silk surcoat, with a silk capuchon lying on his shoulders; but below the gown appeared the grubby padded chausses horsemen wore under their mail. His dark hair and beard were clipped short, and the helm had rubbed a little bald patch on his crown; that was not so smart as flowing locks, but what remained was combed, and as clean as his newly scrubbed face. Margaret looked quickly at his hands. The nails were broken and the fingers calloused; but they also were clean, and very much whiter than his weather-beaten face. That was the mark of a warrior who rode always in gauntlets. On the whole his neat and business-like appearance made a refreshing contrast with the bucolic finery of the provincial knights at Plympton. He halted abruptly before her and bowed. His face was set sternly, but it seemed, from the wrinkles at the corners of his eyes, that his normal expression would be more cheerful.

"That lout announced me incorrectly," were his first words. "I'll tan his hide for him when I have time. Madam, I am one of the King's seneschals, sheriff of Oxford, Buckingham, Bedford, Hertford, Northampton, and Cambridge, castellan of Wenlock and Windsor, captain of the King's crossbows, Falkes de Brealte at your service." He bowed again.

"I would ask you to be seated, Sir Falkes, if the King had remembered to provide me with a stool. Since I am unwilling to share this narrow hutch with a stranger it would be better if I stood also. I am charmed that such a noble visitor should relieve the tedium of my captivity. But I believe this is more than a corporal work of mercy. King John, my liege lord, has the right to make my marriage, and I suppose he has decided that I am to be married to you."

"That is so, madam," Falkes answered unsmiling. "I come to get your free consent to our wedding tomorrow. Or, of course, if you do not consent I shall carry your refusal to the King."

[71]

"And then what would happen?"

"The King has not informed me, madam. Tomorrow I must ride, and I would not witness the result of his displeasure. As it happens, I have seldom been present when the King has punished defiant vassals; Margaret de Braoze died before I was appointed castellan of Windsor, and Count Arthur was alive and well when I left Rouen for the last time."

"Two very neat reminders. But then you have been planning this interview all through supper, while I had no idea of the kind of gentleman I would have to deal with. So it's not really fair. Let us assume that in the end I shall say Yes. Even then, this is a very short wooing. Delicacy demands that I know a little more about you before I fall into your arms. You seem to hold a great many castles, and I remember that one clause of that ridiculous Charter banished you from the realm; so you must be important. That's all I know. Could you tell me a little more, about your family, for example?"

Falkes swallowed awkwardly, as though feeling shy.

"Of course, madam, if my descent had been one of my qualifications for this marriage I would have mentioned it at the outset," he said stiffly, his face sterner than ever. "You may have heard various stories concerning my origin, since I am now famous. But the truth is that my father was a country knight, living obscurely on his manor of Brealte in Normandy; I should add that he never married my mother, a peasant girl who was for a short time his concubine. But he acknowledged me, and brought me up with his legitimate sons. My parents are dead, killed by the invading French. But I am free-born, and the King has knighted me with his own sword. Even the noblest families must have a beginning, and you and I, madam, may found a very noble one."

"This is disparagement," put in Madam Alice, who stood a pace behind her mistress; for an unmarried lady should never be left alone with a man. "Even the King cannot force fitzGerold to mate with the bastard of a peasant girl."

"Be quiet, Alice. No one seeks you in marriage. This is a matter for me to decide." Margaret's tone was harsh, and the waiting-lady pursed her lips.

"But you are not the husband I expected, Sir Falkes," Margaret continued. "At supper there must have been many companions of the King. Were they not surprised at my liege lord's choice of a new master for Plympton and me?"

"They were envious, naturally; but not really surprised. We King's men hold that the King's favor alone suffices to make a man great. That squares well enough with this new-fangled chivalrous nonsense. In France they maintain that knighthood is the only thing that matters, and thus the poorest knight is socially equal to a Count. I don't agree with all their new ideas; I am a warrior, not a jouster. But that would answer the Marshal, or any other magnate who takes chivalry seriously."

"I see. Of course everyone must admit that the King's sword has made you a knight, Sir Falkes. By the way, is your name a peculiarity of your family? I have met many Fulks, but no one who pronounces it in quite that fashion."

"I was baptized Fulk, madam, and Falkes is a nickname. Where I come from it is the peasants' word for 'scythe.' As a lad I was cutting hay in the meadow (I told you we were simple country folk) when a mailed knight rode up and demanded my father's only destrier to replace

[73]

his own lame horse. My father was away, so I took charge. One thing led to another, and in the end I hit the knight with my scythe and killed him. I have been called Falkes ever since."

Margaret was impressed. She knew, from countless recitations of the jongleurs, that even a trained warrior was considered helpless without his mail. This man had not even been trained to arms, or he would not have been helping with the harvest; yet in his shirt he had fought and defeated a mailed knight. He might be a stern master (though so far his manners were not really bad, only too business-like for such an occasion), but he would be a competent protector.

"Your name is honorable, Sir Falkes. You are entitled to bear it proudly. There need be no further discussion. The King has ordered me to marry you, and here in his castle I must obey his commands. When the priest asks me I shall give my consent. There is one further point to be cleared up, though I am sure it will cause no difficulty. My son, on the bed over there, is heir to Redvers. You must support him in a style worthy of his station in life. Will you promise me, on your knightly honor, to treat him well?"

"Certainly I promise. I should be a fool to do otherwise, as I am sure you understand. While I am his guardian I hold Plympton; if harm came to him the whole Honor would go to some Redvers cousin. He is valuable to me, and I shall cherish him."

"I am grateful, sir. I am the more grateful that you have spared me the conventional protestations of a lover. To guard my land I need a brave husband, you seek a rich wife. We seem well suited."

Falkes relaxed; he had been standing stiffly, like a royal doorkeeper at a ceremonial feast; but now his shoulders

[74]

bent and a rather naughty smile played over his features. "We shall soon know whether we are really well suited. But you're a handsome young woman, and I've pleased the ladies before this. There's no reason why we should not be good friends. Now I beg leave to withdraw. The wedding is fixed for the King's morning Mass at daybreak, so we must be ready early."

He bolted the door on the outside, which weakened the atmosphere of friendly cooperation he was obviously trying to achieve. But Margaret, preparing for bed, was not too dissatisfied. The husband chosen for her was certainly not a gentleman, but in daily life he might prove an amusing companion.

In the very early morning the door was once more unbarred, and a page brought a breakfast of bread and wine; by this Margaret knew her marriage was not to be the full Nuptial Mass, for which the bride must fast. Yet she knew also that matrimony, like any other sacrament, should be received in a state of grace; she hoped for an opportunity to make her confession before she went to the chapel. Then two clerks came to see if she was ready. The younger, who seemed to be in charge, was a bustling, vulgar little Norman; but even vulgar Normans did not grate on her like vulgar Englishmen, for the French they spoke was smooth and correct.

"Good morning, madam," he said cheerfully, rubbing his hands. "I am Robert Passelewe, subdeacon, steward to the lord Falkes. This is Father Richard March, priest, of the King's Wardrobe, who will perform the marriage. If you go into that garderobe he will hear your confession. Then we should be on our way to the chapel."

This was a good sign. Her husband had a steward who

knew what ought to be done, which showed that he lived like a civilized gentleman.

The chapel of Cambridge castle was part of the main keep, only separated from the hall by an archway draped with leather curtains. When they arrived it was very crowded, for every official of the royal household used this daily ceremony as a kind of meeting in chambers where the work of the day might be arranged and discussed. Falkes, in full mail, stood by the altar; she noticed that all the other warriors were armed, and the clerks dressed for riding; evidently the court was prepared to move.

For not more than five minutes she knelt beside her husband; the ceremony was very brief, and hardly anyone paid attention; though the buzz of talk was stilled for a moment when the direct question was put to her, so that all present might in future bear witness that they had heard her say Yes. The low Mass began immediately after, the married pair standing in the front row of the congregation. Just before the Offertory, at the last moment which made it technically possible for him to say he had heard Mass that day, the King entered. He also wore mail, which made him look disgustingly potbellied. But perhaps that was not his normal condition, for evidently he was suffering from stomachache. Recognizing Margaret, he winked at her cheerfully; he chose the moment of the Elevation to do it, as though to emphasize his notorious contempt for all the forms of religion. Margaret herself was not especially devout, but on this occasion she tried to keep her thoughts free from distraction. She had an uneasy feeling that she might soon need all the luck she could get, and that it would be rash to go out of her way to annoy her Guardian Angel.

Then they all pushed through the curtain into the

great hall, and sat down at trestle tables for an early meal. Margaret felt her husband take her arm (she was too self-conscious to look at him), and submitted to his guidance. This was the first time in her life that she had dined at an ordinary table, instead of on the dais, and the hall looked odd seen from this lowly place in the middle. But she sank down where he placed her, and heard grace before she took food; though she had no choice over that piece of devotion, for the servants were some time in reaching her.

Dotted about the benches were a few women, including Madam Alice with the baby; but most of the company were male, for clerks have no wives and the warriors had left theirs at home before setting out on such a campaign. Some of these women looked very striking, but Margaret feared it might be dangerous to turn up her nose at anyone in this new environment. Perhaps great ladies of the court always painted their faces like that; it might be a new fashion that had not yet reached Plympton. When a high-colored young woman raised her horn to drink the health of the bride, shouting some catch phrase which made her neighbors giggle, Margaret gravely bowed in acknowledgment. Her husband was more exclusive. He turned to her with a frown:

"This is your first time at court, isn't it? Well, we all serve the King, and we all dine in his hall; but that's no reason why you should drink with Megotta, the common whore of every clerk in the Chancery. I sit in this lowly place because I am a paid soldier. I was once a sergeant doorkeeper; I've got beyond that, and before I die I shall be sitting at the high table among the magnates. In a gathering like this those who offer their friendship are those whose friendship is valueless. I know my way about, and I shall choose your intimates. I married you because you are a great lady, and the more haughtily you behave the better I'll be pleased."

Margaret felt snubbed, and in addition she despised Falkes for his snobbery. When he frankly avowed his mean birth she had been impressed, because then he seemed genuinely indifferent to social distinctions; but perhaps he had only told her the truth because otherwise she would learn it from someone else. After all, she knew very little about him. She concentrated on her food. After dinner they would ride, though no one had yet told her where; it might be a long time to supper.

But silence did not please her husband any more than her previous friendliness. "I don't mean that you shouldn't talk to me. In fact you may talk to any man, though you should assume until you hear to the contrary that every woman you meet at court is no better than she should be. Let's see, you have passed your life in the westcountry. What do you think of us?"

Here was an opportunity to impress Falkes with her good sense and insight; Margaret looked around carefully, thinking before she spoke. "Even at Plympton I heard that the King is a mighty warrior," she said carefully. "He looks all of that, especially in his mail. But surely it must be hard to find horses up to his weight?"

Falkes roared with laughter. "Next time I'm alone with the King I shall tell him how he strikes a stranger. It wouldn't do for the likes of me to tell him now, before all those gentlemen. As a matter of fact, that belly is a new arrival. He always ate enough for six, especially on fastdays, but hard riding used to keep it down. You are now my wife, and you must keep my secrets; so I'll tell you in confidence that his old comrades of the Normandy campaigns are worried about his health. He still rides and fights like the

[78]

Devil his grandfather, but no one would be surprised if he burst at any moment. If that happens Hell will be loose in England, but there will be plenty of work for good crossbowmen. Still, that's no subject to discuss in a crowd. Tell me your opinion of the court in general."

Margaret drew a deep breath, and replied at length. Ever since they sat down she had been trying to fix an elusive impression, and putting it into words made it clearer to her own mind. "My father was a courtier, and to me he seemed the most practical man I knew; though I didn't know him well. But he was a Chamberlain, which made him stuffy about etiquette and set in his ways. These people are quite different from anyone I have seen at Stogursey or Plympton. For one thing, they dress very splendidly, and yet you can see they don't care about their clothes, for they wear them so casually. They talk as though they were enjoying themselves, but obviously they are talking seriously and making important decisions. How friendly they are. Look at that great man on the dais, helping to pass the pheasant. Now old Count William never permits any of his knights to help the servants, because he says it's undignified. I wish I could explain. Everyone seems happy, and busy, and good-tempered in a careless way."

"They are, my dear. There's a war on, and that keeps everyone happy and busy. We know generally what must be done, and we all make arrangements to do it as easily as possible. By the way, this morning I ride for Lincoln, and I am sending you with Robert Passelewe to my castle of Bedford. We may fight a battle, and if we lose I must devote all my attention to running away, unhampered by ladies with infants in arms."

"Why run away, my lord? A soldier wins reputation

[79]

by fighting on until he is unhorsed and taken. The lands of fitzGerold could pay whatever ransom they asked for you."

It seemed wise to remind him at frequent intervals that his wife had brought him a great dowry.

"You've got it wrong, sweetheart. Knights fight until they are unhorsed; then they pay ransom and go home, while the jongleurs praise their courage. Soldiers run away, because no one will grant them quarter. If he caught me Louis of France would hang me, though I offered all Redvers and fitzGerold as ransom. In this hall we are mostly soldiers, and we fight like soldiers. That's why I think the King will beat the chivalrous French knights. But in half an hour I must be on the road for Lincoln; I'm sorry we must part without the really important business of marriage, but I'll join you in Bedford as soon as I can. Before we go, is there anything you want?"

"Anything I want? Why, everything," Margaret answered at once. She must set a proper value on herself, or this preoccupied husband would think of her only as a walking title-deed. "Your own men escorted me from Chiltern to Cambridge. They stole my furs and my jewels, and I have nothing but the clothes I am wearing now. Reginald Croc knows all about it; tell him to return my property."

"I can't do that. It was lawful plunder, and they would desert to Louis if I tried to take it from them. But you must have clothes, of course. I have no money; no one has money in wartime. But there must be weavers and tailors in Bedford. Passelewe will take you around the market there. He is escorting you, and I shall give him instructions. Order what you want, and have it sent to the castle. . . . Rise quickly, the King's on his feet. I'll see you one of these days. Oh, and don't forget you command my household;

[80]

report any sulky or disobedient servant and I'll flog him for you."

Everyone was hustling out of the hall. Margaret saw Passelewe pushing his way toward her, and turned to smile good-bye to her husband; but Falkes was already standing stiffly before the King, receiving his final orders for the march. He did not look back, and Passelewe, catching her eye, shrugged his shoulders; soldiers found war more absorbing than wives.

That was all the wedding feast she had, and it was five weeks before she saw her husband again.

5: *The Coronation*

AT Bedford she was lonely, and a little frightened; the castle was a very strong and modern fortress, with stone walls around both outer and inner baileys. It was manned by a small garrison of sergeants, though there were no knights; and the numerous servants were badly trained. In hall she sat on the dais with only Passelewe and Madam Alice for company; her consolation was to have plenty of time to visit little Baldwin.

Robert Passelewe was a subdeacon, vowed to celibacy. That would not have been sufficient to safeguard her reputation, since she was continually in his company; but he also kept concubines in the town. He was a little wisp of a man, all skin and bone and big brown eyes; but though physically unattractive he was an amusing talker, and could tell her many things about her husband.

They were all a new type to her, these clever, brave,

energetic men who were making a place for themselves in England by their own efforts. The knights she had met at Plympton were eager to increase their fiefs, certainly; but there preoccupation was to safeguard what had come to them from their fathers. Passelewe explained that he also was a bastard, born in the Norman village of Brealte in the same year as Falkes; his father had been the parish priest, which explained why he bore the name of Passe l'eau or Holy Water Sprinkler; the two children, socially a little above the common run of peasants, had naturally been close companions. Passelewe had witnessed the famous exploit with the scythe; earlier the tough little killer had protected his frail playmate from the bullying of village life. Then Falkes, famous in the countryside as the boy who had killed a knight, had gone off to be doorkeeper to the King, and Passelewe had begged and stolen his way through the University of Paris. When the French conquered Normandy the young clerk came to England, where his old friend was already prospering as castellan of Wenlock. That was ten tears ago, and they had been together ever since.

"Falkes has done everything for me," Passelewe repeated as they supped together one evening. "When that French *routier* Lupescar ruled Normandy honest Norman clerks were starving in every ditch; no jobs going unless you had served King Philip from the beginning. Since I reached Wenlock I've dined every day and slept under a roof every night. That means a lot to an exiled bastard with no influence behind him. But, in my turn, I have helped Falkes. You don't know your husband, madam, either socially or in the technical sense" (Margaret reflected with a sigh that these upstarts could never miss a lewd joke), "but when you know him you will love him as I do. All the

[83]

same, he owes his start in life to that lucky stroke with his scythe, and naturally his solution for every difficulty is a stroke of his sword. He needs legal advice. I keep him more or less within the bounds of the law; that isn't as difficult as it sounds. The law is tolerant to a loyal servant of the King."

"But are we ruling Bedford in a legal manner?" Margaret protested. "I know there's a war on, but can we just take what we want from the merchants, as you did when I needed clothes?"

"I think we can. At least if the King wins no one will bother us, and if he loses Falkes will be hanged anyway. English Law is very unlike the Code I learned in Paris, but that wonderful phrase '*in tempore gwerrae*,' in time of war, seems to cover any atrocity. Besides, we gave tallies which the merchants could redeem at the Exchequer if the Exchequer happened to be solvent. That's not quite the same as taking goods without payment, though perhaps it's not very different."

"It will make the merchants of Bedford keen supporters of the King. Only if he wins can they hope for payment."

"Exactly. For us everything depends on winning the war; while Louis will one day be King of France even if he loses. That's why I think we shall win."

"Falkes said as much, more or less, in the only talk I had with him. That was five weeks ago. It's odd to be married so long without sharing a bed."

"He'll come when he can spare the time. You need not fear that he will desert you. Plympton is a rich fief, and they say old Count William is failing."

That was not a tactful way of putting it, but in private Passelewe never bothered to be tactful. Margaret rather

[84]

liked that; he took her intelligence seriously, and talked as though she were his equal.

In fact she rather liked all her new companions, the tough sergeants and grooms who made up the garrison. They were alert and vital, always on their toes; they worked very hard, but they went cheerfully about it, and they always had a smile for the young wife of their lord. Sir Falkes was popular with his subordinates, which to her seemed a strange state of affairs; the sergeants at Plympton were loyal enough, but they took it for granted that every sensible man shirked all the duty he could shirk without punishment. This was a different atmosphere.

Presently Passelewe left her alone on the dais while he went, for the forth time that day, to inspect the sentries. Madam Alice was putting little Baldwin to bed in an upper chamber, where the ladies slept also. For once the hall was completely deserted, save for a single page dozing by the wine jug in case she called for more drink. In this household there was no needlework to occupy the ladies, thanks to Passelewe's labor-saving system of taking what he wanted from the burgesses. Margaret had a great deal of time to kill, and she passed it largely in musing over the new world she had entered.

On the whole she was enjoying herself. She lived in comfort, with very little to do. She might have been bored, but there was her baby, and when he was asleep she analyzed the characters of her companions. She was trying to make up her mind about them; certainly she did not dislike them, but she could not regard them as human beings; they all expected to be hanged if they were unlucky, and killed young in battle after a very good time if all went well. But, of course, whatever happened to *them* the lord Louis would not harm a fitzGerold who had been married

[85]

to a Redvers; and if it came to the worst she could explain that she had never consented to the forced marriage. She was above the struggle, and found it hard to sympathize with men whose dangers she did not share. She hoped they would win, but they were the kind of people who deserved to be hanged; all her upbringing told her that.

Suddenly a horn sounded in the outer bailey; all over the castle other horns took up the signal and the page left his wine jug, snatching sword and shield from the weapons hung on the wall.

"That's the general alarm, my lady," he called, as he ran out. "Keep away from the window. Crossbows can carry the outer wall."

Margaret was halfway up the stairs behind the dais, intent on reaching her baby before the fighting started, when she heard the unmistakable creak of the pulley which lowered the drawbridge. It was a familiar sound, for the bridge was always being lowered and raised again, every time anyone went into the town; the average garrison would have left it down all day, but these professional soldiers never spared themselves trouble. She turned and ran down to the bailey to welcome what must be a detachment of the royal army.

Mounted crossbowmen were filing through the gate to dismount within; they left their tired horses packed very close, as though to make room for a large force to follow. Directing operations from a mounting-block stood her husband, in full mail. Margaret exclaimed in vexation. Since childhood she had played at receiving her lord as he returned to the castle she commanded in his absence; now a genuine opportunity had come, and she had missed it because no one bothered to warn her in time. But perhaps it was not yet too late. She snatched a key from the nearest

[86]

door (it was the door of the arrow-store, and already open, but the form was what mattered); kneeling before the mounting-block she spoke loud enough to be heard above the trampling of hoofs: "Welcome, my lord, to your castle of Bedford, which I have guarded faithfully in your absence." As she caught his eye she continued: "Really, Falkes, the gatekeeper should not have opened without my orders. Please tell him to be more respectful in future."

"Hallo, my dear," Falkes answered briskly. "I'm glad to see you looking so well. Is that the correct way for a lady to receive her lord? Forgive me for not knowing the etiquette. I never had a lady to receive me before. But I shan't reprimand the gatekeeper. When a sentry sees his lord galloping up to the castle he should get the bridge lowered as quick as he can. Knights have been caught before now because a gate wasn't opened fast enough. Louis of France might have been on my tail. How quickly can you have dinner ready for four hundred sergeants and about eight hundred followers? Tell the cooks and the butler. Even if you seem a little surprised they are accustomed to these emergencies. Then meet me in the inner bailey. While the meal is cooking I'll have a bath, and I can tell you the news as I sit in it."

Margaret, hurrying from kitchen to storeroom to buttery, realized that she was the only inhabitant of the castle who had been flustered by this sudden upset of routine. The cooper was opening casks of beef, the cooks were making up their fires, the butler was tapping wine casks into leather jacks, grooms were staggering from the forage-store under loaded pitchforks; her lord's page had already placed the big wooden bathtub near the kitchen in the inner bailey, and beside it a stool. In this busy place there was nothing for her to do, so she sat on the stool and waited.

[87]

Presently Falkes strode stiffly through the bailey, walking with the clumsy straddle of a saddle sore horseman. As he walked he unbuckled his swordbelt, and the page ran to disarm him; but here at last was something a great lady should do for her lord; Margaret pushed the page aside, saying proudly, "Shall I disarm my lord?"

"Thanks, if you know how," Falkes answered casually. Of course she knew how to disarm a knight; it was part of the education of every lady. When the opening at the back of the mail-shirt had been unlaced, the essential opening which the wearer could not reach and which made it necessary that someone else should disarm him, she stood back. He could now pull the mail-shirt over his head, but first the mail leggings must be untied from their attachments high up under the skirt; any knight could do that for himself, and it was not the custom for ladies to fumble inside masculine thighs. But Falkes motioned her to continue.

"Don't be shy," he said, in the same casual tone. "We have been legally married, and tonight we begin our honeymoon."

Margaret felt herself blushing. For more than a month she had been the lady of Bedford, and she had thoroughly enjoyed it; but five weeks was just long enough for her to forget that marriage brought new obligations as well as new castles. However, she had borne a son, and she knew how men were made. This man was more virile than young Baldwin de Redvers, but really there was not a great deal of difference.

Soon Falkes stood disarmed, in sweaty tunic and chausses. He stretched himself luxuriously while the page poured buckets of hot water into his tub. Margaret braced herself for what would come next; the inner bailey was full

[88]

of staring kitchenmaids, but her husband seemed quite un-selfconscious. Then the page fetched a linen mantle, a great circular cloak with a hole for the head; Falkes donned it to undress under its cover; as he stepped into the bath his page spread the mantle to the edge of the tub, and he sat down comfortably, his head sticking out like the ornament on the crust of a pie. Margaret blamed herself for squeam-ish and unnecessary fears; the romances were full of knights bathing in the company of ladies, and she ought to have known that they had found a way of doing it decorously.

"Ah, that's better," Falkes said gratefully. "Yesterday we rode sixty miles and this morning twenty. Nowadays that makes me stiff. Let me see, I suppose you haven't heard the news? No, they didn't know it when we rode in, and since then you have waited politely by my bath. Well, the news is that today we have no King in England."

"Has John fled?" asked Margaret excitedly.

"Not quite as bad as that. He fled once from Nor-mandy, but at bottom he was brave. He died very suddenly, two days ago. They will say he was poisoned, of course, be-cause they always say that when anyone dies without a wound. But in my opinion his belly burst, as I told you it would if he wasn't careful. At the end he saw a priest, so you may pray for his soul if you wish; there's a chance he squeezed into Purgatory. What excited me was his last Will and Testament. The crown goes to little Henry, of course, and there were the usual gifts to religion. They sound quite generous, though there isn't a penny in the Wardrobe and nothing can be paid until we have won the war. Then the old King named the Council which will rule for his son, a most distinguished company: the Legate, naturally, and three Bishops, Winchester, Chichester and Bath; the Mas-ter of the Temple; three Counts, William Marshal, Ranulf de Blundville and William de Ferrers; three lesser English lords, William Briwerr, Walter de Lacy and John of Monmouth; and two representatives of his French fiefs, Savaric de Mauleon for Aquitaine, and for Normandy—Sir Falkes de Brealte, sheriff of Bedford, Buckingham, Cambridge, Hertford, Oxford and Northampton, castellan of Windsor and Wenlock. What do you think of that? A Council of thirteen members, and I am one of them! I am a magnate now, no one can deny that! And Hubert de Burgh is left out, which makes it very much better."

"Who is Hubert? Ought I to know him?" asked Margaret, not because she was really interested but because she could not share her husband's excitement. Of course anyone who married the heiress of fitzGerold and Redvers would be a magnate; Falkes's pleasure at his promotion betrayed his low origin.

"Hubert? You must have heard of him. The Justiciar, who is at present supposed to be holding Dover castle against the French. He holds it all right, but he keeps on making truces with the enemy. He may be getting ready to change sides; the King must have thought so, or he would not have been left out. The point is that he's the only man on our side who has risen from nothing as I have, my only serious rival. Though I bet he never fought a mailed knight with a scythe when he was stripped for work in the meadow. Of course, your father would never have brought him to Stogursey; his name shows that he was born a burgess of some squalid market. He began as a doorkeeper, just like me. He is the standing proof that low birth is no bar to promotion in the King's service. From sergeant to Justiciar, an exemplar to all ambitious mercenaries! He was always just one rank ahead of me, and now at last I have surpassed him!"

[90]

In his excitement, though whether it was joy at his own elevation or hatred of this rival Margaret could not tell, Falkes stood up in his bath, the wet mantle hanging in clammy folds around his body. He pulled it impatiently over his head, and toweled his naked flanks. The kitchen-maids stared, but Margaret was too interested to feel embarrassed. Great events were afoot, and she was hearing of them from one of the magnates who ruled England. That was only the due of her exalted rank, but somehow it had never before come her way.

"Will the Council lead the King's army?" she asked eagerly. "It will be wonderful to see you, my lord, riding before the Leopard banner. We must give a great feast tonight, to celebrate our greatness; or should we go into mourning for the late King?"

"Tonight we shan't be here, my girl," Falkes answered briskly. "As I said just now, there is no King in England. We must crown little Henry before the rebels forestall us by crowning Louis of France. I came out of my way to pick you up. As soon as possible we meet at Gloucester for the crowning, all the loyal magnates and, of course, the whole Council. You shall ride with us after dinner. I hope to God we agree on one lord to lead the army. If all thirteen of us try to do it at once the French will beat us."

Margaret murmured something to show that she had heard her lord's commands and would obey them; then she left the inner bailey and climbed to her chamber. At first she was undecided what to do with little Baldwin; long journeys were dangerous for children and it might be wiser to leave him behind in the care of Madam Alice. But valets were already dismantling her bed, and they told her that the whole household had been ordered to leave before sunset. The castle would be held by a skeleton garrison while the royal army mustered in the west; though Falkes had forgotten to mention it when he told her the rest of his news.

As she directed the packing of her gowns, which were sewn in canvas for carriage on muleback, Margaret did not know whether to feel angry or pleased. It was good that her husband was now one of the greatest men in England, representative of Normandy on the Council and probably already marked to be Seneschal of the Duchy after its liberation; at the coronation she would have the precedence that was her due. On the other hand, Falkes ought sometimes to consult her convenience, or at least ascertain her wishes; instead of telling her to pack everything she valued and be ready to ride across England at three hours' notice. Great ladies often played a prominent part in warfare; Madam Nicolaa de la Haye, for example, was already famous for her gallant defense of Lincoln against the rebels. It would be very pleasant if Margaret fitzGerold (never Margaret de Brealte, of course) won equal renown; but nobody told Madam Nicolaa to pack and ride, or encouraged common sentries to lower her drawbridge without her permission. This war was interfering with her private life, and she felt herself ill used.

The gaiety of the scrambled but gluttonous dinner restored her spirits. There had been no time to cook anything elaborate, but since they were abandoning their stores they might as well feast on the best, without stinting. The only thing measured was the wine. Falkes had arranged to sell the surplus to the tavernkeepers of the town, though all he would get in payment would be his own doubtful tallies. At first Margaret considered this showed a low commercial spirit, but he explained that his object was not to save

[92]

money but to stop his men getting drunk before the journey. Falkes had a military reason for everything he did.

The men were cheerful, surprisingly cheerful for soldiers who were retreating as fast as they could over the breadth of England. When she asked Falkes to explain this he floundered inarticulately; he could not put into words what his sergeants felt, though obviously he shared their feelings. Passelewe, on her other side, was more ready with his tongue.

"Soldiers enjoy a forced march, madam," he said, with a grin, "at least until the saddle begins to cut them in half. When they are tired they know they are getting on with the war. A victory is very inspiring, but the next most exhilarating thing is a defeat; anything positive is better than doing nothing. There is a further reason, which my lord is too loyal to mention. We all liked King John, a charming fellow while he was in a good temper. But there's no denying that he handicapped his own side, always putting himself in the wrong, getting his followers excommunicated and his lands interdicted. Now we are still fighting for Normandy and Anjou, and he can't split our ranks by starving ladies to death or murdering prisoners. At nine years of age little Henry won't have made any personal enemies. Louis of France has no personal enemies either, or he had none when he came here; but whenever he rewards a follower he disappoints two or three envious rivals. At last time is on our side."

When the enormous meal was finished Margaret nursed her indigestion for an hour while the packing was completed, and then the horns signaled to mount. It was a numerous cavalcade, the spare horses ridden by lightweight pages. Margaret asked Passelewe what would become of all these lads when they grew up; surely there was not room for all of them in the ranks? But Robert explained that boys in their teens have very little resistance to disease; sleeping out in wet weather killed most of them before they were old enough to be a problem; there were always plenty of recruits to fill their places, wherever the band burned a village and reduced the peasants to beggary.

Margaret rode astride in the high war-saddle of a well-mannered destrier; though she had in the baggage a padded side-saddle for formal occasions. Little Baldwin's cradle was strapped in the pannier of a packmule; Madam Alice rode beside him, and there were plenty of other women to help in looking after him. Margaret herself was beginning to be a little bored with her son; of course she loved him dearly, but in this new exciting life he might get in her way. If she was to have a good time at court she must make the gallants see her as young bride, not as the mother of an infant in arms. Perhaps it was as well that the baby seemed happier with Madam Alice.

That night the leaders of the band slept in a rustic little hall near Banbury, their followers sheltering in the cabins of the village. There was in the hall a tiny solar, where Falkes and Margaret spent their first night of marriage in more privacy than they would have enjoyed in many castles. In the morning Madam Alice eyed her mistress with great interest, and as she helped her to dress hovered continually on the brink of intimate questions; but Margaret told her nothing.

She could not make up her mind about Falkes. He was not a gentleman, and that grated on her nerves; whenever he wished to he belched or spat, and at table his posture was inelegant. On the other hand, though his language was coarse and sometimes he seemed to be trying deliberately to shock her, he could tell a good story. He might be too outspoken, but he was not, so far, a bore. In bed he had been oddly shy to begin with, the only indication that he felt any awe of her superior rank; but after suitable encouragement he proved competent, and ardent. Of course, a fitzGerold could never love the bastard of a peasant girl, but she could not honestly say that he revolted her; it was possible to imagine a worse husband. She decided to wait and see what sort of showing he made among the great men at Gloucester before she came to a final decision.

Incidentally, at Gloucester she would find the Legate, and King John was dead. Now was the time to seek an annulment. But after that what would happen? While old Count William lived, which by all accounts would not be for long, she might go back to Plympton; but the Honor of Redvers could not remain masterless, and the Legate, or Louis of France if he proved the stronger, would find her another husband. Next time she might get an old man with bad breath and a paunch; and there would be all that honeymoon business to go through again. Falkes was only thirty-one, though after a lifetime of campaigning he looked older; he was short but well made, and as strong as an ox. The Legate would be very busy and reluctant to antagonize a competent leader of crossbows in the middle of the war. Perhaps it would be wiser to make no move until the war was won. And, of course, if for the present she did nothing she would enjoy for a year or two that magnificent belt of castles stretching right across England from Wenlock to Cambridge. Some women would wed a leper to hold such a lordship.

When it was time to continue the journey she rode beside her husband, her eyes meeting his in the intimacy of shared wedlock. He was in good spirits, and seemed glad of her company. Certainly it was heartening to see how popular he was with his men, though he could not prevent them plundering the hall and burning the village before they set out.

The little army spent another night on the road; but they left the Cotswold village unharmed, for it lay in thoroughly loyal country, which had upheld the Angevin cause since the days of Matilda the Empress. Falkes was quick to observe changes in the always swaying public opinion of his band, and he understood that if today he ordered the hanging of a plunderer the rest would cheer the execution; whereas, as he told Margaret, if yesterday he had tried to restrain them they would all have gone over to Louis of France. No one, he explained, could foretell what troops would think tomorrow, but a leader must be perpetually aware of what they are thinking now.

On the morning of the third day they descended Cotswold and entered Gloucester. The abbey was the appropriate lodging for distinguished visitors, and since they had arrived in good time there was still room for the lord Falkes and his lady. The crossbowmen lodged in the town. They were not allowed to choose their own quarters; their leader seized a row of contiguous houses, expelled the householders, and made his men stay in that one place, where he could quickly get them under arms at need. Rather to Margaret's surprise, they obeyed willingly; but she had already noticed that these mercenaries liked living at very close quarters, and seemed nervous and unhappy when parted from the mass of their companions. They knew they had every man's hand against them; knights, even knights of the King's party, hated paid soldiers and were apt to confound them with the despicable routiers of Brabant, excommunicate ruffians whom it was lawful for any Christian to kill when he could. But there was more in it than that.

Any large gathering of magnates might flare up suddenly into civil war, and these men accepted their confinement as an obligation of their trade. Though no one could control them when they wished to pillage, they were proud of their efficiency as warriors and would gladly obey an order justified by military reasons.

On their first evening in Gloucester Margaret and Falkes supped in the guest house of the abbey, with the other upperclass visitors. But on the second day arrived Cardinal Guala, the Legate; he took over the abbot's lodging, where he gave a great dinner to all the loyal lords. Margaret dressed with care in her best tunic and cotte, though she still had no decent jewelry to replace that stolen by her husband's band on Chiltern.

All the same, Madam Alice assured her that she looked as well as any lady there; and probably it was true. For there was little competition. The Marshal was a widower and Count William de Ferrers a bachelor; the clerks, of course, brought no ladies, and Count Ranulf de Blundville had to yet arrived. A few barons were accompanied by their wives, but there were no outstanding beauties among them; and the Queen was such a giggling chatterbox that men soon grew tired of her in spite of her undeniably pretty face. Besides, Queen Isabella was nearly thirty, and middle-aged women never looked well at a feast, where loose teeth must be used with care and weak eyes screwed up against the glare of torches.

But Margaret, at fourteen and a half, was in the prime of youth, though marriage and motherhood had filled out her figure. From the unwilling burgesses of Bedford she had acquired a handsome fur-lined mantle and a pair of pretty red leather shoes; a soft rope of plaited green silk took the place of the usual jeweled girdle at her waist. Before setting out she preened herself in a copper mirror, and was satisfied with what she saw.

Four hours later the ladies left the party, though the men sat on to drink and discuss strategy. As she was undressed Margaret had a lot to tell Madam Alice.

"My dear, at last I have my deserts. This is the life I was born for. All our troubles were worth enduring, with Reginald Croc and then with the King, since they have led me to this. Just think! My partner was the Bishop of Winchester, and the Marshal himself sat on my other side! Of course, I won't have such a good place always, when more ladies come to court. But so long as this regency lasts my lord Falkes is one of the rulers of England. Bishop Peter is a charmer, a gallant knight with the grace of a troubadour. In fact, half the time we spoke in Langue d'Oc; I don't think he knows when he changes from French to Provençal. He is rather ardent in his manner, for a clerk; though they say he is as chaste as a bishop should be, so I suppose it is only his southern courtesy. He declared that he would like to charge the foe with my glove in his helm; but that might be misunderstood, and anyway the Legate wants them all to wear crosses, to show they are fighting for the rights of the Pope and his vassal the King. Then he looked in my eyes and said he would imagine the glove was there anyway, and he would cry my name in the confusion of battle, when the envious could not hear it. At Plympton no one ever spoke to me like that, but then the knights at Plympton never wanted to charge the foe. The Marshal himself spoke to me for a few minutes. He is even more wonderful than the Bishop, though at his age he is a little past courteous devotion. But his back is as straight as a lance, and if it wasn't for his grey hair you might take him for a gallant young bachelor. Unfortunately he did not discuss my looks, like the Bishop. He just said a few words of congratulation on the excellent bearing and discipline of our band; I suppose that was meant for Falkes, and I must remember to pass it on. Tomorrow there's another great dinner, though it's a fish day and they have to keep the rules of the Church on account of the Legate. Still, it will give the Queen's cooks a chance to show what they can do. Then the day after tomorrow we shall have the coronation, and that means the very biggest feast they can manage. I never thought to see so many great functions in one week. What a pity poor Joan is stuck on that barbarous Scottish border to miss it all. I shall get Passelewe to write her a long letter, telling her all about it."

But when Falkes came to join her, in the crowded hall where even great ladies slept on mattresses laid directly on the floor, he was not in a good temper. Although he was dog-tired his brain still raced from the long discussion, and he insisted on sharing his troubles.

"We should gather all our forces and march straight on London," he grumbled. "A pitched battle would finish this war one way or the other, and we stand a good chance of winning it. Supposing we lose, with the Marshal and Lacy on our side we have a safe refuge in Ireland. If we win we can hold a real coronation in Westminster Abbey. But the Legate and all the Bishops are set on holding a coronation here, before we do anything else. They think it will add to little Henry's prestige, and I think they are utterly wrong. In the end I had to give way, though the difficulties are endless. Forty years ago, in the time of St. Thomas the Martyr, it was settled that Westminster is the place of coronation, and that the Archbishop of Canterbury alone has the right to crown a King of England. The Legate says he can dispense from all these privileges, and technically I suppose he can. But our enemies will go about saying the coronation is an invalid, hole-and-corner business. Also we haven't any of the right equipment; no proper vestments, no crown and no sceptre. They were all lost with the late King's baggage, when some bloody fool told him about the short cut across the Wash. All that's bad enough, but there's worse. Count Ranulf is still in his castle of Chester; he's on our side at the moment, but he may be thinking of changing. At a coronation he is entitled to bear the sword and if we carry on in his absence that will give him a genuine grievance. It might be just enough to make him join the French. Why can't they wait?"

"Yet if they crown little Henry the day after tomorrow there will be one solid advantage for us," answered Margaret, now thoroughly awake. If she wanted more sleep she must get her husband into a better temper. "Hubert de Burgh is still shut in Dover. Can he continue as Justiciar if he doesn't render homage at the coronation?"

"God's teeth, I never thought of that! Anything is worthwhile to score off that Hubert. Oh, those blasted chivalrous gentry thought up another difficulty. William Briwerr says the brat must be knighted before he can be crowned. I don't see why. No one has knighted the Pope, yet he is overlord of England. I don't mind the ceremony itself; King John knighted me and it did me no harm. But you see the danger? Who is to knight him? Princes are normally knighted by their fathers, before they become kings. Whoever has the honor, a dozen other magnates will feel themselves slighted. And all this ceremonial is more than a waste of time. It means that the Legate and his clerks want to make little Henry the successor to his grandfather, bound by every engagement that was ever forced out of a previous King of England. It would be much easier for us homeless Normans if we conquered the country with our own swords, and then ruled by right of conquest."

"I don't understand politics, my lord," Margaret said soothingly. She wanted to get back to sleep without further discussion. All her instincts were in favor of as much ceremonial as possible, and she did not look forward to living under the absolute rule of men like her husband and Reginald Croc; but there would be time to go into that in the morning. "It's very late," she continued, "and you should rest. Never mind what is done here in Gloucester, so long as it is done in your presence, with your formal consent. Make sure you are prominent at the knighting, and in offering homage at the coronation. Let the world grow used to seeing you leading the Council, and when at last Hubert de Burgh gets out of Dover you will be far above him."

Hubert de Burgh could distract Falkes from any grievance. As they settled down to sleep Margaret made a mental note to return to this useful subject in future difficulties.

There was really no doubt as to who was most worthy to knight the future King of England, as Falkes would have recognized immediately if he had stopped to think. But fuss about chivalry irked keen professional soldiers as indeed it had irked King John. Count William Marshal had been a famous knight when most of his colleagues on the Council were in their cradles; he had charged beside the Young King in tournament and battle; during the bitter pursuit which hunted the Old King to his death he had unhorsed the Lionheart; he had then buried his defeated and deserted lord and served King Richard faithfully; he had even managed to make friends again with King John after once falling under suspicion. For more than fifty years he had been the best lance in the West, and there was still no knight who could unhorse him. Until Count Ranulf arrived, if indeed he did not intend to join the rebels in London, the Marshal was supreme among the King's Men.

There was the further advantage that he genuinely believed in the code of chivalry, which had been his guide through more than fifty years of war. The solemn knighting was carried out in the great hall of the castle with a devotion and high seriousness worthy of a religious ordination. Little Henry was a handsome and dignified child of nine, who had been trained to bear himself proudly on public occasions; as he bowed his little golden head to receive the accolade many spectators burst into tears. Here was the accumulation of every chivalrous appeal. Here was a helpless child, supported by a beautiful lady in distress; here was the Legate to remind them that their cause was righteous; here was the Marshal to prove that it was the cause of honor and just dealing; here, not least in importance, were the tough and experienced soldiers of King John, to show that wise veterans thought the Angevin cause might prevail. Margaret, standing in the front row of spectators as her rank demanded, wept with a mixture of sentimental loyalty and delight at witnessing such a great historic event. Falkes, standing beside her, disturbed this enjoyable mood.

"That's one way of dubbing a knight," he whispered, "but I prefer the old Angevin method. King John knighted me by whacking me on the backside with a rusty old sword, charging me in future never to rob the defenseless and unprotected unless I was willing to share the proceeds of the robbery with him. Don't take this form too seriously. We are each of us fighting for power, even the Marshal; and indeed there is nothing else worth fighting for."

Margaret frowned impatiently. This husband of hers was impossibly boorish. The trouble was that no one else shared her low opinion of his manners. She had seen him discussing affairs of state with the great men of the land, really great men by birth, like Count William de Ferrers and the lord William Briwerr; they were delighted when he mocked at all that a gentleman should hold sacred, and roared with laughter at his cynical exposition of their own underlying motives. Falkes never pretended to be better than he was; therefore the magnates accepted him as a gay adventurer, on the make certainly, but all the more amusing for that. Perhaps he was right to abound publicly in his lowness, Margaret suddenly perceived; if he had prated of honor and the obligations of a faithful vassal, like a real knight, the gentry would have despised him for a social climber. All the same, she was a fitzGerold and a lady; the Queen was in floods of tears, and she also was entitled to weep at this affecting ceremony.

The rest of the day was devoted to feasting; though there were no special rarities among the dishes, for the Wardrobe was empty and the royal purveyors could seize without payment only the common produce of the countryside. In fact, it had recently been announced that the soldiers must wait indefinitely for their Michaelmas wages, already nearly a month overdue. Falkes left the hall early, to spend the evening in conference with Reginald Croc and other leaders of his band; at bedtime he reported cheerfully that they had all agreed to fight the next campaign on credit.

"They know they will never get their arrears if they leave us, and they trust the promises of the Legate and the Marshal. So do I, the Marshal's promise anyway. He has never broken his word, and if the worst happens he will maintain us on his Irish fiefs. Besides, the lord Louis has no money either, so there's nothing to be gained by changing sides."

But in the morning, when the guest house was full of half-dressed men getting into their best clothes for the coronation, Reginald Croc took Margaret aside to say that the whole band had agreed to follow Sir Falkes wherever he might go. Apparently they were reluctant to tell him this openly, for fear the other magnates might suspect his loyalty; they wanted his wife to pass it on. She dutifully informed her husband, hardly realizing the implication of the message; and she was surprised at his reaction.

"What they mean, the scoundrels, is that it might pay us to join the rebels treacherously, on the battlefield; or perhaps they only want me to ride away and start pillaging at large," he spluttered in genuine anger. "Tell Reginald from me, what I have already told him myself, that King John raised me from doorkeeper to castellan. He made me captain of the King's crossbows, and captain of the King's crossbows I shall remain, whether the King is Henry or John. If they want to be led by Sir Falkes de Brealte, the most skillful plunderer in Christendom, they must stick to the Angevin cause; because wherever the Leopard banner is displayed they will find me fighting under it. Do they really think I would join the French, who burned Brealte and killed my father, and set Lupescar the routier to govern the free warriors of Normandy? I shall serve this little King until the Leopards fly once more from the towers of Rouen. The French indeed! Why, their King Philip can't even ride! There was only one destrier in the world that didn't buck him off, and he rode the poor brute until it was past eighteen years old!"

Here was another facet of her husband's complex character. He was baseborn and a mercenary, but he did not

[104]

fight merely for wages. In England it was easy to forget that the loss of Normandy ten years ago had filled the world with angry and revengeful exiles.

As propaganda the coronation was a brilliant success. In the procession the nine-year-old King sat his horse perfectly, and the very fact that all must be done with makeshift regalia, by deputies lacking authority to act for the customary officiants, changed what might have been a form into an exciting event. Luckily the Archbishop of Canterbury was in Rome, not in the rebel camp; that made it possible to forget that he was being deprived of his rights; and anyway the papal plenitude of power permitted a Legate to perform any of the functions of a Metropolitan. So Cardinal Guala presided; though the Bishop of Winchester bestowed the crown, lest it be said that little Henry had received it from a foreigner. The Sword of Chester was absent from its place at his right hand, and when the vassals did homage more than half of them were missing; even the circle on his head was not truly a crown, since the real crown lay somewhere among the quicksands of the Wash. But at least it was of pure gold, as a crown should be, and roughly the right shape; for normally it kept in place his mother's kerchief. The holy oils were genuine enough, and the anointing performed by consecrated bishops. No one could say exactly what grace or power was conferred by the rite of Unction, but whatever it was this ceremony had conferred it.

Gloucester was already suffering from a shortage of provisions, and the banquet afterward was rather an occasion for formal speeches than an enjoyable party. But the Legate's address was most heartening. He announced that since the King of England was a vassal of the Holy See it was a religious duty to put him in possession of his realm;

the royal army was engaged on a crusade, and crosses would be distributed to the troops before they marched. The magnates were not particularly impressed, for most of them had at some time taken a vow of crusade, and might wear the cross until they had leisure to fulfill it; but the sergeants were very pleased indeed. Some of Falkes's men kept sober long enough to attend Vespers in the abbey, where the crosses were handed out; Reginald Croc wore an enormous cross extending to the edge of his surcoat, and boasted, as the drink rose in him, that when he had driven the French from Normandy he would join the Templars.

The coronation had been so hurried on, to give the Angevin cause a crowned figurehead, that the whole royalist army was not yet assembled. After Vespers, as Falkes and his band left the abbey, another small detachment rode into the enclosure. Obviously it was not a baronial mesnie; the men were too well closed up, and there seemed to be only one knight in the party; though, rather oddly in such a company, there were two clerks. The knight jumped off his horse and ran over to Falkes, who shouted a greeting before he turned to Margaret.

"Here are my brothers from Wenlock," he said joyfully. "You didn't know I had three legitimate half-brothers, did you? This is Sir William, who will hold Brealte when we get it back from the French, and he has brought Nicholas and Colin with him. You see that my family is really quite respectable, in spite of what Passelewe says behind my back."

Nicholas was a priest and Colin a deacon, furtive nondescript clerks who were bashful in the presence of a lady and much too familiar with the sergeants. But William seemed a well-bred knight. He had an easy social manner and a rather pompous way of speaking; his language was the correct French of Normandy, but then even Falkes enjoyed that social advantage. Apparently the brothers never wrote to one another, though two of them were literate clerks; for they had not heard of Falkes's marriage. The news made them very excited, and they could not take their eyes off Margaret. But they were more pleased than surprised, for they thought no one was too good for Falkes. Soon the talk turned to military affairs; it appeared that William commanded at Wenlock, but since the March was quiet at the moment he had decided on his own responsibility to bring most of his garrison to join the royal army. Falkes was glad of the reinforcement, though his subordinate commanders were naturally less pleased to see a rival. Everything was speedily arranged, and when the sergeants had been dismissed to their billets the leaders spread their bedding in the abbey guest house.

That meant a domestic upheaval in what Margaret already considered her own quarters. Even in comfortable Plympton she had longed for greater privacy; now the realities of a soldier's life were brought home to her. In the crowded guest house the three brothers, with Passelewe the boyhood friend of the family, slept two on either side of her, as close as pigs in a litter. Falkes slept on top of her, and she quickly perceived that Sir William, at least, took a keen interest in the details of his elder brother's matrimonial life; from that night forward she felt an intense dislike of all her relations by marriage.

In the morning the Council held a business meeting, from which all spectators were excluded. Margaret was glad of the breathing space. She spent some hours with little Baldwin and Madam Alice, wandering through the October rain beside the banks of the Severn. At midday Count Ranulf at last rode in at the head of a strong following. The

[107]

whole town cheered, for some politicians had begun to doubt that the whole County Palatine of Chester might not go over to Louis and the rebels. At dinnertime the Council was still sitting and Margaret remembered she had no money; luckily the Queen dined in a large tent before the castle and any lady was welcome at her board. This was a queer sort of life, when your husband ruled half a dozen castles and you could not buy a dinner in a tavern. But Falkes was a queer sort of man.

At dusk she slung little Baldwin's cradle from a handy roof beam, where he could not be trampled when the throng settled into the guest house for the night. Presently Falkes entered to fetch her to sup in the castle; but he forgot to ask where she had dined, and she was too proud to raise the subject. He was so full of his own news that he could talk of nothing else.

The question of the high command had been settled. The Council was not dissolved, but after long persuasion the Marshal had agreed to lead them in the field. The foremost warrior in England was the obvious candidate for the post of commander, but by birth the Marshal was the younger son of a not very important family, and there had been a danger that Count Ranulf, the noblest magnate among the royalists, would refuse to serve under him. Count Ranulf, on his arrival, had swept away this difficulty. The Legate, as representing the feudal suzereign, held a more or less honorary preeminence, the Marshal would manage the war, and the Bishop of Winchester would safe-guard the child-King's person. The other councilors might return to their neglected responsibilities.

"And now whither shall I go, my lord?" Margaret asked sharply. It was time to remind her husband of his domestic obligations. "If Bedford is unsafe would Wenlock be better? It's about as far from the war as any place in England. But wherever I go you must give me money. Today I would have gone hungry if the Queen had not feasted all comers."

"Ah, the Queen," Falkes murmured vaguely. "I hope you took leave of her in due form. We shall send her back to Poitou as soon as we can find a ship. There's a woman who can't live without a husband, and if she stays here she will jump into bed with some handsome nobody and offend all the magnates. No one minds if she disrupts the government of Poitou, because there is'nt one; that county lives in happy anarchy. Probably you won't see her again. But money is a problem. I haven't any. I might borrow from Count Ranulf, or from the Bishop of Winchester; but anything they have ought to go to the troops. Why not send the child to Wenlock with Madam Alice and yourself ride with me? We go to Bristol soon for some tiresome Council about issuing a revised version of that Charter; the Legate insists on it; though, of course, it will not bind us once we have won the war. But that will only take a few days, and afterward I have been given rather an interesting job. My band are to raid the roads north of London, plundering rebel convoys and keeping the town short of food, while the Marshal leads our main army against the Cinque Ports. With any luck we shall force a battle while the prestige of this coronation is still fresh; and those rebels who hated King John personally, but don't want a Frenchman for king, may change sides on the field of battle."

"If I ride with our band shall I be very uncomfortable?" asked Margaret, thinking of the crowded floor of the abbey guest house.

"Sometimes, perhaps, if we have to run away very fast. But I am sole commander, and if we halt near a decent hall

[109]

I can take it for our private use. At least it will be interesting. Nothing ever happens at Wenlock; I've held it for ten
years and never lowered the portcullis."

Margaret had noticed how her husband's face had lit
up as she said our band. She was completely in his hands; he
might keep her shut up in a tower and no one would
object. But he seemed willing to take her as partner in his
queer, precarious life, and robbing the Great North Road
would be more amusing than managing even a big castle. It
would mean parting from little Baldwin, but that baby was
sometimes a nuisance anyway.

"I shall ride with my lord," she said, smiling. "A wife's
place is beside her husband. And when you pick up a good
prize I shall be there to remind you that my purse is
empty."

"Good girl," he answered, and kissed her. He was very
proud to see that in such a short time he had won his wife's
affection; though, of course, it was her lands that really
mattered.

6: A Case of Conscience

AS THE January dusk darkened the unbroken canopy of cloud the road began to freeze; Margaret's destrier slithered and plunged until she lengthened the reins and sat loose in the saddle, ready to jump clear if he fell. Falkes, riding beside her, nodded approval of her horsemanship.

"That's the way, my dear. Don't hold him up, then if he comes down it will be gently. He ought to be used to frozen roads, but horses are foolish beasts who never learn anything. All the same, the weather might be worse. Snow would mark our tracks, but tonight it's too cold for snow. Look at the smoke behind us; those damned rebels keep themselves snug."

Margaret turned carefully in the saddle, for a sudden movement might unbalance her mount. To the southward the walls of London had faded into the murk, but a great

[111]

smear of woodsmoke rose straight across the edge of the cloudy sunset; the column of horsemen stretched unbroken into the gloom, traveling at the collected hand-gallop of skilled soldiers in a hurry, thinly spread that stumbling horses should not be knocked into by their fellows. She realized with a thrill of pleasure that she was actually riding at the head of more men than she could see, and her imagination played with the idea that their army was innumerable; though she knew very well that it was made up of four hundred cold, hungry and unpaid mercenaries. As she looked once more ahead, trying to guide her tired horse through the frozen ruts, her depression returned; she also was cold and hungry, and very tired.

"In half an hour it will be dark," she called crossly. "Must we ride through the night? Isn't there some unsacked village hereabouts where we might unsaddle and sleep? The French can't follow our tracks on this trampled North Road and, anyway, they won't pursue in the dark. They have too much sense to leave their firesides in this weather."

"Luton is only twenty miles away," Falkes answered cheerfully. "It's better to be safe, even if it means a long ride. Count Arthur might now be ruling Brittany if he hadn't taken it for granted that even King John wouldn't ride eighty miles in the dark and charge at daybreak. We captured the Lusignans and destroyed their whole army, just because they disarmed and went to bed in hostile territory. When it's dark we can slow to a walk and at Luton we shall sleep late tomorrow."

"I wish I had known what I was letting myself in for when I agreed to make this campaign," Margaret replied. "I might be sleeping warm at Wenlock, two hundred miles from the war. You made it sound so jolly and exciting,

[112]

plundering convoys and holding rich merchants to ransom. I didn't understand that when there were no convoys you would ride all day to burn three huts and a stackyard, and then run away all night for fear of the French. What good have we done, anyway? We have lost half a dozen good men, left behind when their horses foundered; and the rebels will be only a few pennies the poorer. Why not stay comfortably in Luton until you get news of a convoy worth robbing?"

"It annoys the French, my dear," Falkes answered placidly. "They will have heard of our raid as they were sitting down to supper. The peasants will describe us as the whole royal army, because peasants can never count troops. So the French must arm, and drag their horses out of warm stables just as the frost sets in; I bet they lose more horses from coughing than we did by our journey. Probably they will stand to arms all night. But the real advantage is the moral effect of a raid right up to the gates of London. This is a civil war, and a great many people who don't particularly want a French King have joined Louis because they think he can protect them and little Henry can't. We have to prove that we can be dangerous, even if we can't hold our own castles."

"Surely that is another reason for stopping at home and sending our men into garrison. Hertford and Cambridge might still be yours if their garrisons had been stronger. That's two of our castles lost since the coronation, and the King's Men in general have lost at least five others. When Lincoln falls the whole east will be French."

"I didn't like abandoning Hertford and Cambridge, but the Marshal talked me into it. His plan is sound if the magnates are brave enough to follow it at the cost of their fortresses. We might have gathered a band strong enough to relieve Cambridge, but it would have been blockaded again the moment we left, since all that country is strong for the rebels. Hertford could have been held with a little more energy, but it would have been a constant drain on us. It wasn't provisioned, and how could we raise supplies for it? By selling silk mantles for beef? The Marshal is now selling King John's robes to carry on the government. No, surrendering those castles was the only policy. They made good terms and the garrisons went free; so our army is stronger than before. It's a queer sort of war when you think of it, and my part in it is the queerest; because every man I lead is a mercenary, who hasn't been paid for a year and won't be paid until we have won. Yet they follow me. If we are driven from England the King of Sicily or the Duke of Brabant will be eager to employ a captain of crossbows who can get such good work from unpaid men."

"Yes, my lord," Margaret said bitterly. "You are winning great renown as a captain of routiers, and I shall be known as Margaret fitzGerold, the routier's wife."

"On the contrary, my dear, we are Crusaders. It sounds unlikely, but the Legate says so. You are cold and tired at present, but you will feel more cheerful at Luton."

Margaret rode in silence. Talking to Falkes was like talking to a stone wall. He was invariably polite and good-tempered, even when she complained in a way that would have made many men beat their wives; but he was quite certain that he knew best, and she could never persuade him to alter a decision.

For nearly three months she had been constantly in the company of her husband, and she was getting to know his character. At first she had been impressed by his remarkable energy; he was always ready to ride another ten miles, or to get up in the night to go round the sentries. Later she had come to see that was a quality found in every real soldier; what made Falkes unique was his boundless self-confidence.

He talked buoyantly of the great future that awaited them, when the French had been beaten and he was one of the rulers of England; though he left the strategy of the war to the Marshal and cheerfully carried out any mission entrusted to him. Sometimes he would discuss military affairs with the detachment of an onlooker, assessing the chances of a royalist victory as though war were an amusing game, which it would be fun to win but not really disastrous to lose. He would boast of all the foreign princes who would be glad to employ him, implying that he had only come to England to fight for his liege lord, King John, and that it was a dreary country anyway. This annoyed Margaret, who found herself instinctively standing up for her native land; though as a well-born lady she ought to feel quite detached as between the Norman lands of England, Ireland, Sicily, and Normandy itself. Then he would suddenly flare into hatred of the French who had sacked Brealte and murdered his father; and that also was wrong, though at present it might win applause. For it was the essence of chivalry that a knight never hated his antagonists, who might one day be his comrades; only the untraveled lower classes were permitted patriotic sentiment. Through all his flow of conversation, whether it was anticipation of ruling a great kingdom on behalf of a child-King or light hearted chatter about beginning a new life after defeat and exile, ran this irritating vein of certainty that he, Falkes de Brealte, would always find a welcome from the ruling class in any land.

It was justified, and that made it all the more annoying. Margaret had watched him exerting his charm at that gloomy council in Bristol. There the loyal magnates had insisted on issuing a mutilated version of the old Charter which had caused all the trouble in the first place. That proved that they were not so much loyal to their infant lord as unwilling to submit to the rule of any king, even a congenial gentleman like Louis of France. Then the Marshal had been compelled to postpone the attack on the Cinque Ports, since these magnates refused to lead out their mesnies in the depth of winter; the only warriors who would fight for his penniless cause were Falkes's own little band of professionals. Apart from casual raids on neighboring castles, which magnates enjoyed all the year round and undertook even in time of peace, the only operations at present carried on by the Angevins were these attacks on the trade of London. At Bristol there had been a further unpleasantness, at least for Falkes; the presence of Hubert de Burgh, released from Dover castle by a timely truce. Margaret had seen at once why the two men must always be rivals and enemies. Their background was similar; both came from nowhere and had risen by efficiency and loyalty; but their attitude to their betters was essentially different. Hubert was a heavy, dignified, pompous middle-aged man, who dressed in a rich but dowdy style; his manners were excellent, and his courtesy elaborate; though the effect was ruined by the appalling Norfolk accent in which he spoke a very provincial French. At the end of the longest feast he was perfectly sober, still giving sound but obvious advice in his barbarous jargon. Irresponsible young sparks like Count William de Ferrers were awed by his pomposity and treated him with deference to his face, though they made fun of him behind his back; even the Marshal seemed to take him at his own valuation, as an elder statesman who

[116]

understood the institutions and public opinion of England better than any Norman or Poitevin could hope to do.

But Falkes was the life and soul of a jolly party, a privileged mocker at every revered institution, whether English or chivalrous. His clothes were a flashy exaggeration of the latest fashion from Provence, and he sprawled without dignity among the wine-cups. In every sentence he insisted on his low birth, contrasting the opinions of "you noble knights" with those of "us mercenaries." At the same time he had a remarkable fund of campfire anecdotes, and a long repertoire of the sort of marching songs no jongleur recited in a respectable hall. Everyone slapped him on the back and interrupted without courtesy; but at the end of the evening the Council had usually come around to his point of view. In his absence men spoke of "that wicked Falkes, no better than a routier," but they said it as though they liked him.

All this was very galling to Margaret, who had expected the deference due to a great lady and received instead a few casual pinches on the bottom. Since she had consented to marry such a husband she was considered fast, though no one could deny the nobility of a fitzGerold. Falkes was very proud of her; his marriage brought him once more level with Hubert, whose wife, lately dead, had been the widow of Count William de Warenne and herself by birth a Bardolf. Now the rumor ran that Hubert would shortly marry the elderly Isabella de Clare, who had been Queen of England for a brief period until King John repudiated her. Falkes made unkind jokes about the match, but it was a genuine score for Hubert. Margaret suggested, without really meaning it, that he might get level by repudiating her to marry Isabella d' Angoulème, the King's mother. To her surprise, Falkes took this seriously and was shocked; he explained laboriously that their wedding had been regular by Canon Law, and would bind them until death. His character seemed to be composed in two layers; on the surface he was a scoffer who pretended to be more ruthless than in fact he was; but deep underneath lay the lad from a sleepy Norman village, brought up to serve his Duke, fight the French, and obey the commandments of the Church.

It was this same conventional streak that made him take seriously his duties as a husband. He was always polite to his wife, and usually gave reasons with his orders, unless he was in a great hurry. He fussed over her safety, and would have fussed over her comfort if he had not taken it for granted that in wartime the whole human race was indifferent to hunger and hard lying. As far as Margaret could see he was even faithful; though she did not look very closely, for the most that a lady could expect was that her lord should not flaunt his mistresses in her presence. If only he had been more staid and respectable, and less of a buffoon at the council-board, she would have no cause for complaint. As things were, they got on together as well as any other pair of strangers suddenly compelled to live in close intimacy.

Now, as the weary destrier slowed to a walk that called for no attention from his rider, Margaret retreated into her own thoughts. She could inhabit at will her favorite dream, seeing herself mistress of a great castle, welcoming the King and his court to the knighting of her son; she saw little Baldwin, grown to sturdy manhood, kneeling to receive the accolade bestowed by the Marshal; Counts and Bishops congratulated her on her cellar, and the Queenmother praised her embroidery; Passelewe arranged an impressive Te Deum in the chapel, and Reginald Croc commanded the strong mesnie in flashing mail; at the feast she sat between Count Ranulf and the Bishop of Winchester, who each begged for a token to wear in the tournament; while Hubert de Burgh, from an unimportant seat in the midst of the hall, nodded approval of her excellent housekeeping. The reverie was inhabited by every distinguished personage she had met. Then with a guilty start she realized that her husband alone was missing. She tried to fit him into the picture, but he would not go into it anywhere. Perhaps this was a sin, to be mentioned next time she went to confession; but there was no denying that what she wanted from life were Falkes's castles, his power at court, and his strong mesnie; but without Falkes.

She rode on beside her husband, under his orders, sharing his dangers and hardships; and yet living in a different world.

Long after midnight they stumbled into Luton, the unfortified market town which was base and headquarters for their cautious blockade of the much stronger rebel army in London. Though unwalled it contained a few stone-built houses; the largest boasted an upper chamber, quite distinct from the hall and reached by a genuine stone staircase, where the leader of the band might dwell with his wife in as much privacy and comfort as in the greatest castle. At a pinch they could summon reinforcements from the west, and it served as a permanent address to which the Marshal might direct his messengers.

When great men rode out at the first streak of dawn, and inefficient candles made it difficult to do business after sunset, midnight was a very late hour to retire. Margaret slept late, snug in the great marriagebed which filled the chamber. When she awoke the room was full of people; since she was naked under the coverlets she peered out cautiously, knowing that she could not get up until the council of war was finished. Falkes had no qualms about revealing his nakedness to casual messengers; it was tiresome for his wife, but he never permitted her convenience to interfere with military affairs.

Now he sat on the edge of the bed, pulling on his shirt; before him stood in a row, holding themselves straight to show they were on duty, his brother William, Reginald Croc his lieutenant, and a messenger wearing the badge of the Wardrobe. Robert Passelewe, who never stood straight or paid any heed to military etiquette, squatted cross-legged on the floor reading aloud from a despatch. As Margaret looked out he rolled the paper again, and threw it casually in a corner. "We needn't bother with the rest," he said carelessly. "Extracts from the Legate's last exhortation proving, by quotations from the Fathers, the Code and Canon Law, that we are engaged on a righteous war, with all the privileges of Crusaders. We knew that already, and it didn't need a messenger to tell us. So the only part that matters is the first sentence, about the Marshal's need for money. That must genuinely be urgent or they wouldn't have written at all."

"If whenever I wanted money I sent a messenger to say so, every horse in Christendom would be foundered," said Reginald Croc. "Of course the Marshal needs money. Who doesn't? We haven't any, and if we had we should keep it to pay the men. Must we waste parchment to say as much?"

"Shut up, Reggie," said Falkes. "No one would ask you for money. The Marshal would just hang you as a robber if he thought you had any chattels worth taking. Robert, is that all there is in the letter? Are you sure? Then the Marshal really needs it badly, and we must do something for

[120]

him. But 150 marks seems a very small sum. Can it make a difference to the war?"

"It might," answered Passelewe. "The Marshal and Lacy depend for supplies on their Irish fiefs, so they must have secure communications through Wales. One hundred and fifty marks would buy some Welsh chieftain who won't take our tallies because he doesn't think we shall win. As I have told you, there is nothing else in the letter. He must need it, desperately. Oh, he ends up by reminding you that in the eyes of the law you are still sheriff of Hertford; so I suppose he wants you to raise it lawfully, by levying distress on the fief of some rebel."

"If we could hold a rebel fief we wouldn't be here," put in young William de Brealte. "We can't take Hertford castle by assault, and if we blockade it the French will come out from London and drive us away. What chance have we of a surprise attack on London itself? If we got on to a bit of the wall we could threaten to burn the whole town unless they paid ransom."

"No good, William," Falkes said decisively. "Last week we might have managed it, but after yesterday's raid they will be on the alert. Anyway, if we got the ransom the French would catch us as we retired."

"This needs thinking out," Passelewe murmured slowly. "Is there anyone in the County of Hertford who would have 150 marks in ready cash? Let's attack it from that end."

Margaret had an idea. Suddenly she saw herself as a great influence on the civil war, the lady who planned campaigns while she lay in bed; that was even grander than wearing a steel cap and defending a castle, like Nicolaa de la Haye at Lincoln. These foreigners might know every defile on the roads, after long years of warfare; but they could not carry the whole countryside in their heads like a native. She would show them. Next time Falkes held a council he would let her get dressed and take her proper place in it. "Try in the Abbey of St. Alban," she called from her nest among the coverlets.

The idea was well received. Falkes leaned over the bed to give her a smacking kiss on the mouth, while the others began to talk at the top of their voices. Croc, Passelewe and Falkes were strongly in favor, though young William was doubtful. They had passed by the great abbey, crowning its hilltop beside the main road to Chester, a dozen times that winter; but the Legate had given strict orders that Church property should be spared, and they had not touched it. The question was whether the new letter overrode their previous instructions. Passelewe pointed out that they could not expect the Marshal to command the sacking of an abbey in a letter which might later be produced against him; he would be very pleased if Falkes used his own initiative, though he might have to go on record as condemning the sacrilege. Reginald's only doubt was whether the money could be sent to the Marshal or whether the sergeants would keep it for themselves. William said that a true knight might not rob God's Church; Count Ranulf had knighted him last year, to please King John; William had been very much impressed by the unexpected honor, and talked of chivalry and the obligations of his rank as though he were the only knight in the Angevian party. Passelewe replied that taking money from an abbey to give it to the Legate was not robbing the Church; it was merely a sensible measure of centralization. The messenger, of all people, intervened to clinch the matter. He came from the Wardrobe, which was interested in finance; he had heard that last December Louis of France had taken an aid from

[122]

St. Albans, though the local inhabitants had not informed the Norman strangers of this important piece of news. Passelewe was deighted to hear it.

"That's what the Marshal meant by reminding you that you are still sheriff of Hertford. St. Albans has comforted the King's enemies and therefore it lies in the King's mercy. You, as sheriff, have the duty of levying the amercement. It's not even a forced loan, but a legitimate punishment which can be entered openly in the Exchequer records. I should have thought of something like that long ago. When shall we start?"

That led to a discussion about the best way of breaking into the abbey, which was complicated by the fact that no one present knew the way of life in a Benedictine community. They wanted if possible to catch the monks asleep, or in the refectory; it would have a bad effect on the spirit of the troops if they invaded the church during the office, and gave the Abbot an opportunity to excommunicate them from the altar. Reginald Croc suddenly remembered that one of his sergeants was a runaway Benedictine novice, and proposed to question him. But at last Margaret protested that it was time she got up and the council adjourned to the hall below.

In this crowded bivouac there was no proper dinner, because the hall was always full of men sleeping after night duty. Margaret passed the day in her chamber, where a page brought her black bread and bacon, the best food to be had in the ravaged countryside. She felt bored sitting still without needlework or feminine gossip to pass the time; but boredom was a part of campaigning, to be endured like hunger and cold. In the afternoon a sergeant put his head around the door to say that Sir Falkes wished her to be ready for supper at nightfall, and that they would be riding through the night. So she went back to sleep while she could, like any other seasoned warrior.

Over supper Falkes explained his plan. "According to this renegade novice there isn't an hour, from midnight to sunset, when you can count on the church being empty. In winter black monks eat only once a day, but apparently one of their strict rules is to go to bed early and get up at midnight. So if we break in through the main gate just before midnight we ought to catch them all in the dormitory. That's important. I don't want my men frightened of the wrath of God, and of course there will be a certain amount of cursing and threatening of hellfire. But monks probably look as silly as everyone else when they are suddenly roused from sleep and frightened into the bargain. We shall leave our horses at the bottom of the hill and creep up quietly on foot. William has volunteered to climb the wall and unbar the gate from the inside. Then we all run in swiftly and put a strong guard on the church door. We herd the community into the chapter house and settle down to talk business. They must pay, or we burn the whole establishment. We never enter the church, so the boys can't put themselves in the wrong by plundering a shrine, or lose their nerve because they see themselves excommunicated with full ceremonial. Raiding a holy place with excitable mercenaries is always tricky; they may start killing everyone in sight, or worse still one of them may fall and break a leg, and start shouting that St. Alban is after him. I'd like you to come with us, right into the chapter house. That will show we mean peace. We don't want bloodshed, though of course we must have the money."

Margaret listened carefully. She was gratified that her casual suggestion, thrown out when half-asleep, was enough to set in motion the plundering of a great abbey; but her sense of power would be increased if she reminded Falkes of the ghostly perils he must face.

"Of course I shall come with you," she answered, "and I shall do my best to restrain the men. You know why there is an abbey at St. Albans? It is one of the most holy shrines in England, the tomb of the first Christian martyr in the island. What you do there will be known all over the country. But, of course, you are not plundering; you are merely levying an amercement as sheriff of the county."

Her husband's single-minded concentration on the war sometimes annoyed her; that ought to make him consider the fate of his own soul; for he was intelligent enough to realize that she and Robert Passelewe would not be continually insisting that he was only doing his duty if the matter was not in fact very doubtful.

That night the band rode in silence. They feared what they were about to do, and there lay the danger; for an access of hysteria might lead them to kill without mercy, just to prove to themselves that they were not afraid. They were men who habitually broke all the Commandments (except that they seldom worshipped graven images); yet they had been reared in the framework of Christendom, and to their material minds the material aspect of religion loomed large. During King John's quarrel with the Pope they had been excommunicated; and that had not bothered them a bit, for it had been done in some distant church while they were busy fighting; but if they saw a venerable Abbot dash out the candle that symbolized their hope of salvation they would at once begin to feel the undying worm gnawing at their souls. Then they might pillage and slay until the Legate was compelled to disown both them and their leader. Margaret herself worried about the outcome, though she was gratified she had originated the enterprise.

From the bottom of Holywell to the abbey stretched a little unwalled township, sound asleep at such a late hour. Some burgesses may have looked out at the armed men who tiptoed up the street, but they were too frightened to raise an alarm; anyway, from Compline to Prime the abbey was cut off from the world by the Great Silence, as it had been every night since it was founded by King Offa; if they took to their heels they would not think of hiding in it.

Before the main gate the band closed up and halted. Margaret, standing beside her husband, admired yet again the silent efficiency of these skilled craftsmen whose craft was war. A single crossbow twanged as its bolt carried a knotted rope over the wall. Young William de Brealte swarmed up, fully armed, and there was a soft hiss as Falkes drew his sword from its oiled leather scabbard. A cry rang out, ending in a gurgling scream; Margaret clutched at her husband's arm, but felt only the smooth surface of his shield. All held their breath. But the alarm was not repeated. The gate swung open and four hundred men poured silently into the sacred enclosure.

Margaret, surrendering herself to the press, was borne through the darkness across the cloister. In the dormitory a light winked and a voice called inquiry. It was answered with a great shout of "King's Men," and she felt Falkes push her into a corner. "Stay there, my dear," he whispered. "In a moment arrows may fly. But unless they fight now they won't fight at all. In five minutes come to the chapter house."

The press of excited bodies frightened her more than the chance of an arrow. As she drew aside someone whispered urgently, "Is that Margaret? For God's sake speak for me when Falkes learns what I've done. I killed a monk who saw me on the wall. I had to do it, but Falkes will be angry."

How like William, thought Margaret. He was the legitimate heir to Brealte, proud of his knightly rank and anxious to fulfill all the duties of chivalry. Yet when he was excited the bad blood of that low family came out, and he slew as a frightened cur snaps. At the moment he was panting his foul breath into her face, and she must soothe him to get rid of him. She murmured, and he disappeared into the confusion.

In a surprisingly short time the soldiers had vanished to their posts. The gate once more was barred, and the wall held in force; though there was little fear that the burgesses would attempt a rescue, for the subjects of every monastic township notoriously disliked their masters. Lights glowed in the chapter house and Margaret wandered over to peer through the open doorway. The enclosure had been broken by the entry of the band, but she did not wish to make the outrage very much worse by intruding, a woman, into the presence of the community.

The chapter faced facts without useless recriminations. As recently as last month they had been held to ransom by the rebels, and they knew that the only thing to do when armed men broke in was to pay them, as quickly as possible, to go away again. This band could not be frightened by solemn anathemas, or they would not have entered in the first place. Round the walls sat grave figures, their faces muffled in cowls; but at the far end the Abbot and the cellarer were counting money on a table with Falkes standing before them. The monk nearest the door made a gesture of violent revulsion at sight of a female, and Margaret, to spare his feelings, strolled out again to the cloister.

In an hour the raiders withdrew. As they walked down-hill to their horses they could hear the first note of Prime; in the winter midnight another monastic day was opening, and St. Albans stood unharmed. Falkes gave his wife a hug, saying cheerfully, "That's that, 150 marks for the Marshal, no bones broken, and no hard feelings. The Abbot admitted that the sheriff of the county was entitled to amerce him for giving money to Louis. Of course, he protested at the amount, and the manner in which I levied it; but he dared not excommunicate us for fear of a row with the Legate. It has passed off peacefully, and the men won't be upset by superstitious fears."

"Peacefully?" said Margaret sharply. "Your brother William told me he had killed a monk."

"He killed a man who stood between him and 150 marks. That shows he is a true Brealte. Luckily the fellow was not a choir-monk, only the Abbot's cook, a lay brother. When William told me I took the offensive, threatening to report to the Legate that the monks of St. Albans loitered by the gate during the Great Silence; the Legate would assume he was waiting for his girl. They explained that the man was the Abbot's cook, who sat up all night brewing potions because Abbot Warin fancies himself as a physician. William says the man took him by the shoulder, using force. So we can report to the Marshal that at the capture of the monastery one layman was killed in battle. At the worst that is bloodshed within the enclosure, a fairly mild sacrilege; not nearly so bad as killing a monk. William was lucky."

In silence Margaret considered, not for the first time, Falkes's attitude to the law. Like all the old servants of King John he knew it thoroughly, and was always conscious when he broke it; but he had a real genius for twisting it to his advantage. Did these quibbles satisfy his conscience, like the quibble that the plundering of the abbey was really an amercement? Or was he so used to justifying himself before a hostile public opinion that he must do it even to his wife? She still did not understand him.

Before dawn they rode into Luton and Margaret, exhausted, went to bed. Falkes joined her as soon as he had eaten and sent off the money. He fell asleep almost at once, but presently she was disturbed by his groaning and tossing. Was he ill? Then she would put him in the care of Abbot Warin of St. Albans, the most eminent physician in the neighborhood. That should be an amusing situation.

For she would be gald to embarrass her husband. There was no one particular reason for her annoyance; it was an accumulation of little things. On campaign she was physically ordered about much more frequently than if she were living at home in a castle; she was often cold, hungry and tired; the sergeants had grown impudent and did not treat her with the respect which was the due of a fitzGerold. The real cause of her dissatisfaction was that Falkes had grown used to her, and now took her for granted. She was a very important and nobly born lady, not a piece of baggage to be dragged across country by a band of soldiers. It was time she did something to make them remember her greatness.

Falkes sat up in bed with a great cry. As the sentry ran in with drawn sword Margaret also sat up, hastily pulling the covers over her naked shoulders. That brought to mind another grievance: her husband kept her in this masculine establishment without a waiting-lady to hand her a bedgown (though it was by her own wish that Madam Alice remained at Wenlock with the baby). Falkes shouted at the sentry to get out and stay out. There was nothing the matter; it was outrageous that a tired captain couldn't murmur in his sleep without being disturbed by half-wits. But when they were alone he remained sitting erect and clasped his wife's hand.

"Margaret, don't go to sleep, I must talk to you," he said in a low, urgent voice. "I have just dreamed the most disturbing dream, but we must discuss it quietly without upsetting the men. Perhaps I was wrong to rob St. Alban. These confounded English saints have no kindness for Normans."

"St. Alban wasn't English. He is older than that. He was a Roman," said Margaret sleepily, because she was in the mood to pick holes in any statement. "But you haven't told me the dream."

"Shut up and don't argue. Listen carefully, and then tell me what you think I should do. I dreamed that I was back in the abbey; but it was daylight, and I entered the church to offer at the shrine. The monks were in choir and there was a great crowd in the nave. As I stood before the shrine I looked up and saw the keystone of the vault falling on my head. The monks laughed horribly, and as the stone crashed on me I awoke. Now is that a warning from Heaven or just a nightmare? And if it is a warning how can I escape the vengeance of St. Alban?"

Margaret nearly answered that if he came home in the small hours and then stuffed himself with cold bacon before going to bed that sort of nightmare was to be expected. But the memory of her wrongs decided her that a little more worry would be good for his soul.

"Some dreams are warnings from Heaven," she said, in a didactic tone which would be sure to irritate any man. "Others have a natural explanation. You won't know which kind this is until the stone actually falls on you. To be safe you should send back the money; but you can't, because it's already gone to the Marshal. So there's nothing to be done. You boast that you serve the King at the risk of your life. This makes the risk a little greater, but it can't be helped. I suppose they will find me another husband. It's for the Marshal to choose, and he doesn't hold with disparagement. Next time I shall probably get a gentleman."

Falkes smacked her hard on the jaw.

"You little devil. If I am bewitched I know you had a hand in it. I shall tell Passelewe to see you burned if I die suddenly without a wound. Now talk sense. I can't send back the money. How am I to show penitence and earn the forgiveness of St. Alban?"

Margaret was not physically afraid of her husband because it never occurred to her that a mercenary would dare to lay violent hands on a fitzGerold. She answered shortly, "There's nothing I can do. Consult Reginald Croc, your lieutenant, and Passelewe, your clerk, or even brother William the gallant knight. They have more experience of sacrilege than I. It was a thing that never came my way before I married you. Oh, all right, don't hit me again. The wisest thing you can do is call on the Abbot, explain that you can't make restitution, and perform any penance he enjoins. I suppose you will have to visit the martyr's shrine, out of common politeness. You can go fully armed and hold your shield above your head as though storming a breach. But I can't tell you how to dodge the vengeance of the greatest saint in England, neither can anyone else."

In a towering rage Falkes jumped out of bed, pulled on his shirt and left the chamber. The sentry was despatched to order the whole band to parade immediately. There were no orders for Margaret, so she remained where she was. When the band had ridden forth she sent a page to fetch

[131]

bread and cold bacon, drank several cups of wine, and settled down to sleep away the afternoon.

In the little chamber there was no hearth, but at nightfall the page brought a brazier of glowing charcoal. Margaret, in a thick padded bedgown, sat staring into the coals, a jack of wine beside her. Presently she heard horses and knew the band had returned. She waited nervously for her husband. She had tried his patience very highly; in fact, she had teased him when he was in great need of sympathy. If he beat her with a stick no one would blame him. But a woman has no weapon except her tongue. She had deliberately jumped into a very risky situation, as Falkes had jumped into a risky situation when he tackled a mailed knight with that famous scythe of his. Now she must face the consequences.

When at last the door was flung open it was not Falkes who entered. Robert Passelewe grinned at her broadly and bowed with an exaggerated flourish.

"Madam, I am to inform you that for a few days you must lie alone. Sir Falkes is indisposed and will rest on a mattress in the hall. My dear girl, I don't know how you did it, but you should come downstairs to see your handiwork. Falkes told me that it was by following your advice that he came by his not very honorable wounds. Don't start. He's not seriously hurt and he has plenty of company on his mattress, for all the other knights in the band received the same injuries. Now do please satisfy my curiosity. I shan't pass it on, but you must tell me what happened this morning."

"My lord was threatened by the vengeance of St. Alban," Margaret answered in a completely expressionless voice. "He could not restore what he has taken, so I advised him to beg the Abbot for absolution, performing any penance enjoined."

"Hm, theologically sound and morally unobjectionable. You would have made a good clerk, madam. I suppose you foresaw the outcome? My lord commanded his knights to accompany him to the chapter house of the abbey; he wanted me to come, too, but I explained that I am a subdeacon of the diocese of Paris, and the Abbot of St. Albans is not my Ordinary. So I peeped in through the door. It's not often I am so sensible, but then it's not often Falkes is so foolish. Well, he and his knights knelt before the Abbot in full chapter, expressing their repentance. There could be only one answer. The novice-master fetched his heaviest scourge and every choir-monk in the place laid on in turn. There are seventy choir-monks in St. Albans though, of course, some are handier with the discipline than others. I must say our knights took it very well. None flinched or cried out. Then the Abbot led the whole party into the church for absolution. So far, you must remember, no one had spoken since the scourging began. In the choir the Abbot paused, obviously waiting for his money. But Falkes spoke up firmly. 'Lord Abbot,' he said, 'I came to do penance because of a dream, and because my wife so advised me. What I repent of is killing your cook. As to the money, it was a lawful amercement. I cannot render it, and I would not if I could. Will you grant absolution to my comrades and myself?' That was not what anyone had been expecting. We had all taken it for granted that Falkes had somehow got hold of 150 marks, or would give land to St. Alban instead. But it was cleverly done. Abbot Warin is a graduate of Paris, like myself, not one of those children of the cloister who take the cowl at the age of seven and think of nothing but the material prosperity of the community. If

[133]

he refused absolution it would look as though he valued money more than repentance. That would have spoiled a very dignified occasion, which will enhance the prestige of St. Alban. The cellarer squirmed in his stall, but the absolution was granted. So if St. Alban threatened vengeance because the blood of his Abbot's cook cried to Heaven, that danger is averted. But if he loves money, Falkes still owes him 150 marks. You can take it as you will. Now what do you think of it? Isn't Falkes unexpected? Next time he beats you, as I suppose he does from time to time, you can console yourself with the recollection that once your advice got him seventy strokes with a novice-master's scourge. You will be the envy of every down-trodden wife in England."

Margaret had listened with close attention. Passelewe was right; you never knew what Falkes would do next. She saw what had been in his mind; the amercement was legal, the murder of the cook a sin; now the sin was wiped out by the scourging. But understanding afterward the reason for his action was not the same as knowing beforehand what he would do.

Passelewe had not yet finished. In Paris he had studied rhetoric and he enjoyed delivering long speeches. "The funny thing is that St. Alban, or the Devil, or some other supernatural power who looks after mercenaries, did us a good turn as we rode back here. The men were most impressed by it. Roger de Colville, a knight who had set up on his own as a brigand, sent a message to ask if his band might join ours. They were thrilled to hear we had robbed the great abbey, since for months they had been hoping to do exactly that as soon as they were strong enough. Falkes agreed and we returned to Luton stronger by sixty well-armed ruffians. It's a very good omen."

"It makes nonsense of the fiction that Falkes is sheriff of Hertford, collecting amercements from lawbreakers," Margaret said hotly. "He should remember my feelings. The company of Reginald Croc is bad enough, but at least he calls himself a mercenary, not a brigand. If they expect me to be civil to this robber I shall go off to Wenlock."

"Well, yes, I see that," Passelewe continued, his grin broader than ever. "Though you can't go unless Falkes permits it. This may have been done on purpose to annoy you. Your advice got him a thrashing, and as he groans on his mattress he may be comforted to see you sharing a dish with a notorious brigand. Suppose you regard it as payment for your score off him. You get off very lightly, for Roger is a knight of good family, with charming manners."

"I understand, Master Robert. You come as go-between to reconcile husband and wife, which I suppose is part of the office of a sub-deacon. Of course I shall submit to my lord. The flogging was not entirely my fault; his dream sent him to St. Albans and the Abbot chose the penance. But I shall come down to the hall and entertain his guests. Remind him that I did not offer advice until I was asked for it."

Falkes never again related his dreams to Margaret and she never volunteered spiritual counsel. Only Robert Passelewe seemed to remember the incident, and showed his admiration for her intelligence by frequently consulting her.

At the end of January the roads north of London had been so harried that there were no more convoys. At the same time came news that the Marshal had gathered an army for the projected attack on the Cinque Ports, and Falkes led his band south to join the Leopard banner. But this would be a campaign of swift marches and hard fighting; he looked about for a secure base in which to leave the women and the heavy baggage. On Candlemas Day the 2nd February, he took his advisers, including Margaret, on a flying visit to Bedford.

Bedford castle was still in the hands of his weak garrison, though only because the rebels had been too comfortable in London to march out and besiege it; for winter storms had undermined part of the bailey wall and in its present state it was almost indefensible. That was easily remedied by turning out the burgesses for an unpaid corvee; but there was also a lack of dressed stone. Falkes gave orders that the nearest masonry building should be demolished, and the easily handled freestone built into his wall. In vain the burgesses protested that the nearest masonry building was the revered parish church of St. Paul; when Falkes had threatened to hang them up by their thumbs they did as they were told. Next day the knights rode back to Luton, leaving Margaret and Passelewe with the followers in the castle.

Once more Margaret found herself mistress of a great household, and now without the distraction of little Baldwin. She thought of fetching him from Wenlock, but Passelewe advised her that the roads were unsafe. The child would soon be Count of Devon, for old Count William had taken to his bed and would never rise again; even a loyal magnate might be tempted to kidnap such a valuable ward.

She found it difficult to occupy her time. There were few visitors to what was now a dangerous frontier post, and even the stable offered little amusement, since the best horses had gone to he scene of war in Sussex. The obvious distraction for a bored lady, with no company except a clerk, was churchgoing; the most notorious evil doers, even

King John and his captains, enjoyed choral High Masses and elaborate processions, where they heard better music and saw more sumptuous robes than the greatest layman could command. But when she proposed to celebrate St. Valentine's Day and the opening of spring by visiting the neighboring nunnery of Elstow, Passelewe demurred.

"It's a public Mass and they do it very well," he said doubtfully. "The ladies of Elstow are famous for their singing, and you hear the latest love songs from Provence in the procession afterward. I should like to go there. But this year we would not be welcome. You see, the Abbess has a special devotion to St. Paul, and she was very angry when we pulled down his church. But she was more annoyed with St. Paul for permitting it than with Falkes for doing it, since no one expects better behavior from a captain of mercenaries. When Falkes rode away unharmed she took steps to remind the Apostle of his weak-spirited submission to injustice. In her chapel she has a big image of him with the usual attributes. She took away his sword and told him in front of the whole community that he wouldn't get it back until he revenged himself on the despoiler."

"In that case we can't visit her. I wish Falkes wasn't always in such a hurry when he sees something that needs doing. I don't like being on bad terms with the neighbors."

"It's because he does things quickly that he's such a good soldier. The Legate says we are Crusaders, so perhaps St. Paul is glad to lend us the stones of his church; but Falkes is making influential enemies in Heaven. He owes St. Alban 150 marks and a church to St. Paul. That may bring bad luck."

"The castle needed repairs and our cause is just," Margaret answered, undisturbed. She believed, of course, that miracles might happen; but none of her acquaintances had been miraculously punished or rewarded, and it would be very odd if Falkes alone were picked out from among so many sinners. "He never relies on good luck, anyway. He is a well-trained soldier."

But he had feared the vengeance of St. Alban, there was no getting away from that. Perhaps the Abbess was a rebel, making her gesture to spread dismay in the Angevin ranks; all the same, Falkes would be worried when he heard of it.

7: The Tournament at Lincoln

DURING March and April there was plenty to think about, if not very much for a solitary lady to do. For the war moved swiftly. The Marshal had managed to collect a strong field army, a difficult operation in that widespread war; the rebels and their French auxiliaries, though their total numbers were much greater, were scattered all over the country, defending their own castles or attacking those of their neighbors; they could put no equal force in the field.

Falkes sent frequent letters, and Passelewe scratched on the dinner table a rough map of southern England; though Margaret found it difficult to follow the campaign, for rebels and Angevins seemed inextricably mingled among the close-set fortresses of the south coast. Then the rumor spread that Louis had crossed to France to gather reinforcements, and Passelewe was elated.

"You see, madam, both sides have been starving one another between Winchelsea and Rye, at the bottom of the table here. At that sort of game we are bound to win, for we have the trained professional soldiers. The French are better men in a joust, but when it comes to enduring cold and hunger our fellows stick to their banner while the rebels ride home to their warm castles. Now Louis has had enough, and whoever he leaves in command will not get loyal service from hot-tempered magnates who don't really want anyone to be King in England. In a few months we shall rule in Westminster and your husband will be one of the rulers."

"That's all very well," Margaret objected. "If you say we are winning I'm sure you are right. I've never seen Sussex and I can't understand how these little towns can be so close to one another and yet take different sides. But this is a poor sort of life for me. I don't expect my husband to stay at home in wartime, but somewhere there ought to be a gay court, and I should be part of it. Now the Queen is back in Poitou someone must be teaching the little King to behave like a gentleman; in fact, there must be a court, and I've a good mind to go there, even without my husband's permission."

"Be patient, madam," answered Passelewe. "You know that I advise you for your own good. Ever since that remarkable coup at St. Albans I have admired your intelligence and I wish you to be one of the greatest ladies in the land. If you defy Falkes you may be imprisoned for the rest of your life, for once we have won his word will be law. I suppose that as our side grows stronger courtiers will gather around little Henry; or, at least, the warriors will keep their ladies at court, where they can visit them between battles. I shall write now, in your name, to ask if you can leave this isolated castle and join the little King."

Margaret was patient, for it really seemed that she would not be stuck much longer in her dreary front-line post. Louis returned to England, with more French knights; but public opinion now backed the Angevins to win, and some of the more flighty rebels began to change sides. Young William Marshal, the Regent's son and heir, rejoined his father's banner; it was not an important gain, for his tenants had argued that they were not bound to follow him in rebellion against his natural lord, and he had a very small following. But Count William of Salisbury came over at the same time, and he made a considerable difference; he was a bastard son of the Old King, notorious for his skill in choosing the winning side. There were now in the royal camp enough magnates of good birth to make a good display, and it was publicly announced that at Pentecost, 1217, the Little King would wear his crown in state, according to ancient custom. (Even his supporters called the child who had been crowned at Gloucester the Little King. It was doubtful whether he should be numbered Henry III or Henry IV, depending on whether you counted the Young King, the eldest son of Old King Henry, who had been crowned without reigning. To any middle-aged man "King Henry" meant Henry fitzEmpress, and Young Henry meant that son of his.)

The crown-wearing would take place at Northampton, within easy riding distance of Bedford; and the whole royal army had moved north to be present at the festival. Margaret did not wait for permission, and Passelewe agreed that Falkes would probably expect to find her there. Passelewe was in general helpful and anxious to oblige, and Margaret, after puzzling over his character, thought she now understood his attitude. He was not in the slightest bit in love with her, which was disappointing; but then, though he lived very unchastely for a deacon, he was never moved by love; the low concubines he kept did not affect his conduct in the daytime. He really loved Falkes, as a comrade; he thought that a well-born and handsome wife would be an asset to his adored leader; and ever since the flogging at St. Albans he had admired her brains. He was determined to keep her as a friend and ally; though he was always careful to remind her that no woman could be the equal of a man, and that if they quarrelled her husband could hurt her while she could not hurt him. Perhaps he thought that one day she would make Falkes very happy, if they reamined on good terms until peace came. Perhaps she would; about that she would make up her mind when the time came.

Now she was going to Northampton to see the great world. The castellan of Bedford had collected the handsome dresses from the burgesses and enough jewelry of sorts to make a show, though it was unworthy of a fitz-Gerold. The garrison could not spare an escort, but she rode swiftly by night, with only Passelewe and a couple of grooms, to reach the court on the Friday before Pentecost.

On the same day the royal army rode in. After three days of feasting the ceremony was held with all its old splendor. All the Council of Regency renewed their homage, and when Falkes knelt before the Little King he made a most impressive figure. He had changed, and changed for the better. He was no longer a gay young tough who masked his inferiority by mocking at everything sacred; now he took his own grandeur for granted and bore himself toward other magnates as an equal. It was said that he had done very well in the campaign of the Cinque Ports, though as far as Margaret could gather, he had not especially distinguished himself in the actual fighting; it was rather that he had kept his followers contented and efficient, although they had nothing to eat and no prospect of another payday. He treated her as an old and tired companion.

On the evening of the great feast, when the bedcurtains had been drawn and they were alone until the morning (for Falkes de Brealte was now great enough to have a little chamber to himself), he opened his mind to her.

"You know, my dear," he said cheerfully, "jongleurs talk a lot of nonsense about noble birth. When you come to think of it the noblest blood must be very widespread. King John ravished a peasant girl wherever he happened to stop for the night, and I dare say earlier kings did much the same. My mother was a peasant, yet Duke Rollo may be among her ancestors. It's really a matter of being shy and awkward; if you are nervous you make everyone else feel nervous, too. But these great lords don't want to snub the new men if the new men behave with self-possession. That's where poor old Hubert de Burgh always goes wrong. He is so touchy that everyone feels impelled to insult him, since that is what he is waiting for."

"But there must be something interesting about Hubert," Margaret answered. "No one likes him personally, yet everyone seeks his opinion. I should like to see more of him if ever he leaves that strong castle of his."

"It's not his castle. Dover is a royal fortress, held at the King's pleasure. Though I foresee that if Hubert holds it long enough he will begin to think of it as his own, like some other castellans. I saw him at Pevensey last month. Now he is shut in once more with the French battering his walls. Down there in the south he is out of touch with the court, while my influence grows. But if he hangs on to

Dover he will take a lot of shifting after we have won the war."

"The clerks admire him, if the gentry don't," said Margaret doubtfully. "Passelewe thinks that one day he will give us trouble."

"Oh, that's because he is so busy being a native-born Englishman. He pretends that English Law is a mystery no Norman can grasp, and talks heavily of the welfare of the realm. What he means, of course, is that we ought to abandon the Normans and make peace with King Philip. Clerks and burgesses like the idea, but it won't appeal to magnates whose fiefs across the Channel have been stolen by the French. Hubert is a nuisance, I grant you; but if we win the war here in the midlands while he is stuck in Kent, people will forget his existence."

"Then let us forget him now, my lord. You began by saying that at last the magnates accept you as one of themselves. In that case you must live like a magnate. Is it really necessary to have men like Reginald Croc and Roger de Colville dining with us in our hall? Why can't they lodge apart with the sergeants?"

"Because my power depends on their loyalty. You must be gracious to all my men, and so must I. I can't pay them and they only follow me from affection. They could ride away tomorrow and get a little money from the rebels, though luckily Louis can't give them much; or they could go to Italy or the Empire and be paid in full every month. It's hard work keeping their obedience, but if they follow me in the coming battle I shall have done more than anyone else to put the Little King on his throne, and the Marshal will remember me when the rewards are distributed."

Everyone took it for granted that there would be a

[144]

great battle before the army returned to the south. The war had continued for nearly two years of sieges and truces and countermarching, and there seemed no reason why a battle should be fought now; but these moods come to armies suddenly, and the mood would bring its own fulfillment.

Whit Monday opened a week of strenuous campaigning. A strong force of rebels and French had occupied the disloyal town of Lincoln and settled down to a leisurely seige of the castle; but Louis himself was battering Dover, so the hostile army was divided. The Marshal led his forces northward.

It was not only the royalist army that marched, but the whole Angevin party. The three Counts, Chester, Salisbury and Derby, and the Bishop of Winchester who led a larger mesnie than any Count, were for once united under the Leopard banner, instead of wandering off to capture the castles of their neighbors in private feud. The Little King was there, with Sir Philip de Aubeny his tutor, and the clerks of the Chancery and the Wardrobe. The Legate and his great household, with the wives of most of the fighting men, trailed behind the army. Margaret rode with the court, for Falkes had never told her to go back to Bedford.

From among the families of the mercenaries she had collected four moderately respectable women. Decently dressed (in stolen clothes) they could pass as waiting-ladies, especially because they were French-born and spoke more elegantly than the noblest Englishwoman. The sergeants were delighted with this promotion of their concubines, for as a general rule the women of soldiers were even more despised than their men; and in the relaxation of morals that always accompanies campaigning the genuine waiting-ladies of the court were civil to them. Falkes had never thought it could be done, for he underestimated the

English value of a good French accent; he himself spoke good French, and so did the lowest of his grooms. He was very pleased with the effect on the morale of his band.

While they rode to battle there were naturally a great many quarrels among the magnates, for a battle was the most formal social occasion that any of them would see. Every jongleur knew by heart the exact order of precedence of both armies at Bouvines two years ago, and a man's daughters would marry more nobly because he had been near the right of the line in the coming fight. The Norman exiles claimed the post of honor on the general ground that everything French should take precedence of anything English; Count Ranulf de Blundville claimed it also, as a privilege of the County Palatine of Chester. When the army reached Newark on the evening of Friday, the 19th of May, the rival claims were formally laid before the Regent.

Luckily the Marshal could always decide a point of chivalrous etiquette. He explained that against the French the men of Normandy had the privilege of striking the first blow, and the men of Chester against the Welsh. These claims would now be recorded in the public roll of the Chancery, that in future they might never be disputed. But they only applied to battles against those particular foes, and then only when the King of England led the knight-service of his realm; this was to be a battle against English rebels, and on account of his tender years the King would not take his place in the line. A mere Regent, waging war on such an undistinguished enemy, might draw up his men as he would; and solely with a view to efficiency, without prejudice to future precedence, he would allot the first place to Count Ranulf and the men of Chester. After a certain amount of grumbling the Normans accepted this plan.

[146]

Falkes and Margaret had been among the suitors who heard the judgment, as was their right; Falkes as one of the Council, Margaret as lord of the Honor of fitzGerold. Margaret was keenly interested; this was the sort of military incident that a lady could understand; and she approved of the solution, since Count Ranulf was the most nobly born magnate in the Angevin army. Falkes made no effort to hide his contempt. But what really annoyed him was that everyone spoke as though the knights of the vanguard would strike the first blow, ignoring the part allotted to his band. At supper he indignantly explained his grievance to Margaret.

"I have just pulled off one of the greatest feats a commander of crossbows has ever been asked to perform. Now a silly dispute between Count Ranulf and some other silly knights looks like hiding it from posterity. This afternoon, as we laid our plans for tomorrow's battle, Bishop Peter pointed out that we would be in a nasty fix if the French knights ride out from Lincoln and charge us downhill while we are fording the Wytham." (Margaret noted again, but still with surprise, that this foreign husband of hers carried in his head every defile and fortress he had ever passed in his ceaseless travels with the mesnie of King John.) "We shall avoid that by marching west, crossing the stream out of sight of the town. But what no one would say, though it was in every mind, was that even on a level field French knights will probably ride down these Anglo-Norman half-breeds. The Marshal thought of a way to break the French charge, if I could persuade my men to do it. Can you guess what my band must do tomorrow? We ride in front of what Count Ranulf calls the van, and when the French appear we are to kill our horses, use their

[147]

carcasses as a barricade and turn the charge with arrows from our crossbows. *And* my men have agreed to do it."

Margaret did not grasp the significance of the agreement. "It sounds reasonable, my lord," she said indifferently. "Don't our crossbowmen usually fight on foot, though on the march they ride to keep up with the knights? It seems a good way of getting rid of their horses."

"*Their* horses, exactly," said Falkes with emphasis. "Don't high-born ladies ever think of money? Those horses are the private property of my men, who haven't been paid for a year and a half. They are to kill them for the good of the cause before the battle has even begun, when they don't know which side will win or whether there will be any booty afterward. I put it to Reginald Croc; not because I thought there was the slightest chance of the men being willing, but because the Marshal gave me a direct order to try it. Reginald also thought the proposal absurd, but he talked it over with his favorite veterans. I have never been so proud in my life as when I took back their answer to the Marshal. The old soldiers of the Norman war said they would stab their mothers, let alone their horses, if I commanded it; and though they couldn't vouch for Colville's recruits who hardly know me, they were pretty sure that if I stabbed my own horse and stood in the front rank not a man would desert me. Think of it! None of the men care whether England is ruled by an Angevin or a Frenchman; they fight only for pay, and even that I can't give them; they are bound to me by no oath. Some mercenaries are sticky about dismounting at all, until they see which way the battle is going; they want a good start if they have to run away. These men will stand by me, dismounted between the armies. I tell you, there has never been a band like mine."

"Or a captain like Falkes de Brealte," put in Passelewe, who had come up to stand behind his lord when he saw him gesticulating excitedly. "From your eloquence I thought you must be asking my lady to change sides, or flee with you to Outremer. But after all you were only boasting; that will sound better tomorrow than tonight. All the same, madam, it is a great achievement, and it should be remembered. So I have told the whole story to that busy trouvère who is composing a poem about the Marshal, ten times as long as the Aeneid. He has promised to fit it in somewhere, if he can find room for anything else besides a catalogue of the foemen slain by his eighty-year-old lord."

"Surely the Marshal will not lead the charge?" asked Margaret in surprise. "Though I must say he looks younger than eighty."

"He will lead us," answered Falkes. "He must do it or all the magnates will dispute for the first place."

"Besides, he probably is younger," added Passelewe, with a smile. "After a certain age well-preserved old gentlemen boast themselves older than they really are. I wonder if one could fix the period when the change comes? Men of forty-five say they are thirty-nine; perhaps seventy is the crucial date. But that kind of speculation is more interesting to a student of Paris than to a captain of crossbows."

"Before I was born he rode with the Old King," grunted Falkes. "He has never lied in his life, and if he said he was a hundred I should believe him."

"Oh well, he is a gallant leader and our cause is just," muttered Margaret, in the perfunctory manner of one saying the right thing. "Now where would you like me to go tomorrow? Shall I watch the battle from as close as I can, or hide in some strong castle in case we are beaten?"

"Not in a castle," Falkes answered with decision. "If

we are beaten tomorrow all England will be lost. The Little King will go back to Nottingham; his guardians think he should have a forty-mile start if things go badly. You had better do the same. The court will get early news of the battle, but if you like I will bring Robert along, and send him back as soon as there is anything to report. If it's news of defeat I may not be able to join you. Then if the Legate offers you protection, accept it; otherwise ride hard for Chester and take boat to Ireland. Of course, you will pick up little Baldwin, and then, with Redvers and fitzGerold to bargain with, you should get fair terms from Louis."

"And you, my lord? Oh, I see . . ." said Margaret, rather shaken. Falkes took it for granted, without boasting as a chivalrous knight would have boasted, that if the Angevins were beaten he would be among the slain. Most captains of mercenaries fled early from a lost field, but she already knew that Falkes was faithful to the memory of King John.

That night there was little sleep. In the morning the army would march east and the train west; Falkes worked on into the dark, inspecting equipment and horses, while Margaret collected the women and children of the band and arranged their transport. Most of the concubines were reluctant to be parted from their men; some were genuinely in love with their protectors, and others feared they would be abandoned if they were absent. But the trouble which Falkes never spared himself brought advantage in the morning, when the band marched out while the baronial mesnies were still saddling up and quarreling about precedence: Margaret got her convoy on the road by sunrise and reached Nottingham in time to requisition good quarters.

That evening she sat in the public room of an inn by the east gate, to get early news from any messenger as he arrived. In a few hours she would know whether she was wife to one of the rulers of England, or a fugitive widow. She said a few prayers for victory, because that seemed to be the duty of a supporter of the Angevins; then she found herself praying fervently for Falkes, and was surprised to discover that she cared for his personal safety. After a few months of marriage it was difficult to imagine life without him; without his unruffled good temper, his efficiency, his calm certainty. He was a scoundrelly mercenary, a low-born hired soldier unworthy to mate with a fitzGerold. He was also her partner in the difficult struggle for existence, a very brave man who took it for granted (there was the supreme flattery) that she was brave enough to share the risks of his hazardous life. It was hard to imagine that already a French lance might have snuffed out that abounding energy and competence.

There was continual traffic through the gate, and each arrival brought fresh rumors. Crowded Nottingham was on edge, for it was known that battle had been joined near Lincoln. And such a battle! The whole royal army against the stronger part of the rebel and French forces! The war between Angevins and French had continued for a generation, but it had been a war of sieges and truces and swift raids by a handful of hard-riding knights. Not since Hastings, a hundred and fifty years ago, had two great hosts contended on English soil for the crown of England. Every peasant wife who brought in a basket of eggs was questioned as to whether she had seen the smoke of ravaged villages or a band of defeated warriors riding hard in flight.

It was already known that the French had remained behind the shelter of the town walls, to await attack. There had been no downhill charge as the royal army approached and no need for Falkes to stab his horse and fight on foot.

[151]

The risk he ran was no greater than the danger faced by every other knight.

As dusk fell lookouts on the church towers reported no fires to the eastward. So the Angevins had not been defeated and pursued; presumably the battle had ended in the usual draw. Wars went on and on because it was so hard to win a clear-cut victory when the first thought of every combatant was to avoid capture and the ruinous ransom that would be the price of release. For weeks, during the last campaign among the Cinque Ports, two armies had been in close contact; but their leaders had feared to risk all in one great gamble, and they had drifted up here to the midlands with nothing decided.

On one thing all the rumors agreed. The royal army had ridden right up to the gates of Lincoln, and no fugitives had come back. As the last streaks faded out of the western sky Margaret and the knowledgeable she-mercenaries who posed as her waiting-ladies could be certain that the day had not gone against their lords.

Then, as they sat munching the usual campaigning supper of cold bacon and biscuit, the lookout at the east gate blew his horn and the guard turned out. In a few moments they could hear, even in the inn, the trampling of approaching horses. Margaret ran out.

There was a blaze of torches, and some cautious veteran had lit a great fire just within the wall to heat pitch in case the town must repel an assault. It was impossible to see into the gloom beyond the light. The portcullis had been lowered, though men stood by the windlass to raise it swiftly if the new arrivals were friends in need of refuge. But the rhythm of the hoofbeats was reassuring; these men rode fast, but there was none of the frenzied patter of horses driven in desperate flight. Then the visitors halted beyond the gate and there came the mellow call of a brazen trumpet; not the urgent grunt of a horn, sounding alarm or defiance, but a pealing merry noise of rejoicing. Amid breathless silence all heard the clear voice of a trained herald, chanting: "Open to the mighty prince, Count William of Pembroke and Striguil, Regent of King and Kingdom, come to announce to King Henry the great victory God has granted to us."

Margaret saw the Regent in the firelight as he rode under the raised portcullis; still wearing full mail, save for the helm on his saddlebow, the old man who for fifty years had been the best lance in the western world sat erect and slender as a lad of twenty. His long white beard flowed over his surcoat, but above it his face was one huge grin; on his shield was a jagged scar where steel had ploughed the painted leather, but he himself was obviously unhurt and almost drunk with the joy of victory.

Behind him rode only a small escort; the royal army had evidently remained in conquered Lincoln. Then Passelewe, his scholar's gown conspicuous amid burnished mail and painted surcoats, dismounted and shouted: "Where is the lodging of the lady Margaret de Brealte? I have news for her."

When he was comfortably squatting on a cushioned stool, his legs stretched out to the fire of the inn's best room, he looked carefully around his audience. "Is Annie here, the sweetheart of Reginald Croc? Poor little darling, you must seek another protector. Your man is dead on the field of honor, nobly slain by a noble French knight. All you other ladies may take heart, for no other of our band died in the great victory."

Little Annie, a dirty, snub-nosed slut of fifteen, rose at once, grief lending her dignity. Luckily she was very proud of being a real sinful concubine, and thought it childish to display her sorrow. "So Reginald has cheated the hangman," she said. "It's a better death than will come to most of his comrades. I shall ride to Lincoln at once. I may get there before they rob his body and I know where he carried his purse. I must seek the main army anyway, to pick up another friend. Good-bye, ladies."

"That's right, child," Passelewe called after her. "Keep your gaiety and some sergeant with a load of booty will be glad to take care of you. My lord Falkes has guarded the body, and you may find the purse. Since the only knight slain was Reginald they talk of giving him a slap-up burial in the cathedral. . . . Now, ladies, listen to the story of the great fight at Lincoln where the band of Falkes de Brealte won immortal glory."

Passelewe had seen it all, and he was a trained rhetorician who enjoyed telling a tale. Margaret lay back with closed eyes, the better to see what he described. She knew Lincoln and every man mentioned, at least on the Angevin side, was a personal acquaintance; this was more immediate and exciting than any trouvère's account of battles in Outremer; she could follow it as though she had been present.

Falkes had obviously played a great part in this successful engagement. She knew enough about mercenary crossbowmen and what was expected of them to see where the band had done its bare duty and where it had displayed outstanding devotion.

The lady Nicolaa de la Haye, hereditary sheriff and castellan of Lincoln, was holding the castle for the Little King, while the French and their rebel auxiliaries battered her wall where it faced the town with engines they had set up in the cathedral square. When the royalists had crossed the Wytham and knew that the French intended to await attack behind the town walls, Falkes and his men were sent on in advance to enter the castle by its western gate. A jongleur could make that sound very fine, since they went before the van of the main army; but Margaret saw it was merely common sense to use crossbows to hold stone walls dismounted, instead of exposing them to the terrible French charge.

Then the Bishop of Winchester rode into the castle and out again by the gate facing the cathedral. It was characteristic of that undisciplined jouster; even when the army was led by the Marshal, the stainless veteran whom any knight could follow without loss of dignity, Peter des Roches would ride in front to seek adventure. It was also characteristic that he should have discovered an old blocked gate, unguarded by the French; and ridden back at once to tell the Marshal where he might break into the town. For Bishop Peter was more than a bullheaded champion (though he was that among other things); he was a sound tactician with an eye for country. Of course, as he rode beyond the castle walls he had been covered by the crossbows; so far Falkes had been useful, but no more.

Then Passelewe described the arrival of the main army. The old Marshal rode a length in advance; his great helm covered his beard, and he might have been a lad in his teens, so straight he sat his destrier. Bishop Peter (of course) rode as near him as he could get, and while others shouted "King's Men," their regular war-cry, he called, "God aid the Marshal." The French prepared to meet them at the narrow gate, but at that moment Falkes sallied from the castle, at the head of his handful of mailed knights. The French turned to meet the new attack and the Marshal entered the town against slight resistance.

[155]

Passelewe did not dwell on it, but Margaret understood that this was a desperate and devoted feat of arms.
French knights were the best jousters in the world, and
even English nobles of good birth, trained to the destrier
from childhood, met their charge with decent fortitude,
but expecting to be unhorsed. Falkes had not learned to
ride until he was a grown man who had killed with that
famous scythe; his bachelors, robbers and outlaws who had
somehow acquired mail and destriers, chose to call themselves knights, but were essentially just as untrained. And
this little group had spurred into the cathedral square to
encounter the young Count of Perche and the best blood
of France!

Of course, they were sent flying in every direction, as
soon as the lances crossed. Equally, of course, no one was
killed, or even wounded; for knightly mail was constructed
especially to avoid that danger. The next move, in an
ordinary combat, would be for a few sergeants to dismount
and collect prisoners for ransom. But no ransom would be
taken for Falkes and his bachelors. They had been fighting,
bumptiously, against their social superiors; rebel preachers,
to counteract the Papal Crusade preached by the Legate,
had enlarged on the atrocities committed by these mercenaries; Louis and all the French leaders had sworn to hang
them. Margaret already knew that all ended happily, but
none the less she caught her breath as she understood the
danger.

As an exhibition of reckless courage the deliverance
was even more remarkable than the first unfortunate
charge. The crossbowmen on the castle wall saw their
beloved leader lying helpless in danger of the gallows; on
foot, in leather jerkins, they sallied out against the mailed
and mounted French. Given time the knights would have

[156]

hustled these miserable infantry up against the castle wall and cut their throats to the last man; but there was no time, for meanwhile the Marshal and the Angevin knights were filing through the unblocked gate and forming for the charge. A few French horses were shot down by the cross-bows, and the other horsemen feared to find themselves dismounted before they had struck a blow in the important and honorable battle which would begin when the Marshal was ready; they withdrew across the square, leaving Falkes and his followers where they had fallen. The crossbowmen carried them into the castle. Then the Marshal charged.

"But you said Reginald Croc had been killed," Margaret objected. "Was he so rash as to charge again?"

"Reginald charged again, as I shall tell you. I saw it with my own eyes, and I'm pretty sure he was killed only because he was a mercenary thrusting himself into a quarrel between gentlemen. In fact, he was murdered; but not before he had murdered one of his enemies. That was why I got rid of little Annie at the start. I didn't want her to hear the story, though the rest of you may as well know it."

Passelewe squirmed to ease his aching buttocks and paused to collect his thoughts.

"I saw the Leopards overthrow the Lilies, a few feet from my post on the wall," he continued. "That's a very fair sight to an exile from Normandy. I can't describe to you how the Marshal fought, though every trouvère will rack his brains for adjectives to describe it. It's enough to say that he didn't behave like an old gentleman of eighty. Horses reared, lances splintered, swords flashed, French men tumbled down like ninepins. But you must remember it was very like a tournament, a first-class tournament of course; no one was seriously hurt. Then the French recoiled

[157]

and some of them began to ride down hill toward the bridge and the London road. But the young Count of Perche, not twenty years old and commanding his first army, was determined to win renown by covering the retreat of his men. He could pay a good ransom when he was taken, and if he unseated the Marshal he would be famous to the end of his days. By the west door of the cathedral he turned his horse for another joust. A few friends backed him up, though his army was already retiring. Just then I saw our Reginald ride forth from the castle, lance in hand and shield on neck. He had been knocked over in our first charge, but it seems he got hold of a new lance from Madam Nicolaa, and perhaps he thought he might pick up a rich French prisoner. Or he may have been genuinely eager to win knightly fame, poor man. I could have told him that if he fought more gallantly than Roland no trouvère would sing the exploits of such as he! He came up with the Angevin knights just as the whole battle paused to watch the joust between Perche and the Marshal. What a crash it was! Both horses kept their feet, though the shock brought them to a standstill. Dropping his shattered lance, young Perche tugged out his sword; but our Marshal, though the blows he received would have sent most men sprawling, decided he had already won the fight. He also dropped his lance, but he never touched his sword. Instead he leaned over to seize the Frenchman's helm. Twice young Perche swung his sword, but the Marshal's helm was strong, and he did not flinch. Perche was forced half out of the saddle; in a moment his head would be on his horse's withers and the Marshal would lead him captive, as long ago at a tournament in Champagne he had led captive his grandfather. The other knights had reined in; they sat fascinated, watching this amazing old veteran

[158]

conquer yet again. They our Reginald decided to lend his assistance. I was too far away to see clearly, but I was told all about it afterward. He pushed forward until his horse was only half a length behind the Marshal's, and thrust at the Frenchman's head. It was a well-aimed thrust, and quite unnecessary. Young Perche, stone dead, reeled from the saddle; the lance had entered the slit of his vizor and penetrated the brain. The Marshal, in disgust, pulled back from the fray. Then the remaining French knights spurred against Reginald, and the English sat quietly watching until he was dead. After that the battle, or rather the tournament, was carried on with great spirit until most of the French had been captured."

"You mean that when they might have saved him they allowed Reginald to be killed?" Margaret said sharply.

"That is exactly what occurred, my lady. Of course, he had killed a young Count who would otherwise have been taken unharmed, so perhaps he deserved his fate, for being so bloodthirsty. But the real reason, I am sure, was that both sides resented the intervention of a mercenary in a struggle of gallant gentlemen."

"But Reginald also was a knight, though I know nothing of his birth," said Margaret. "Chivalry has been outraged, and I shall take it up with the Marshal. Look here, Robert, you know the code of knighthood as well as I do. I know it by nature, because I was born a fitzGerold, and you because you are an educated man. Knighthood is a personal quality, you admit? Most knights are nobly born but noble birth does not in itself confer knighthood. Before the coronation even the Little King had to be knighted. Yet any knight may grant knighthood to a warrior. My lord Falkes was knighted by King John, and he knighted Reginald Croc, as I have often heard him say. So if these rules

[159]

of chivalry mean anything Reginald was the peer of the Count of Perche, or of the Marshal himself for that matter. The whole point of knighthood is to make good warriors of every rank equals and comrades. What did my lord say when he heard of it?"

"He was very angry, madam. But he expects you at Lincoln, and I shall say no more, lest I aggravate the quarrel."

"Nonsense. I don't need to hear more. My lord's followers have been treated with injustice, which is an insult to fitzGerold as well as to Brealte. First I shall visit the castle here to have it out with the Marshal. Then, without waiting for daylight, we all ride for Lincoln. Give orders to have the horses ready in an hour."

But in the castle it was difficult to raise a grievance, however justified; for such a victory called for celebration, and practically everyone was already drunk. Margaret pushed past riotous sentries and doorkeepers until she strode unchecked to the dais in the great hall. The Marshal sat in the place of honor, still wearing his battered mail; he was talking excitedly to his sovereign, and indeed his account of the decisive battle was exactly suited to the understanding of a nine-year-old boy.

"So our four hundred and six knights went up against their six hundred and eleven," he was saying as Margaret bobbed a perfunctory curtsey and stood over him, her whole posture charged with anger. "We charged them and chased them from the town. A stray cow blocked a contraption the burgesses had fixed on the London gate to make it easier to collect their tolls, many fugitives got stuck behind her, and more than four hundred knights were left captive in our hands. The remainder are in full flight. But the great moment was when young Perche spurred against me. You must remember that years ago I overthrew his grandfather. On that occasion, when they sought me afterward to award me the prize of valor (a remarkable carp which had been caught that morning) they found me with my head on an anvil, while the blacksmith knocked the dents out of my helm. Old Perche had struck so hard that I couldn't get it off as it was. Now see what young Perche did." He stroked the battered helm on his lap. "Feel those dents. That's where his sword landed, twice, while I grasped his helm and strove to lead him captive. I would have done it, too, but some low sergeant killed him. A pity. I can't recall another knight who has captured the grandson of an adversary of his youth. The trouvères could have made a good song of it."

"But he was not a low sergeant," shouted Margaret, as the old man paused for breath. "He was Reginald Croc, a knight of my lord's mesnie. Sir Falkes de Brealte was knighted by King John, and Sir Reginald Croc was knighted by Sir Falkes. Why didn't your mesnie stand by him when the French attacked?"

"Let me see, I don't recognize faces as I used to. Ah yes, you are Margaret de Brealte, daughter of poor old fitzGerold the Chamberlain. I remember you perfectly, it's only a little weakness in my eyes. Is there anything I can do for you, madam, or any grace I can ask the King on your behalf?"

He shifted in his seat, as though to rise. But though he had been for many years a very courteous gentleman he was, after all, Regent of King and Kingdom; he took it for granted that she had motioned him to keep his seat though, in fact, she did nothing of the kind.

"All I seek is justice," she said angrily. "Your mesnie saw my lord's knight killed before their eyes. Perhaps the cowards cannot be punished now, but you should rebuke them publicly, for hanging back in the charge."

"Knights do get killed in battle, though perhaps not very often," answered the great man, his happy boyish grin fading to the wary expression of an experienced politician. "This Reginald rode most gallantly in the forefront of the melee, and the French slew him. It might have befallen any brave man."

"And, of course, if he was one of the Brealte mesnie the other knights would take him for a routier," put in the Little King, anxious to show that he was following this grown-up conversation.

"*Ex ore infantium et lactentium*," Margaret quoted grimly.

"How absurd. I am a knight and a King, and I was weaned long ago," said the child, who knew his psalter.

"There is no more to be said, my lord Regent," Margaret continued, ignoring the King as rudely as she could. "By prime I shall be at Lincoln, where I shall tell my lord that his followers can no longer expect help and protection from the mesnie of the Marshal."

It was a very long ride over crowded roads in the dark, but rage is a wonderful source of energy. Passelewe, who had ridden to Lincoln, then to Nottingham, then back to Lincoln, within a day and a half and practically without stopping, groaned and set his teeth; but he just managed to keep up with his fiery young mistress. Some women of the band fell out by the wayside, but it was obviously important for a soldier's companion to be on the spot as soon as possible after a remunerative victory, to get her share of the plunder before her man gave it to another girl; those who were strong enough rode with her, and as the sky reddened in the east a considerable company entered Lincoln.

[162]

There was a strong smell of charred timbers, but most of the fires had been extinguished. The city gates were open wide and the streets filled with riotous sergeants. But it did not seem to be a real bloody sack. The victors were enjoying themselves, but they had not massacred the burgesses; although the city had been taken by storm and the laws of war entitled them to that diversion. Margaret rode in by the blocked gate which Bishop Peter had opened for the entry of the royal army, for she had a natural curiosity to see the ground of the famous battle. The cathedral square was littered with dead horses and broken weapons, and the cathedral itself stood doorless and windowless, though no one had tried in earnest to burn it; the cloisters were in a particularly bad way, for the chapter had supported Louis of France. But there were limits to what an army of Crusaders, led by a Papal Legate, could do to a cathedral; now sentries stood guard over the enclosure, and peace of a kind reigned in upper Lincoln.

By the river, where the prisoners were guarded, there was still considerable tumult, with several houses burning. It was not a district where ladies might wander for sight-seeing, though Margaret would have liked to count the prisoners; after a glance at the famous turnstile which the cow had blocked she rode to the castle.

Here all was quiet. Clean and correctly dressed sentries watching alertly, their wound crossbows in their hands. After a winter of campaigning Margaret could recognize military efficiency when she saw it, and it hardly needed a glance at the banners on the keep to see that here Falkes had fixed his headquarters. Three banners waved side by side; the tattered old battle-flag of Nicolaa de la Haye, who had commanded during the siege; a large embroidered standard bearing the arms of William fitzHenry,

Count of Salisbury; and the grubby little half-moons of Brealte. But all the sentries were Brealte men, who recognized her and stood smartly at the salute as the portcullis was raised.

Margaret was still very angry. Reginald Croc had been a ruffian of unknown origin, the professional plunderer who had captured her on Chiltern; but for that she might now be married to some Frenchman of noble birth. But he had died alone and unsupported because he was a follower of her husband, not because he captured ladies. Against Falkes she stood on her gentle birth, but against the world in general she supported her own lord. She demanded fiercely to be led to the lord Falkes de Brealte, and the guard commander, impressed by her rage, sent a sergeant scurrying before her.

The leaders were still talking in the great hall, too elated for sleep on such a night of triumph. Madam Nicolaa, a fat old lady with a weather-beaten face under a very odd kerchief, sat at the head of the table, the Count of Salisbury on her right and the Bishop of Winchester on her left; below the Bishop sat Falkes, and these four discussed affairs of state among themselves, though lower down the table a few knights and captains yawned and drank. The discussion seemed heated.

"God's toenails," Madam Nicolaa declared in anger, "I am sheriff as well as castellan. I know we are all on the same side, but I can't sit here drinking while your men sack my town. To restore order we must send out strong patrols. My garrison are worn out. My lord Bishop, have you any disciplined men fit for duty?"

"Not one who is sober tonight, dear lady," Peter des Roches answered cheerfully. "I'm not all that sober myself. Damn it, we've won the war and the burgesses were on the wrong side. They deserve to see their wives raped and their shops pillaged. Rebel property is forfeit by the laws of warfare."

"If you want men to restore order, madam," interjected Count William, "I can lend you as many as you like. But they must use this castle as their headquarters. The burgesses won't believe they are serving the sheriff unless they lodge here."

"I am grateful for your kind offer," Madam Nicolaa said stiffly. "Unfortunately the Marshal himself ordered me to lodge Sir Falkes and his band here, and that leaves no room for your mesnie. Oh, who is this lady? Be seated, madam. Have you come to offer ransom for a prisoner?"

Then Falkes ran toward her, looking genuinely pleased; Margaret noted that he had changed completely into the garb of peace, a fine linen surcoat over a warm cotte. Count William and the Bishop were still in the padded tunics which they had worn under their mail, and the Marshal had ridden all the way to Nottingham in full armor. That was one difference between chivalrous knights who made a hobby of fighting and a professional soldier who regarded war as work.

She had expected Falkes to share her anger at the death of Reginald Croc. But while she had thought of nothing else during a long, dull ride, he had been planning how to follow up the victory, and it is hard to remain in a bad temper while doing interesting work. He was surprised, and rather alarmed, to see her so unexpectedly; but when she had explained that no disaster brought her from Nottingham and that she wished to speak with him in private he strolled by her side in the misty dawn that filled the inner bailey. A castle-dweller who desired privacy usually

[165]

sought the open air; it was difficult to be private in a crowded fortress.

She finished her recital of their wrongs by saying that now was the time to threaten to join the French, or to seize the castle of Lincoln and hold it against all comers. He answered politely and patiently.

"Of course, Reginald was not given the help any knight should expect from his comrades," he said easily. "But he must have known, before he charged, that he could not rely on them. Don't you see, my dear? We, all the Brealtes, my family and my followers, can never hope for common fairness and comradeship. Our enemies hate us and our allies are ashamed of us. If I had been captured when we sallied from this castle the French would have hanged me; and the Marshal would have been rather pleased. Because it would be easier to reconcile defeated rebels to a respectable government that employed no mercenaries. Now they must endure me in peacetime, when there is no war to keep me busy in the field. What it amounts to is this: we must always do very much better than any respectable knight, and expect a very much smaller reward. If it had been Bishop Peter who charged from the castle every trouvère would say he had won the battle single-handed; because I did it no one will mention it, while all will sing the Marshal's joust. Well, never mind. I am the best soldier in England, my band are the best mercenaries in Christendom. If we get only half of what is due to us that will still be a great reward."

"Then you will ignore the wrongs done to you and remain faithful to the Little King?"

"Certainly, my dear. Did you hear the discussion you interrupted, about restoring order in the town? There is a lot behind it. The Count wants to get his men into Lincoln

[166]

castle, on the pretext of helping Madam Nicolaa. Then he will turn her out and hold it for himself, in the King's name, of course. The Marshal put me here to help Madam Nicolaa against Count William. We all hope it won't come to open fighting, civil war within the victorious army which defeated the French yesterday; but my men are in the castle and the Count's in the lower town. You see, the Marshal still trusts my loyalty. It's going to be very difficult, and I shall never get my full deserts; but I have already come a long way from the hay meadow at Brealte, and while I keep within the law and obey the Regent nothing is beyond my reach."

Margaret did not bother to answer. Instead she went off to rest in a little turret chamber. But she was too tired and too excited for sleep. She was also too angry. Thanks to their splendid victory Falkes would now be one of the greatest men in England, but nothing she could say would spur him to demand his rights. His low birth must always be a handicap; but she had married him, and the husband of a fitzGerold should be good enough for the most noble company.

His trouble was his complete loyalty; the King's Men could count on him, so they never bothered to placate him. Look at the task he had now undertaken, the safeguarding of Lincoln from the Count of Salisbury. It was an unpleasant job which was bound to make him enemies. The Marshal was a much-loved leader, but would any other magnate in the royal army have taken such orders without protest? Could you imagine the Bishop of Winchester interrupting the celebration of victory to take measures against one of his colleagues, a Count of the highest birth, a son of the Old King himself?

Count William was an example to all ambitious magnates. Unlike her silly old Redvers father-in-law, he was brave enough to fight for his own profit, and a good enough warrior to be worth buying. He changed sides without scruple, but he chose his time carefully; a moment when the two parties were equally balanced, and his own adhesion made his new allies the stronger. He would never make the mistake of sticking to one lord through thick and thin, or of joining the winning side when it was already so strong that he was not especially welcome. If he wanted Lincoln now it would be wise to help him take it and earn his gratitude.

The band of Brealte might be the best soldiers in the world, but would they serve their lord faithfully and contentedly when they saw that he was unwilling to protect or avenge them? It was all very well to say they were baseborn, and so must try harder than noble knights; that was contrary to the rules of chivalry; but she did not really believe in chivalry, and it was a good thing to keep the baseborn in their place. Yet the sergeants might not see it in that light. How much would Count William fitzHenry protect one of his followers? Would he without protest see him murdered in the melee?

The fundamental question, which hitherto she had shirked asking herself, was this: when peace came, as it must soon come after this great victory, would she do better to remain a faithful wife or to join the enemies of Brealte who would gather from every side when the best captain of crossbows in Christendom was no longer needed to protect them from conquest by the French?

She lay on her pallet, staring at the stone ceiling and trying to make up her mind. This was a very ugly thought, and she wished it had never occurred to her; but now it was there it must be dealt with.

Her inclination was to leave things as they were. She liked Falkes, both as a husband and as a companion. He could never be her equal, but in some ways that made her married life even more pleasant. She feared her husband's anger, as was the duty of every wife; but she could not help despising him in her heart, as he very well knew; and the interior glow of that inward contempt was a comfort whenever he commanded her to do anything she would not have done of her own accord. Little Baldwin could not have a more competent guardian. As Falkes's wife she was the partner of his greatness, and every gentleman, every trouvère, would expect her to follow his fortune. If she deserted him she might be called recreant, and that would be a shocking thing to be said of a fitzGerold. Of course she would be true to him. It was her duty.

But then, if you really thought the matter to its conclusion, perhaps she was not his wife after all. In the chapel of Cambridge castle she had consented to marry him; but it had been only an outward consent, inspired by fear of King John. Later she had grown to like him, but at the wedding she had been basically unwilling.

Oh well, the time to raise that point would be when he did something silly or insupportable, not when he had just played a chief part in winning a decisive victory. It was something to store at the bottom of her mind, waiting on the uncertain future. The death of that revolting Reginald Croc had led her thoughts a very long way. She was the Lady of Brealte, wife and partner of one of the greatest of the King's Men; she would serve him loyally, as her blood demanded; and as her blood demanded she would be splendidly rewarded.

8: Christmas at Northampton

AS THE splendid procession left the chapel Margaret slipped from her place and ran up the wooden outside stair. From that point of vantage she could oversee all her household: the sergeants of the garrison, waiting to cheer at the word of command; the steward posed with his wand at the hall door, pages and servingmen clustered behind him; a trouvère gulping down his meal preparatory to entertaining the company (and two unauthorized jongleurs tuning their lutes in a corner in case the Little King should be bored by the earnest and improving call to the Crusade which was the principal item in the repertoire of their eminent colleague); the cook's boy peering around the kitchen door, a wooden clapper clasped nervously in both his hands, lest it should go off by mistake and cause the meal to be dished up too soon; the underbutler standing over the faucet near the stable, from which two casks of wine would flow for the entertainment of the lower orders when the King drank his first cup and not a moment earlier; the choir, ready to strike up the anthem *Christus Vincit*, the solemn music which must be sung whenever a King of England wore his crown in state. Everything seemed to be in order.

Of course it was raining heavily and blowing a gale. Velvet cottes would suffer from the walk across the bailey. But this was Northampton on the 25th December 1217, and such weather was to be expected.

What made the occasion especially nerve-racking for the fifteen-year-old chatelaine was that her staff were strange to the place. Falkes was sheriff of six counties, besides the Honor of Redvers which had at last come to him on the death of old Count William. He had planned to keep Christmas at Bedford, his favorite hall. It was only at the last moment, a few days ago, that the Little King had signified his desire to honor his faithful counselor by keeping Christmas under his roof, and Northampton had been an unexpected place for him to choose. All the skilled servants, and the pompous gentlemen who supervised them, had ridden from Bedford at very short notice. To arrange such an elaborate function was a great deal to ask of a young lady most of whose married life had been passed on active service. Margaret felt that someone had been unfair to her, but it was difficult to identify the culprit. Her husband had received no more warning than anyone else, it was absurd to blame the Little King who always did as he was told, and somehow it seemed as hard to be angry with the Marshal as with the Saints in Heaven. Very likely it was his fault, but then he was a gallant old gentleman who only really came alive when his shield was on his neck; probably he imagined that every castle in the land had a feast ready in the kitchen every day in case the King should happen to drop in. It was nothing more than normal male thoughtlessness.

Anyway, the hard work was done, and she might as well enjoy herself; if the cook couldn't make the fire burn, or there was not enough wine in the buttery, it was too late to do anything about it. She came down the stairs and entered the great hall with the last of the procession.

As she took her place at the high table she was pleased by the evident pleasure of her husband. Falkes had as usual inspected the sentries, turned out the guard, and checked the working of the drawbridge; but he did as much whenever he visited a castle under his command; the royal visit had caused him no extra trouble. And it was a signal honor, the final confirmation that the unknown bastard from Normandy was now one of the magnates of England. The King had not visited Dover, even to congratulate Hubert de Burgh on his gallant defense.

The whole government of the realm was concentrated in this hall. Margaret sat between the Regent and the Little King, the real possessor of power and the titular head of the state. It was impossible to imagine a higher place, or one more worthy of a fitzGerold. Even if young Baldwin had lived he could not have placed the Countess of Devon in such a seat. She must admit that Falkes gave her something that no one else could offer.

She did this grudgingly, for she was a little annoyed with her husband. On this important occasion he was not behaving with due decorum. The trouble was that he had no reverence for outward form; if a man was powerful he deferred to him, but if he merely held a great position without ability, like the Count of Aumale who had such charming manners and so little sense, Falkes treated him as a nobody. That was wrong and unfitting in a magnate who had married the daughter of a chamberlain. A Count who had inherited from his father must be greater than a successful bastard from Brealte, even if one could win battles and the other could not even manage his estates.

It was very easy to see, now that all the magnates were assembled in Northampton castle, that the late civil war had left two factions in the realm; they might be friendly at present, but they looked at affairs from different viewpoints. The old comrades of King John were drinking heavily; they carried themselves with a reckless air of bravado, and seemed not to mind if they upset the ordered progress of the feast by getting drunk before the last course was on the board. The nobility, of whom some had supported Louis, some held aloof, some come in at the last moment on the Angevin side because, after all, they were Normans who could never accept the rule of a Frenchman, were conversing decorously among themselves about the prospects of peace and the administration of the kingdom. The two groups did not mix, though for the present they sat together on friendly terms.

Of course, Hubert de Burgh spoke only to magnates of the very highest birth. Margaret looked down the table to where he was expounding the best method of raising money to pay off Louis and end the war with no hard feelings. (That unnecessary payment was the pet hobby of the Marshal, who argued that any course would be cheaper in the long run than putting down perpetual revolts of discontented rebels; but to Falkes it seemed a wicked waste of money. It was for the losers to pay the cost of the war, and if they rebelled again that actually increased the King's resources, since the fiefs of rebels escheated to the crown. Yet the Marshal, who could do no wrong, proposed this

[173]

payment. High policy was a difficult subject, too difficult for the understanding of a young lady.) Hubert knew all about finance, which may have been why he had risen to be one of the wealthiest men in the land. Now he was talking earnestly and looking as though ten generations of his ancestors had been great Counts; he had even assumed the popeyed look of a jouster who has taken too many knocks on the head, though he had never in his life fought except at sea or behind stone walls. On the whole Margaret preferred her husband's attitude. If you were a successful young warrior who had risen by the sword it was better to be reckless and gay and slightly shocking than to give such a convincing imitation of respectability.

The Little King was addressing her in the careful tone of a self-conscious child who knows that his elders are watching his behavior. "I would like to signify my pleasure at this noble entertainment, madam," he said graciously, "but my Regent tells me that I shall have no pleasure of my own until I am grown. So I cannot reward you."

This was interesting. Had the Little King a will of his own, and was he irked by the Regent's restraint? But before Margaret could lead him on to further indiscretions the Marshal himself, sitting on her other side, disposed of the topic.

"Sir," he said, with a gracious smile, "the late King your father, on his deathbed, devoted his last thoughts to the welfare of his realm. He entrusted his castles to brave men of his own choosing, and it would seem impious if you altered his arrangements so soon after his death. Besides, you are not of an age to dispose of your own fiefs. This should be known as widely as possible, so that greedy magnates leave you in peace."

The Little King looked annoyed, as was natural after

[174]

such plain speaking. But Margaret knew that the Marshal was too great-hearted, and too loyal, to care that he angered his young lord when he did what was best for the realm. His conscience was clear, and in a few years he would be dead. Almost any other leader in his position would have seized the crown. The Kingdom of England was hardly a hereditary fief; William the Conqueror had won it by the sword, and in the hundred and fifty years since the Conquest William Rufus, Henry I, Stephen, and John himself, had taken it by force from rivals with a better hereditary claim. Little Henry should consider himself very lucky that one day he would enjoy the possessions of his father.

But there was another point, more immediately important to the Brealtes. Margaret turned to the Marshal, ignoring the boy's muttered grumblings. "Do you mean, my lord," she said with interest, "that it is the policy of the Council to leave fiefs and castles in the hands in which they were placed by the pleasure of King John? Does Falkes hold his shrievalties and castles until the King comes of age, and do the magnates admit that they cannot take them from him?"

"I am no lawyer, madam. I suppose the Council of Regency might do anything a King can do. But it is as you say. Our policy is to make no changes."

"Yet by the terms of your treaty at Kingston the rebels will get back their castles as soon as they have sworn fealty and done homage. May it not happen that the same castle is sought by two claimants?"

"That can be arranged with good will on both sides. There are many castles in England and few lords great enough to hold them. If there is any case we cannot settle then the matter must be left unsettled until I am gone and the King is old enough to decide."

[175]

Margaret smiled polite agreement, and then bent her head over the dish to think in silence. Here was the weakness of the Marshal and of all these chivalrous knights; they enjoyed fighting and they enjoyed making peace afterward; but because they never hated the foe they forgot that some wars, at least, are fought to decide a definite issue; their terms of peace never settled the question in dispute.

Perhaps that was not quite fair. The Treaty of Kingston had settled that England should be ruled by the House of Anjou, not by the House of Paris. But how many warriors on either side had fought solely from loyalty to their lords? Probably only the Marshal himself. The others fought to keep their castles, or to win more; and after the great victory of Lincoln all disputes should have been settled finally in favor of the King's Men. The Marshal's magnanimity would keep quarrels alive for a generation now that rebels had a chance of getting back in peace what they had lost in war. But Falkes could look after himself. Her business was to see that the servants brought on the second course and kept the cups filled, at this great feast which did honor to her husband and to herself.

Her only regret was that the honor had come too soon, while young Baldwin could not take part in the proceedings. The Little King was already a knight, and probably he would be charmed if he were asked to knight someone even younger than himself; she had suggested to Falkes that the infant be brought in to receive knighthood at the King's own hands. But he had answered that a knight who could not stand unaided would be nothing but a figure of fun. So her son, head of Redvers and fitzGerold, remained with his nurse. He did not even know that he was host to the King of England, and though she would tell him of it as soon as he was old enough to understand, this great honor might never again come his way.

Where Margaret sat the party was dull. After a few cups of wine the Marshal always felt sleepy, as was natural at his age; but not only was he silent himself, he had angered the Little King, who took refuge in sulky silence; until Joan Nevill, sitting on his other side, worked hard to put him in a better mood. Margaret glowed with pleasure to think that her sister was now a poor relation. Hugh Nevill had been altogether too neutral in the late war; his fiefs had not been forfeited, nor was he compelled to renew his allegiance; but he had been deprived of everything he held at the King's pleasure, and would never again be trusted by the government. All the world knew that Joan and her husband were passing the winter with Margaret for reasons of economy.

Now Joan did her duty as a dependent, making herself pleasant to a sulky guest. "I am interested to hear that you, my lord, have a Pleasure, separate from yourself, which has now been removed and will one day be returned to you. What do you think it looks like? Has it matter and form? Why not ask the Doctors of Paris to define it? I see it as a small image of a King, smiling broadly most of the time, because after all it is a Pleasure; but turning purple with rage whenever you plan to remove some wicked castellan from his fortress."

"Ask the Marshal to show it to you, madam. He keeps it in his wallet," answered the King. But he smiled at the conceit and began to sketch a shadowy royal manikin on the tablecloth; he was very fond of sketching and always carried a stub of charcoal.

At the far end of the table, where Falkes sat among the Norman exiles and other King's Men, the party was

[177]

more than jolly; it was boisterous. That was the trouble, from a lady's point of view, with these holy days in midwinter; it grew dark so early that no one tried to hunt after dinner; and unintellectual warriors, who did not care for chess or backgammon, were tempted to sit drinking at the board until supper was brought in. It was no good signaling to the trouvère to recite the Lay of Antioch; Master Robert had already twice begun it, to cease in a huff when no one listened; probably he would go away and compose a satire on the boorish manners of the English court for the amusement of his French audiences. Margaret resigned herself to a few hours of boredom, only thankful that Falkes was sitting among men who agreed with him on public affairs, men who were unlikely to quarrel with him even in drink.

But this was not the hard-drinking court of King John. After barely two hours the Marshal begged to be excused; at his age he needed an afternoon nap, even in the short days of winter. The Little King, squirming in his seat, was eager to examine a carved tomb in the nearby church of St. Paul. The other guests rose, respectfully, and as King and Regent walked together to the door there occurred a little scene which Margaret remembered for the rest of her life.

No on was paying any attention to Hubert de Burgh, who sat prosing away about finance to a few like-minded colleagues. Evidently he thought the time had come to impress his personality on the public once again. He called, as the Marshal passed: "My lord, before you withdraw will you give instructions about the gathering of a force to deal with Robert de Gaugi? Everyone is here, clerks and commanders. If you tell us what you have in mind the plan will be made out, ready for your approval, by suppertime."

The Marshal, who was very sleepy, blinked as he

[178]

struggled to summon his wits. "Robert de Gaugi? Oh, the castle of Newark. Well, this is the season of peace to men of goodwill. Let it wait. Next time I see Robert I shall talk to him severely."

"But Newark is a fief of the Bishop of Lincoln," Hubert persisted. "Our suzereign at Rome will be angry if we permit Robert to detain the property of the Church."

The Little King flared up, principally because he was annoyed at the prospect of a long discussion while there was still light enough to examine an interesting tomb. "I command," he said fiercely, "that the knight-service of England be mustered to destroy that castle unless Robert yields at the first summons."

"Don't be so bloodthirsty, my little lord," Falkes called across the table in a mocking tone. "The Bishop of Lincoln was a rebel and Robert won that castle from him during the war. These recreants must have their castles restored to them by the terms of your precious Treaty of Kingston. But the King's Men will not willingly make war on a loyal knight in the interests of a rebel clerk. Robert has promised that one day he will leave the castle. Give him another six months to pack his booty."

The Little King pursed his lips in silence. He was bitterly angry; but he knew that he could not gainsay the decision of his Council, and it was less humiliating to give in at once than to argue without hope of success. The Marshal, thinking of his nap, never observed the King's anger; he heard what Falkes said, but the jeering tone escaped him; he only realized that Hubert de Burgh was again making trouble, while Falkes de Brealte was for once advocating peace. Peace is good, particularly for old gentlemen, particularly at Christmas. The Regent gave his decision: "Robert de Gaugi shall have one more summons

[179]

before we make war on him. As Falkes says, he is a loyal knight, and I expect he has a great deal of heavy baggage in Newark. Justiciar, when we meet for the Easter crown-wearing you will send him another writ. Then if at Pentecost he still defies us we must take strong measures. Any of you gentlemen who meet Robert in the next few weeks might pass on a hint that next time we shall really mean business."

The Marshal withdrew, the scowling King in his train. As Margaret climbed the stair to visit her son, Passelewe overtook her.

"Did you hear what that trouvère was saying as we passed?" he called softly. "He is a clever poet and his words will be repeated. He was muttering over to himself, 'King Henry of England wished to make war on Gaugi, but Falkes de Brealte counseled peace, and peace there was. Falkes the Bastard, Falkes of the Hay Meadow, is greater than the King of England. That will make me a good song.' "

In the afternoon little Baldwin slept, as befitted his age. Margaret sat by his couch murmuring lullabies. She thought the nurse looked at her curiously, and realized that under her breath she was crooning a single verse: "Falkes of the Hay Meadow is greater than the King."

9: *Law and Order*

ON THE 18th of June 1219, her seventeenth birthday, Margaret looked closely in her silver mirror. Since popular love songs and romances all praised the beauty of fourteen-year-old maidens she feared that her age might be beginning to show. But the mirror reflectd only a few wrinkles of worry, natural in a chatelaine. She felt encouraged, her only regret that on this auspicious day she must wear mourning. For her chaplain, assisted by one of the best choirs to be found in a private castle, was about to sing a Requiem for the great Marshal, dead exactly a month.

The Mass was magnificently rendered; it took most of the morning, and afterward she went straight to dinner. She sat alone on the dais, watching her large household enjoy excellent food and making a very good dinner herself. Here in Bedford, her permanent home, she had trained her cooks thoroughly.

In her life there was nothing lacking. She was undisputed ruler of Bedford, town and castle; she held as many fiefs as any lady in England, and would be rich in her own right if Falkes died tomorrow; she had but one child, and it seemed certain that her present husband would give her no more; yet that one was a boy and already a great Count; she could not be reproached as a barren woman, and the omission must be the fault of her husband. She had wealth, power, the respect of her peers and the envy of her elder sister. She was very lucky indeed. At Mass this morning, after she had prayed for the Marshal's soul, she had tried to think of something to ask God for her own benefit; and she had been unable to think of anything.

With a slight shudder she moved her right hand in a sketchy Sign of the Cross. Everyone knows that complete happiness and satisfaction is a dangerous tempting of Fate. Quickly she adjusted her mind to dwell on something unpleasant.

Perhaps the only unpleasant factor in her life, apart from the empty cradle which could not be her fault, was her husband. She did not hate him, in fact, she liked and admired him. But there was no getting away from it; he was a nuisance.

She had been born into the ruling class. She took it for granted that if a lord inherited castles from his father the castles would always be there, defended by castellans and administered by hardworking stewards. If a great lord needed some other amusement than hunting, feasting, and making love, it was all to the good, and helped his reputation with the jongleurs, if he displayed his courage in battles and tournaments. But he ought never to worry over money, or politics, or the government of the realm. Of course, his opinion should be asked on weighty questions of state, for that was his due as a magnate; but he ought not to work at such things.

Falkes worked harder than anyone else on the Council of Regency (except Hubert de Burgh who wasn't a gentleman, anyway). He rode with the court on the ceaseless journeys which had become the tradition of Angevin government since the days of the Old King, the Little King's grandfather; at first he had expected his wife to ride with him, getting wet through whenever it rained and seldom halting long enough to unpack her best gowns; soon she had stopped that, pleading that she could not bear him an heir unless she rested for a few weeks in the same castle, and protesting that she must oversee the rearing of little Baldwin, the future Count of Devon and Wight. Now she was permitted to remain at Bedford, which Falkes regarded as his home. But she never knew when he would turn up unexpectedly; and when he arrived he brought a train of dreary politicians who talked about nothing but money and the policy of the Pope. What was the good of being a great lady, wife to the greatest man in England, if she never was visited by amusing guests and her husband was too busy to entertain her? Day after day she toiled at the unending task of keeping the great building comfortable, healthy, and defensible, driving the stupid and checking the dishonest. And all went to waste in solitude. Yes, she thought to herself, she was very lucky, but all the same she had a cross to bear, her husband's neglect. That would be something to remember when she was examining her conscience. Refreshed and cheered by this discovery, she gave the signal to finish dinner, and ascended the stair behind the dais.

Margaret was abstemious and she also disliked waste. When she was in command of Bedford everyone stayed remarkably sober. But that only made worse one of the chief problems of a castle-dweller's existence, what to do with the afternoon. The mornings were not long enough for all the housekeeping and store-counting that must be done every day, and very often, as today, there were special services in the chapel as well; in the evening the whole household must be allowed to linger over their wine or ale while a trouvère or a troupe of traveling jongleurs sang of the Crusade which was the chief duty of Christian men. The afternoon was in theory devoted to amusement, but a lady was hard put to it to amuse herself alone.

Margaret was still extremely fond of hawking; it was the best pastime for a lady, sufficiently strenuous to bring her home tired, but not so exhausting as galloping through the woods after a stag. But June was a bad season for the sport. The bushes were full of young fledglings, and the hawks, satiated with easy kills, soon grew sluggish; even more important, this year the season was late and the hay not yet gathered; a crowd of falconers riding through the water-meadows would do serious damage. Of course, she was entitled to hawk over the land of her villeins, and she made a point of doing it at least once a year at the most inconvenient time, lest her rights be forgotten; but in this degenerate age money was more important than sport, and it would be a great nuisance if she were compelled to buy hay to feed the destriers through the winter. Better not go hawking this afternoon.

There was always the nursery. Reluctantly she climbed the steep winding stair to the top floor, where temporary partitions divided the great stone-floored room into solar, bower and chambers for herself and her son. Little Baldwin was delighted to see her. He sat entranced at her feet to listen to an exciting story about very wicked men who were

[184]

pursued to their lair in the greenwood by the holy statue of an avenging saint. But the nurse frowned, whispering "Elstow," and the story dwindled to an extemporized close. The nurse was right; though the servants were forbidden to mention the public protest of that tiresome abbess, little Baldwin was sure to hear of it sooner or later, and his dreams would be nightmares if he got it into his head that his stepfather was pursued by a statue of St. Paul. The child was too easily frightened for one of his noble birth. Even now he sensed that his mother was recalling an unpleasant memory; he wandered over to a corner of the large room and whimpered over a broken toy horse. He was always whimpering, and when he was smacked for it he bawled hysterically. Perhaps that was because everyone in Bedford was a little nervous about the future. But what else could you expect in a castle garrisoned by unpopular foreign mercenaries?

It was very wrong for a mother to be bored and irritated by her only child; Margaret loved him dearly, but he would not behave as a son of hers ought to behave, and she could not always hide her disappointment. She reminded herself that he had never known a father's care. He must grow up with the calm self-possession of the nobly born, and for that he should be much in his mother's company. But not when his mother was angry with him; that only increased his regrettable timidity. Margaret strolled downstairs and out to the stable.

Looking at horses and discussing their welfare with a knowledgeable head-groom was a pleasant way of passing the time. She noted that once again the steward had permitted the villeins who brought forage to dump it by the stable door, instead of carrying it on pitchforks into the basement of the keep; that saved them trouble, and since carting forage was an unpaid labor-service they were always as slack as the steward would permit; it also saved the understrappers trouble when they carried hay and straw to the stalls. But the stable was a lean-to, built against the inner wall dividing the two baileys; Falkes had pointed out, when last he visited Bedford, that this wall was part of the defenses of the castle, and that to pile inflammable stores at its base was a breach of sound military practice. When the whole realm was at peace it was hard to think of defense (perhaps that was the real cause of her boredom; she had grown up in a time of perpetual war). But it was her duty to rule his castle as her husband wished, even in his absence. She rated the head-groom, telling him to have the forage shifted at once.

Now it was impossible to pass the afternoon chatting in the stable. The head-groom was offended at what he considered unnecessary fuss; he answered her queries with Yes or No, and if she stayed much longer he would say something impertinent that must be punished. To think that only four years ago she had dreamed that to rule a great castle was the summit of human happiness, and now, on her birthday, she was bored and lonely!

She wondered whether to go for a ride, though that would mean a considerable disturbance of everyone's routine; an escort to be called out and armed, her waiting-ladies to be summoned and suitably dressed, a change of clothes for herself. Perhaps it was too much trouble, and she would order an early supper instead. Then, as she hesitated, standing bored and alone in the dusty bailey, she heard a sentry's challenge and a moment later the creak of the moving drawbridge. Her maid came running with a fresh kerchief, and she stretched her mouth into the smile of a gracious chatelaine receiving welcome guests.

[186]

The smile faded when she saw it was only her husband with a small escort. She had hoped for a company of young knights, perhaps even a Bishop with a train of witty clerks. She knew exactly what Falkes would say in answer to her greeting and, of course, he said it.

"Good evening, my dear. They got the bridge down smartly, but not smartly enough. I might have been running for my life; it should be done in the twinkling of an eye. Well, I shall watch them practising it tomorrow. H'm, that forage must be moved, but you have noticed it yourself. Give the carters a whipping next time they come here. Otherwise everything seems in order. Only fifty extra visitors for supper, and six at the high table. Why do you wear mourning? Oh, the Marshal? The month's mind, I suppose. At court that is stale news; dead rulers are soon forgotten. Well, I must wash. We can talk at supper, for there is a lot I must tell you."

He had brought no one interesting, except Passelewe, whom she was always glad to see; the others were his brother William, that tiresome and pompous ass, and three bachelors who were familiar but scarcely distinguishable figures in battered but well-kept mail. There were no clever young clerks or gay knights of noble birth. She had been bored with her solitude, but this would be as dull as any other intimate family party. She took it for granted that they would stay only for one night, since Falkes was always on the move.

But although the talk at supper was not gay it was important. The realm was still at peace, but the death of the Marshal had brought possibilities of change, and Falkes was taking precautions.

"The Council govern the country until the Little King comes of age." he explained carefully, as they sat over their

[187]

wine, "and I am a member of the Council. But who is its head? There must be one. We all served the Marshal because he was obviously the greatest man in England. The story goes that as he lay dying he named the Legate as his successor; in any case the representative of the Pope, the Little King's suzereign, has a pretty good claim. But a clerk can't rule a Kingdom. Bishop Peter of Winchester has actual possession of the King's person; he's a clerk, I suppose, but he's a warrior first, and quite capable of leading us. I like him and he likes me. We should do well under his rule. But, of course, he can't give orders to the Legate, because the Legate is specially commissioned to give orders to all Bishops. Perhaps we would be better without the Legate, but I don't know. The Council looks weak, as indeed it is; without him perhaps no one would obey us."

He had not yet mentioned the man who must occupy the forefront of his thoughts. Margaret helped him out, as a wife should; besides, she herself was curious. "What about Hubert de Burgh? Is he still one of the Council?"

"Our Hubert? You can be sure he is. Nothing can be done without his advice, as he would tell you himself if you asked him. King John named him Justiciar, and he maintains that he must continue to be Justiciar until Little Henry is old enough to make a change of his own free will. I can't see that myself, but it doesn't really matter, at least so long as the Legate and Bishop Peter do most of the Justiciar's work."

"But it is one of the important factors making for peace," put in Passelewe, and Margaret turned eagerly to hear his lucid explanation. "You see, madam, the Council can't do whatever they like. They are bound by all sorts of previous decisions and tacit understandings. First, the dear

[188]

old Marshal made his treaty with the rebels; he was a gallant knight, but he never would think straight. It was agreed, and sealed in writing, that rebels who did homage and swore fealty should get back their castles. He may have meant the castles we took in the last year of the war; but what about the castles which King John escheated, and granted to his faithful followers? Can the Council take away what was granted by a real King? They may have the legal right, but there would be a lot of fighting before it was recognized."

"That would mean calling out the knight-service of England to make war on our friends in the cause of our enemies," added Falkes, with a snort. "An absurd project, as I told Hubert."

"Quite so, my lord," Passelewe assented. "If the Little King is to rule when he comes of age the old party of the King's Men, who won the war for him, must keep their fortresses. But you know Hubert's new catchword, that only native-born English are fit to administer the queer laws of England. He fought for his lord"—"When he wasn't making truces," Falkes interjected—"he fought for his lord, but he never approved of his lord's faithful servants. The only way we could keep the peace was by decreeing that the pleasure of King John must stand unaltered until the new King is old enough to alter it himself."

"Which boils down to this," Falkes said fiercely. "Every castle must remain in the keeping of its present castellan until we have a real King. No magnate will surrender a castle except to superior force, whatever the law may say; and once fighting starts the discontented will call in Louis again. I myself enjoy war, and no one has ever called me coward; but for the next few years the Council must put up with anything to keep the peace."

"Fair enough," William put in, "if you treat everyone the same. But poor Robert de Gaugi lost Newark, just because he was too loyal to hold it against the Leopard banner."

"Yes, that was a mistake," his brother agreed. "But he had defied the Marshal and insulted the whole Council. Besides, it never actually came to drawn swords. He yielded without fighting when we sat down before the castle."

"If he had fought I might have joined him," William answered. "Newark was entrusted to him because the Bishop of Lincoln, who used to hold it, was an open traitor."

"Yes, and our suzereign, the Pope, ordered us to give it back to the Bishop, who was entitled to it under the terms sealed at Kingston. For God's sake don't start that old argument again," said Falkes wearily.

"Peace on earth to men of goodwill," Passelewe murmured sardonically. "That is the motto of the new rulers of England. Anything to keep swords in their scabbards, for once they are drawn no one knows on which side they will strike. But it's not enough to say, 'Brethren, love one another.' We take our precautions. Has my lord told you, madam, why he is riding this way?"

"Oh, that," said Falkes vaguely. "A dirty business, but it's not really secret, and anyway people will soon guess. Just another breach of the pleasure of King John, which we have all sworn to keep undisturbed. After that battle at Lincoln good old Nicolaa de la Haye couldn't restore order in the county which is her hereditary shrievalty, and I'm not surprised. So the Marshal made Count William of Salisbury sheriff of Lincoln; to reward him, I suppose, for not changing sides again in the middle of the battle. He put his men in the town, but Nicolaa stuck to the castle she had defended so gallantly. Now the Count's men prowl around her gate, complaining that they can't rule the county without her castle. They might slip in one dark night and defy us to turn them out. So the Council agreed that I visit her, with three knights and a few sergeants. It's a bore, but a compliment at the same time. They know that Count William will think twice before breaking the peace if it means fighting me. Of course, after I have gingered up her garrison he won't get in by surprise; he must display his banner and levy open war."

"You see, madam? Anything rather than open war," said Passelewe. "Luckily all dread it equally, King's Men and rebels. So we may keep the peace until our Little King is old enough to fight for his own."

That night, lying beside her husband in the great marriage bed, Margaret explained how bored she was in lonely Bedford; she begged him to stay a few days instead of riding on to Lincoln. When she thought of Falkes in his absence she never particularly wished to see him again; she remembered his rough manners and the low view he took of human nature. But when he was present she was refreshed by his vitality; and even though she disapproved of him it was impossible for her to feel bored in his company. But Falkes explained that Madam Nicolaa was in genuine danger, and that it was his duty to carry out the mission entrusted to him by the Council.

It was a new idea to Margaret, that one "more powerful than the King" had duties which might not be neglected. Her father had spent much of his time riding with the court; but then, though he was a very distinguished nobleman, he was also the King's personal retainer. Count William de Redvers had been a great magnate, and he had sat quietly at Plympton governing his tenants. She knew that Falkes would like to do the same. Nothing gave him more pleasure than turning out his own sentries, inspecting his own stable, sitting in his own hall to watch his own servants minister to a large company. It gave him the reassurance he needed, proof that the bastard in the hay meadow had really climbed to a position of power and dignity. No, it was not restlessness that made him leave his favorite castle after only one night at home. If he worked so hard it was because he thought the work must be done.

He tried to explain, though she did not pay much attention. During the civil war she had followed politics with care. But the Tournament of Lincoln had destroyed the power of the King's enemies. The old servants of King John were firmly in the saddle, there was no faction in the countryside that would dare to fight them, and they even enjoyed, most surprisingly, the support of the Church. Her husband and his friends ruled England and public affairs were no longer a menace.

But Falkes would not let her sleep until he had told her his views, and at length she began to understand that the House of Brealte was not so firmly founded as it appeared.

"So long as the war raged I was the only captain who could hold unpaid mercenaries to the Leopards," he told her, leaning on his elbow and prodding her to make her stay awake until he had finished. "The Marshal and the Legate needed me, Count Ranulf likes me, and the other magnates were willing to keep me in a good temper. In a way it's a pity we beat the French so thoroughly; if they were still a menace I should still be courted. But even after the war was won the Marshal needed a competent soldier to capture any castle that still defied him, and I know more siegecraft than most Englishmen. And there was no doubt about who was head of the Council; the Marshal had no peer. Now he's dead and there is no Rector *Regni et Regis*. But what has really upset the balance of force, as it was after Lincoln, is Hubert's victory in that sea fight. Hubert is Justiciar by the same title that gives me my castles, the pleasure of King John. If I turn him out I hazard all I possess. That didn't matter while I was the greatest soldier in England and he was only a stubborn defender of stone walls. Now there are asses going about saying that Hubert is my equal as a soldier, and an Englishman born who understands their ridiculous law. Yet he is as tender to the rebels, from sympathy, as the Marshal was from chivalry to a beaten foe. Hubert never was wholeheartedly on our side. I do what I can to put it about that he murdered Count Arthur with his own hands, though I happen to know King John did it himself. But people forget very quickly; half of them answer, 'Who was Count Arthur?' Hubert aspires to be Regent, and the rebels, the clerks, and the native English would rather be ruled by him than by a Norman. That's why I must remind the Council that I am indispensable. And also why we must keep the peace at all costs. If war breaks out Hubert might overtake me."

"But why should any magnate care whether Falkes or Hubert is Regent, or at least care deeply enough to risk his fiefs in civil war?" Margaret objected. "I suppose you both serve the Little King? In less than ten years he will be ruling by himself."

"When he grows up he will rule this country. But what about Normandy? That is the root of the quarrel. Hubert is an Englishman who thinks of Normandy as a foreign land. He doesn't really expect us to drive out the

French. But I want to strengthen the Little King here in England until the whole knight-service of the land is at his disposal for a campaign across the Channel. I want to make him as absolute as the King of Sicily, so that he can hire a great army of mercenary reinforcements with his tallages. It's the only way to rescue my Norman cousins from French oppression. The French sacked Brealte and killed my father. Probably they killed my mother, too, though no one bothered to report her death. Ask Passelewe. His father was priest of Brealte, and he was there when Lupescar burned it. If I could sack Paris and defile the shrine of St. Denis I should die happy. Perhaps that's too much to ask. But Normandy must be freed, and only an absolute King of England can free it."

He grasped her shoulder so firmly that she cried out, but he was too excited to notice. It was odd that she should learn his great obsession, the mainspring of his life, only after nearly three years of marriage. But then she knew very little about him and she was not especially eager to learn more. He was one of "the Norman Exiles." Most people envied them the good positions they had found in England; it was a new idea that they saw themselves as maltreated men, burning for revenge. But it was not important. If Falkes wanted to liberate Normandy he would probably accomplish it, as he accomplished everything he undertook. He was a satisfactory husband, but she had been forced to marry him on pain of death; she could not be expected to share his projects for a country she had never seen. She kissed him firmly on the mouth to make him forget politics. Soon they were sleeping side by side, and whatever filled the dreams of Falkes Margaret saw in her sleep only a greater and gayer castle of Bedford.

In the morning she complained once more of the

loneliness of her position. She hoped that Falkes would leave Passelewe to keep her company, for she found the clerk amusing. But the result was unfortunate; she found herself saddled with brother William, that silly would-be chivalrous oaf whom she considered so ridiculous. Her husband gave her no choice in the matter; it seemed that he had brought William intending to leave him as castellan of Bedford though he had not bothered to inform his wife until he was about to leave.

"It's because the Marshal is dead, my dear," he said airily. "The times are disturbed. I must ride wherever the business of the Council calls me; but this is the head of my Honor, and it should be commanded by a good knight. I know you think William a fool, and in some ways I agree with you. But he had a sound training under me, the best castellan in Christendom. If trouble comes he will hold Bedford gallantly, and since he is my heir no one can bribe him to desert me, since that would be to rob his own inheritance."

"Heir to what?" Margaret answered sharply. "Your shrievalties are held at the King's pleasure, and my son will hold Redvers and fitzGerold when he is free of your guardianship."

That was true, and very galling to her husband. He was one of the rulers of England, perhaps even "greater than the King"; but he held nothing in fee, to be transmitted to his heirs; all his castles were held either in right of his wife or at the King's pleasure.

Falkes never lost his temper unless there was some tactical advantage to be gained by a display of rage; it was one of the most irritating things about him. Now he answered gently: "Heir to my band, and to the name and war-cry of Brealte. You brought me land, but my faithful sergeants hold it, and if I fell dead on the way to Lincoln they would follow William against all comers. Should the King ever propose to take back what I hold at his pleasure a great many experienced soldiers would advise him to think again. Even Hubert is aware of that."

So she was left to endure the undiluted company of Sir William de Brealte, who had all his brother's faults of social behavior and other failings which were his alone. For one thing, he was of legitimate birth and his mother had been respectable; so he was intolerably patronizing to a mere Anglo-Norman, whose blood must have been weakened by a hundred and fifty years of the influence of this inferior island. Margaret despised him for a ruffian, and he despised her for a provincial; it made social intercourse uncomfortable.

But his worst fault was a maddening insistence on the duties of chivalry and a ridiculous deference to the high-flown opinions of jongleurs who did not themselves follow that impractical code. He was absurdly generous, very quick to resent slights from the neighboring knights whom he regarded as his equals, and much too lenient with the peasants because it pleased him to pose as one indifferent to money. He was an efficient castellan and a strict commander of the garrison, thanks to his training under Falkes; his sergeants liked him, for soldiers are always happier under a strict captain, though they may sigh for a slack one; but the gentry of the countryside laughed at his posturing. He was very lucky to have been knighted, and knighted by a King; it filled his thoughts.

To Margaret he was distant but correct. He was aware that she despised him, and he revenged himself by sneers at the unwarlike qualities of the Counts of Devon. But she was the property of his adored brother and he guarded her with the zeal he displayed in guarding every asset of the House of Brealte. He was fanatically loyal to Falkes, so loyal that there was no room left in his mind for friendship with anyone else.

10: Public Opinion

DURING the next four years Margaret came to terms with life. She was reasonably content. William remained castellan of Bedford and she did not see much of her husband, who was busy with the government of an increasingly restless country; but occasional visits to court broke the monotony of her provincial existence. Anyway, she was not so isolated as her sister Joan, stuck in a tower among the Nevill fiefs on the Scots border, and no lady had a better life unless she rode every day with the ever-riding court. Margaret preferred to stay in one place, even though she might be far from great affairs.

Little Baldwin was growing up, which should have been interesting; but he was a disappointing child. At six years old he began learning to ride like a knight; which meant putting him on a well-mannered, elderly destrier, for it was a waste of time to practice on hackneys. But he made slow progress, and Margaret grew very angry when William suggested that his lack of skill might be due to nervousness. It was impossible to imagine a Redvers afraid of a warhorse. All the same, he behaved as though he were afraid. Perhaps because he was an only child, with no younger brothers to bully and impress, he had remained very babyish. He did not want to grow up, and he genuinely disliked pain and hardship; he even asked to come in from hunting if it was raining heavily. Occasionally you met soft children like that, even among noble families; the best remedy was to make them into clerks, but for little Baldwin that was impossible. He had no brother and he must become Count of Devon and Wight, a knight trained to defend his fiefs, whether he liked it or not. Margaret realized that Falkes could feel no sympathy for a weakling; she kept him out of the way of his stepfather.

For a lady, the most interesting event of those years was the Little King's second coronation, at Pentecost of the year 1220. When the project was first proposed Falkes was against it, for it might seem to reflect on the first scrambled ceremony at Gloucester; that irregular coronation was the main title of the King's Men to govern in the name of their lord, and if it was held invalid the next thing to be questioned might be King John's will, setting Falkes on the Council. But Hubert was anxious to please the Archbishop of Canterbury and the monks of Westminster, while every bored magnate who saw an opportunity for a lavish party was strongly in favor. As politics it might be unsound, but as a function it proved most enjoyable.

In the event it did no harm. Passelewe foretold that during the festivities Hubert might try to get the Little King declared of an age to govern. Then the King's pleasure would once more dispose of castles and shrievalties, and the whole world knew that the King's pleasure was really Hubert's. But little Henry was only twelve and childish for his years; it was obvious that he had no will that was his own. The Legate made no move and it was for the Legate, representative of the papal suzereign, to declare when the boy came of age.

Margaret came to Westminster for the festivities, since for a few weeks the court would remain in that one place, like the ideal court of King Arthur in the romances which never left Camelot. It was the kind of life that suited great ladies, and Margaret was perfectly content. But then there was trouble in the north; the whole administration took the road to deal with the insubordinate Count of Aumale, who refused to surrender the royal castle of Rockingham which had come into his hands during the civil war. The government had argued for three years before resorting to force; luckily, when at last the knight-service of England marched on the disputed fortress Aumale submitted before any discontented magnate had the chance to join him. But while the court stopped at York to oversee the siege that tiresome Hubert scored a personal triumph.

The Little King's sister had been betrothed to King Alexander of Scotland, and it was convenient to celebrate the marriage while the Council was in the north. Margaret had not gone to York because she could not afford to make another state visit in the very month after the coronation. At Bedford she heard, with disgust, that Hubert de Burgh had taken Alexander's sister in marriage, with the County of Kent as endowment for his new status as brother-in-law to a King. That put him definitely a rank above Falkes. Margaret considered herself just as nobly born as any Scottish princess; but Hubert was now a Count and Falkes only sheriff and castellan.

There was another alarm in July. The knight-service of England mustered in the far southwest, where Count Henry of Cornwall claimed to hold the Stannaries in fee, not at pleasure. But when the army was assembled Count Henry, though as a grandson of the Old King he was of the turbulent Angevin stock, also submitted without fighting. So far the Council had just kept the country under control; the provincial knight-service came when summoned, and there had been no display of a rebel banner to attract the discontented.

For discontent there was, much of it directed against Falkes personally. In Devon he had been granted, as guardian of his stepson, all the rights of a Count, including the Third Penny of all amercements. The county court should have brought him a considerable income. But the freeholders of Devon entered into a sworn agreement never to bring suit before it. The agreement was publicly concluded and Falkes wished to treat it as open defiance; but Hubert maintained that it was not repugnant to the Law of England, which he alone could interpret; if people wished to keep away from the law courts, settling their differences by friendly arbitration, no one might hinder them.

In every county controlled by Falkes there was trouble. The old Marshal had never stopped to think before offering repentant rebels their old fiefs; many of these fiefs had been declared forfeit by King John and granted to loyal knights in recompense for their loyalty. It was too much to expect that the victors in a civil war would impoverish themselves to make restitution to defeated rebels. But the law supported the rebels; Hubert had devised a special writ, "*de tali saisina habenda*," and when a plaintiff bought that from the Chancery a loyal sheriff found himself in a difficult position. Of course Falkes always disregarded the writ,

[201]

telling the plaintiff to go away and win the Battle of Lincoln before trying to take back the fruits of victory. But then the freeholders of the county muttered that he was breaking the law.

There was one particular case, concerning the wood of Norton in the county of Northampton, which gave an infinity of trouble. King John had granted it to the sheriff of the county, to cut timber for repairs to his castles; the sheriff was Falkes, and after cutting the timber he naturally pastured his pigs in what was left. But the wood, before it was forfeited for rebellion, had belonged to John Marshal. He brought to bear all the influence of his great family, and appeared in court with a copy of the writ. Falkes refused to hear him, expressing himself forcibly on the value of royal writs issued by a child too young to rule. He kept the wood, while John Marshal bought further copies of the writ and threatened to appeal to the Council of Regency. Since Falkes sat on the Council that was a hopeless undertaking. But the story of his contempt for the King's writ was widely told, and it was rumored that little Henry had been deeply offended.

Margaret herself witnessed the outbreak of the next war, at the Christmas feast of 1220. When threatened with outlawry the silly Count of Aumale had surrendered Rockingham and Sauvey; but he still clung to the castle of Bytham, which was also spoil of the civil war. He had been ordered to render it and there had been various schemes for a peaceful settlement, including the desperate expedient of sending him to Gascony as Seneschal, to get him out of the country. But no one wished him harm, and if he had sat quiet he might have died lord of Bytham. However, he grew tired of being badgered to surrender his booty, and in the middle of the feast at Oxford cried out that there was a plot to ruin him; he rode north by night to display his banner in rebellion. Nobody took Aumale seriously, but it was the old business of Rockingham again. The Council felt so weak that it must crush rebellion before the rebels crushed it. The Christmas feasting was abruptly broken off and everyone rode north.

Hubert and the Legate, who worried about finance, seized the opportunity to impose a scutage for "the war of Bytham." That was a pity, for once the government recognized a state of war important legal consequences followed from the suspension of the King's Peace.

But the trouble blew over. Aumale escaped from Bytham and took sanctuary at Fountains; his garrison immediately surrendered and were granted free pardons. Since no one had been killed no one cried for vengeance, and the leaders of both sides were old comrades of the civil war. Aumale presently came out of sanctuary to pass the rest of his life quietly on his own fiefs.

When the Christmas court dispersed Margaret rode back to Bedford. Nowadays she seldom saw her husband except at the three great courts, Christmas, Pentecost and Michaelmas. Falkes was always on the move, either riding with the King and Council or dashing off to preside over one of his numerous county courts. When he came to Bedford, either to harry John Marshal over that disputed wood or to ensure that the Abbess of Elstow lost any case to which she was a party, he might sleep in Margaret's bed; but all day he would be riding the countryside, delivering royal writs and testing the sentiments of the local knighthood, as was the duty of a conscientious sheriff. Naturally he had a deputy, for the law assumed that a sheriff was always on the spot, in spite of the modern custom by which half a dozen shrievalties were given to one trusted soldier. Equally naturally, since what Falkes looked for in a subordinate was loyalty rather than skill in legal matters, the deputy was William de Brealte; William sometimes forgot to deliver his writs, but he dealt firm and extremely partial justice in any case that concerned a pardoned rebel. Margaret still found him a bore, but he took his duties so seriously that he had built himself a wooden solar in the inner bailey, where he might work undisturbed; often he took his meals there and she might not see him for days on end.

Her life was lonely. Other great ladies lived at home while their husbands rode on campaign; but most of them had large families of growing children, and travelers dropped in frequently. Margaret blamed Falkes for her solitude; it was his fault that Baldwin was her only child, and that travelers of noble birth and interesting conversation avoided her castle, spending the night in some nearby Abbey. Falkes was extremely unpopular with the local gentry.

But whenever she saw her husband, his good spirits, his charm, and his energy won her again, as they had won her at the beginning of their married life. For Pentecost, 1221, the King wore his crown at Winchester, and she rode south to join Falkes for the feast. In the great hall of the Bishop's castle (for the rival fortress was avoided by loyal King's Men, since Count Saer of Winchester had been a prominent leader of the rebels) her husband came forward to greet her. He was dressed as splendidly as ever, but there was something strange about him. She looked again and saw on his shoulder the big red cross of the Crucesignati, the warriors under vow to journey to Outremer.

She was delighted. A journey to Outremer was the best kind of pilgrimage, especially for a lady; it was extremely valuable for the forgiveness of sins, and the luxurious magnates of Outremer always gave western ladies a very good time. As she embraced her husband, she whispered: "I see you are under a vow. I hope you will take me with you. Under that sacred sky I am sure you will quicken my womb." (That ought to decide him if he had been thinking of leaving her behind; he wanted a son to succeed him more than anything else in the world.)

But his answer was disappointing.

"This cross?" he muttered. "I took it some time ago, last Ash Wednesday, and by now I meant to be oversea. Unfortunately I have been compelled to alter my plans, but they won't let me take it down until the vow is fulfilled. Come over to the window and Passelewe will help me to tell you all about it."

So he had hoped to go without her, without even letting her know he was going! He would have wasted little Baldwin's inheritance, traveling as a gay, unattached bachelor! Still, he had not in fact escaped her. She smiled dutifully as she sat facing him in the window seat, with the inevitable Passelewe, always called in to smooth over awkward interviews, standing at her shoulder.

"Bishop Peter asked me to join him," Falkes began nervously. "We heard that the lords of Outremer had captured Damietta in Egypt. They needed reinforcements, and they offered to make Peter Archbishop of Damietta if he would join them with a band of the victors of Lincoln. I was to command his crossbows. But just when we had taken our vows the infidels recaptured Damietta and the lords of Outremer sued for a truce. Bishop Peter went off anyway to have a look at the wars, because being a Bishop in peacetime bores him dreadfully. But he didn't hire mercenaries, so I could not go with him unless I paid my own expenses. I should like to give up the whole idea. But

[205]

it seems I can't. I have taken a vow, and in the end it must be fulfilled. Perhaps if I wait someone else will offer to pay the passage of a skilled professional captain."

"Anyway, my lord could not go at this crisis of his affairs," Passelewe said smoothly. "I told that to the Legate, and there is no danger of the excommunication which is the penalty of a neglected vow. Meanwhile the status of a Crusader carries certain advantages. You see, madam, we can now plead almost limitless essoins if anyone tries to bring us before the King's court; we cannot be excommunicated, except by the Pope in person, or his Legate; and by strict Church Law no creditor may distrain on the lands of a Crusader, though I'm afraid the King's judges won't recognize that immunity unless the Crusader is actually oversea."

"That's true," Falkes said, with a comfortable chuckle. "Next time John Marshal sues for Norton wood I can meet him with a new delay. I am essoined until I return from Outremer. John may be dead of old age before his confounded plea is heard."

"That sounds most satisfactory, my lord," Margaret answered, smiling. "You must give me plenty of warning before we start, so that I travel in fitting state. Perhaps if we delay long enough my son will be ruling in Plympton and you will not need to appoint a castellan for the fiefs of Redvers." (That was a nasty reminder. She saw him squirm.) "As for your other responsibilities, they are all held at the King's pleasure. When our Little King is old enough he can appoint other sheriffs. Then we shall be free as air, free to devote our lives to the liberation of the Holy Sepulchre."

"Of course, I shall have fiefs of my own one day. In fact, I expect them to be granted at this very court. That's what Passelewe meant when he spoke of a crisis in my affairs," Falkes said with some annoyance.

"Yes, my lord. The Little King will be fourteen on his next birthday, and some say that makes him old enough to have a pleasure of his own. You can only be sure of your castles until October." That was Passelewe, evidently continuing an argument which had been interrupted by her arrival.

"I swore to King John that I would defend my fortresses in the name of his son, until that son came of age. I never promised to hand them over to Hubert de Burgh because the Little King was old enough to start shaving. It's absurd to say that by next October he will be capable of ruling. He is so childish that he won't rule of himself in ten years' time or twenty. If Hubert wants my castles let him come and take them, with his banner displayed. I shall show him how we wage war in Normandy."

"Yes, yes, my lord," Passelewe interrupted. "That is all very true, but the King's hall is not the place to say it. United, the Council can only just keep the peace; if you divide into factions the King will never reign."

Falkes swore briefly, and then swung away from the window to greet a party of newcomers. Margaret saw, with surprise, that he was worried. On the night before Lincoln, expecting defeat and death, he had been calmly at ease; she had never seen him anxious, and she looked inquiringly at Passelewe.

"You must comfort my lord and yours, madam," said the clerk, gazing after his master with a smile of loving tenderness. "All his life he has seen his duty plain, and done it at great peril of his body. Uncertainty is new to him, and he can hardly bear it. You see, he is loyal to the memory of King John and cannot bring himself to make war on the Little King. But he sees plainly that Hubert means to take away his castles. How to be loyal to Henry and defiant to Hubert; that is a hard task for one who has always charged the King's enemies without inquiring into the quarrel."

The horns blew for supper and Margaret saw no more of Passelewe that day. Sitting beside Falkes she marked once more his irritability and depression, and found herself sympathizing with him in his trouble. Her first duty was to her son, and Falkes was not the partner she would have chosen if she had been free to choose; but it was hard to be indifferent to the troubles of such a gallant knight. Although she had never been in love with her husband, like most of his intimates she was fond of him.

Winchester Castle was extremely crowded with all the magnates of England lodging under one roof. The Brealtes were important enough to have a little chamber to themselves, with a rather mean bed for the lord and his lady. Passelewe, the knights of the escort, and a couple of pages, slept all over the floor; though Margaret's tirewoman must lie in the female dormitory, to avoid scandal. As Margaret lay in wakeful silence, listening to the rumble of masculine snores which reminded her that she was paying an enjoyable visit, far from solitary Bedford, she seemed to hear on the stairs outside more than the normal activity of any sleeping fortress. A castle never closed down completely for the night; there were always reliefs for the sentries, captains doing their rounds, and servants replenishing the fires, to clatter down winding stairs and stumble through dark passages. But this evening there seemed to be more movement than usual, and she heard the suppressed whispers of excited men. As someone hesitated outside their door she nudged her husband.

[208]

Falkes was instantly alert, like any other veteran accustomed to night alarms. He listened carefully and called softly to the knights of the escort. Their snoring stopped abruptly and Margaret heard the faint squeak of oiled leather as swords were loosened in their scabbards. Then the grunting resumed and Falkes spoke to her quietly.

"You were right to wake me, but that was an unarmed man and well dressed. I could hear the rustle of his long cotte and the pad of soft leather shoes. When he heard us he crept away. Perhaps he was only a butler on his way to the hall to steal wine, or perhaps he wanted to make sure the Brealtes were still here and asleep. But he meant us no harm; and if he did an unarmed man could not harm us."

That was comforting. Falkes was so certain that no one could harm him except in open war, and the confidence of a brave and successful soldier was pleasant to a nervous lady. All the same, something was doing in the castle, something more than petty thieving or amorous intrigue. All night she heard coming and going, and now that she knew what to listen for she realized that these night walkers were great men, wearing the furred cottes and pointed shoes of the nobility. Perhaps they were only holding a secret council. Even so, the exclusion of the lord Falkes, a member of the Council of Regency, ought to be looked into.

In the morning the whole court assembled in the cathedral for the High Mass of Pentecost. Falkes had not been in his place five minutes before Ralph Musard, another Norman exile, told him the news. Margaret could not overhear what was said, but she saw her husband stiffen. He turned to Passelewe, making some signal; the clerk raised his eyebrows in surprise, then nodded to show he understood. Immediately he left the cathedral and Margaret was aware that throughout the long, excessively choral Mass knights and sergeants of Brealte one by one unobtrusively slipped away.

When, at last, the blessing was given and the whole court walked out in solemn procession the band of Brealte was waiting, fully armed and ready to move off, just outside the New Minster. Margaret's own destrier was ready saddled and a page held Falkes's mail for his lord to arm. At once Passelewe came up, leading his horse, to show Falkes a small token. She heard him say under his breath: "This is Peter's signet. I saw him ride out by the west gate. He was free and unharmed."

"Very well," answered Falkes. "We leave by the north gate. Get mounted, madam. Bid no farewells. You are not to take leave courteously, even of the Little King."

"But where are we going? Can't we breakfast before we start? I left my jewels scattered all over the chamber. Must we miss the jousting after dinner?" cried Margaret in surprise and disappointment. The crown-wearing of Pentecost was one of the greatest social functions of the year.

"We shall dine by the Thames and sup in Bedford, if our horses can carry us so far," Falkes answered curtly. "We are on campaign. You may breakfast as we ride."

There was a short delay while Falkes armed, but Margaret was too angry at these sudden orders to ask for an explanation. She wanted to sulk; a fitzGerold should not be moved about like a serf. But she changed her mind when she felt the tension which ran through the whole troop as they approached the north gate. Sergeants hitched around their shields and fingered their sword hilts, and the crossbowmen looked to it that their weapons were wound to the full; the party were obviously preparing to cut a way out.

[210]

She still did not know the cause of this excitement; but it was something serious, and she would be safer if she kept close to her husband and obeyed him with alacrity.

The guard at the gate turned out fully armed, nervous at such a warlike approach. The portcullis wavered in its groove as the watchman prepared to release the winch, and the knight in command could be seen looking earnestly down the street for a signal to prevent the departure of this unfriendly force. Then he shrugged his shoulders and waved cheerfully. "Good-bye, Falkes," he called impudently. "You seem to be in a hurry, and no one has told me to stop you. See you in the buttery next Michaelmas; unless before then I am ordered to break a lance on your shield. But go in peace and I hope you return as peacefully."

At last, while they galloped steadily northward, Falkes and Passelewe remembered to explain to her. Both spoke at once, very angry, but in complete agreement.

"What you heard last night was Hubert's first serious attack on the Norman exiles. He laid his plans very secretly, and by God's toenails the rascal has succeeded so far. But he won't catch me unawares. I am armed and free, and I shall never enter his presence without my sword. The tailed, twisting scoundrel of an Englishman! At supper last night I saw him embrace Peter de Mauley, after the whole bloody plot was already hatched."

"Not bloody," Passelewe contradicted. "That is the one good thing in this dirty business. I saw Peter ride free."

"Of course he rode free," shouted Falkes. "If he had been dead, or even in chains, I would have burned the Minster and cut down the Little King before the altar. I wonder if Hubert realizes how nearly he lost his lord and figurehead. I'll show him the way we Normans hit back when men threaten them!"

"Won't someone tell me whether we are at war, and if so, why?" cried Margaret in great exasperation. "I obey my lord's orders, but I could do it more intelligently if I knew who were his foes. Be quiet, Falkes. You only splutter when you try to talk in one of your rages. Robert, you tell me, calmly, from the beginning. I suppose it has something to do with all that coming and going last night, though you didn't take it seriously when I woke you to warn you."

"Exactly, madam," said the clerk, pulling himself together and arranging the story in his head. "What you heard was Hubert and his accomplices going down to the cells to interrogate Peter de Mauley, castellan of Corfe and sheriff of most of the west."

"And the Little King's guest, who had come in peace to renew his fealty," Falkes interrupted. "He knew nothing of a charge against him until he was hauled out of bed and carried down in chains. The torturers were standing by, with their irons hot, to persuade him to answer. There had been no defiance. It was black treachery."

"Just like the good old days of King John, now in Abraham's bosom," said Passelewe, with a grin. "Really, Falkes, you take this too tragically, just because for once a friend of yours was answering the questions instead of asking them."

"Count Arthur was taken in open war and Matilda de Braoze was wife to a declared rebel," answered Falkes. "King John was cruel, but only to his foes. He didn't pull faithful servants out of bed to answer false charges. But you go on, Robert. I am too angry to talk straight."

"There was a charge against Peter, madam, quite a plausible charge, though I myself think it was false. Hubert may even believe it, and anyway it came in very handy to strip a Norman exile of his castles. Peter was responsible for the safe custody of the lady Eleanor of Brittany. Now assume that everything his enemies said was true, and see how it all hangs together. Bishop Peter of Winchester is Mauley's close friend, and he is now stopping at the French court, on his way to Compostella. Suppose Eleanor was spirited away from Corfe, taken to France, and married to a French lord? That would give Brittany to King Philip; it would also give her French son, if she bore one, a pretty strong title to England; after the Little King and his baby brother she represents the lineage of Anjou. Well, there you are. Peter could have done it; he could have done it easily. We know he is a faithful King's Man, but if you think, as Hubert does, that Normans and Frenchmen are very much the same, you might be genuinely frightened."

"Hubert is ass enough to be frightened of anything," Falkes growled. "What matters is that he got his way. Since the death of the old Marshal there have been factions in the Council; but we could work together because it was agreed that every castle should remain in the keeping of the lord to whom it had been entrusted by King John. Now Hubert has ruined Peter de Mauley. Who will get Corfe? For that matter, tomorrow who will get Bedford? Every stronghold in England is now held at the pleasure of Hubert de Burgh, or it is held by the sword."

"Then we shall hold Bedford by the sword," said Margaret without hesitation. "Is this war, my lord? We ought to send our formal defiance, in writing, from our next halting-place. It would have been better manners to defy the Little King before we left Winchester; but I suppose we could not trust Hubert to observe the rules of chivalry and allow us to go free. The trouvères will understand."

"Oh no, madam," said Passelewe, "we must avoid dependence on the sword. Hubert has worked on these silly English magnates until they are terrified that we loyal Normans aim to seize the Kingdom for ourselves. Let him display the Leopard banner and all the knight-service of England would gladly ride against us. At present we have the law on our side. At all costs we must keep it there."

"Do you think Peter would have yielded Corfe if he had a chance of holding it?" asked Falkes scornfully. "I am not defying the Little King. I am merely withdrawing from the court, in a very marked manner, to show my disapproval of what has passed."

"Anyway," said Passelewe soothingly, "Peter de Mauley is free and unharmed, so we are not bound in honor to avenge him. Presently the English magnates will see that they cannot rule without the help of the King's Men from Normandy. They dread civil war, and all will be patched up somehow."

"In fact, we have left a very pleasant feast for no particular reason," Margaret said sharply. "You know how I look forward to these great feasts; as you would, my lord, if you sat for months at Bedford. Couldn't we go back now that you have made your protest?"

"Sorry, my dear," said Falkes shamefacedly, "I lost my temper, I suppose. But I can't go back now. We continue to Bedford."

They did. It was a very toilsome journey, though the swiftness of the march would impress every warrior with the mobility and discipline of the band of Brealte, so perhaps the discomfort brought some advantage. But Margaret had food for thought. Falkes had lost his head. She had never considered her husband capable of a foolish act, even when he was led by a generous impulse to stand by an old friend and fellow-Norman. In a husband whose first duty was to safeguard the inheritance of his infant stepson it was a fault. Henceforth she no longer trusted his judgment.

It was also disturbing to see, what Passelewe had made very plain, that somehow, for no one particular reason, Normans were now suspect in England. Of course they were the old King's Men, the supporters of John in his tyranny. But Hubert had been a King's Man also; in fact, he was accused (untruly) of the actual murder of Count Arthur; yet everyone trusted his moderation and fair dealing because he had been born in Norfolk. Oh well, the world was a foolish place. One must bow to its judgments as facts while recognizing that they were nonsensical. But it was no longer quite certain that to stick to her duty as a loyal wife would be the best way of keeping the County of Devon for little Baldwin.

11: Choosing Sides

 IN EARLY SUMMER Peter des Roches, Bishop of Winchester, returned from his pilgrimage. He soon made peace in the divided Council; Falkes rode once more with the court, the most trusted commander when trouble threatened. Margaret lost interest in politics, because it seemed that the most significant causes produced no tangible effects. Knights rode in mail, vowing war unless their friends were pardoned; a month later they sat down with their foes to work out a way of dealing with Llywellyn of Wales. In fact, when there was something to be done the competent Norman soldiers who were the sword of the government could work with Hubert de Burgh; it was only when they saw too much of him socially that his pompous manner made trouble.

In July 1222 little Baldwin celebrated his sixth birthday. There was no fixed age at which a tenant in chief attained his majority, but with a friendly Chancery and a stepfather on the Council he might be enfeoffed at fourteen; so far all the Redvers lands were loyal and obedient, and there might be only eight years to go. Margaret looked back to the disturbed year of his birth, when the whole realm was at war and respectable widows could not travel without being kidnapped. Then the inheritance of an infant had been precarious indeed; Falkes had preserved it until the worst dangers were past. But it would be a great pity if he now endangered all he had guarded by some ridiculous political mistake. There crept into her mind the idea of asking for an annulment of her marriage; of course, it was absurd, for even if at the time she had not consented her free consent had been given again and again during these years of peace, when a Legate ruled in England who might have heard her plea. But the idea remained in her thoughts, a safe escape from any disaster that might threaten the House of Brealte.

Although she had given up the study of politics as too difficult since causes brought no consequences, she still kept in touch with events. Robert Passelewe was steward of all Falkes's financial affairs; he spent much of his time with his lord, trying to keep him within the tolerant limits of the law as it was applied to the actions of a powerful sheriff; but from time to time he visited Bedford to go through the tallies and receipts of the fief. In July he came to check the offerings and reliefs which had been rendered at Pentecost. He was as usual full of wise and cynical explanations for every political happening, and it amused him to give Margaret a picture of the state of England; for she was inclined to see everything in black and white, with each magnate either a trusted friend of her lord or an unrelenting foe.

"My dear lady," he said smiling, "there are other

questions which agitate the Council besides the welfare of Sir Falkes de Brealte. About these royal castles there is a genuine problem. King John entrusted them to faithful King's Men, who swore to hold them until his little son came of age; and most of them have managed to keep their oath, though Peter de Mauley was unlucky. But you know as well as I do that King John, if he had lived, would not have trusted the same castellans to all eternity. There ought to be some peaceful way of changing a castellan and the Council is trying to discover it. Furthermore, there are not two parties only in the Council. I can distinguish at least four points of view. My lord and his friends wish to keep things as they are, except that they would like to see the Justiciar less powerful. Hubert wants to take into his own hand every royal castle. But it is possible to dislike Hubert without loving the Norman exiles, which is the standpoint of the Archbishop of Canterbury. He wants to see every castle surrendered, including the Justiciar's own fortresses in London and Dover; he has a scheme for lending them to the Bishops in whose dioceses they lie until the King is old enough to make his own decisions. Or it is possible to like the Norman exiles and still regard Hubert as a pretty competent Justiciar, which in fact he is. Count Ranulf wants more power for the Council. He is not unfriendly to the Normans, but he would like to compel them to surrender if ordered; and in less important matters he would leave Hubert to run the country."

"I suppose you are right, Master Robert," Margaret answered casually. "You always put things very clearly. But I can't be bothered to understand it. All I know is that after the Tournament of Lincoln my lord seemed a safe guardian for my son, and now he has powerful enemies. My son comes first. If Falkes seems to be leading us to disaster

I shall leave him. At all costs I must save Redvers and fitzGerold. I can't tell him that, but you might find a way of letting him know, tactfully."

"A true wife should not speak so, madam," Passelewe said sternly. "I stick to Falkes, the companion of my youth. But you were at the beginning an unwilling wife, and it is not my business to train your inclinations; I am a mere deacon, and that is the duty of your confessor. However, it *is* my duty to give Falkes a true picture of the world, and I shall make him aware of your feelings. Yet the conflict may never arise. Falkes has been very successful, and all successful men incur the envy of the weak. If only there were a danger from abroad! Then Falkes and Hubert would lead a united realm against the foe."

Shortly afterward Falkes and Hubert rode together, though it was not a foreign foe who menaced the realm. At the end of July a messenger summoned Sir William de Brealte and the band to meet their lord in London, where the Justiciar needed their help to suppress a dangerous revolt. A wrestling match between the men of London and the men of Westminster had developed into a faction fight, which nobody minded. But a prominent burgess, Constantine fitzOlaf, led the Londoners against the Abbey to the cry of "St. Denis and our lord Louis"; and that dreaded watchword had brought Hubert and his most competent captain at full gallop right across England from the Welsh March. The ringleaders of the rebels were hanged and the Londoners in general were roughly treated; though Hubert so arranged matters that Falkes carried out all the executions, while the English-born Justiciar, who had ordered them, ostentatiously pardoned a few culprits to impress the public with his clemency.

That winter the Council, once more united, made an

unsuccessful attempt to increase its power; but because the attempt was unsuccessful its power was, in fact, weakened. Orders went out to all sheriffs to inquire from a jury concerning the King's rights as King John had enjoyed them; in other words, what would be the rights of the Little King if the Charter did not exist. There was unanimous opposition from the knights of the countryside, and the writ was hastily withdrawn. The Charter had come to stay, and the Council must govern in accordance with its provisions.

But for how long would the Council govern? Little Henry would be sixteen in December 1223. Surely that made him of age, even if he were still very childish for his years? Then the death of King Philip of France caused a crisis in foreign affairs, and everyone was too busy canvassing the possibility of freeing Normandy to bother about the government of England.

The new King of France, Louis, had sworn in the Treaty of Kingston to restore little Henry's French fiefs. That was the sort of thing sworn in treaties and no one expected him to carry out his promise of his own accord; but little Henry was a papal vassal and the Pope might be induced to forbid the coronation at Rheims until right had been done. Envoys ran busily to and fro, and everyone worked very hard; but it had been a forlorn hope at the best, and King Louis was crowned with Normandy still under his sway.

At harvest, when everyone was feeling rich and prosperous, there was a round of feasts and tournaments to entertain King John of Jerusalem, who was touring Christendom to beg support for his threatened realm. Unfortunately the feasts and tournaments were so expensive that no help could be offered after they had been paid for; but the festivities gave Margaret an excuse to visit London and the court.

She found Falkes little altered physically, though she had not seen him since the previous spring; he was still the gallant warrior who could outride any knight in England, and still a clumsy jouster who avoided tournaments; but the responsibility of government was changing the cast of his mind. He had become unsure of himself; he could not tolerate disagreement and he was absurdly suspicious of treachery. During the London riots Hubert had lodged the band of Brealte in the Tower, a very striking proof of trust; now Falkes refused to enter it as a guest, fearing he might be seized and thrown into a dungeon. His quick temper made him very difficult to live with.

But he still had friends in plenty. Hubert had annoyed nearly every magnate on the Council, and a faction was forming to compel the Little King to dismiss him as soon as the Regency ended. Hubert countered by breaking off the festivities without warning and taking the King off to Gloucester, ostensibly to deal with Llywellyn of Wales; Llywellyn was a genuine nuisance, but the real reason for the journey was to get the King away before the assembled magnates lodged a formal complaint.

With the King of Jerusalem sent empty away and little Henry far off in the west there was no reason for the magnates to remain in London. But Count Ranulf of Chester suddenly began to entertain on a great scale, and no one was willing to go home while he was giving such amusing parties.

Count Ranulf had assumed leadership of the opposition from pure public spirit, or perhaps from an inborn dislike of any government of all. Hubert de Burgh did him no harm and, in fact, no one could harm him, since he was by far the most powerful lord in England; probably more powerful, if it came to open war, than the Regent with the Leopard banner behind him. In the Honor of Chester the King's writ did not run; the Pope, who recognized the the King of England, the Prince of Wales, and the Count of Chester, as though these three potentates were equal; his first wife had brought him a claim to the County of Brittany and his second the formal title of Constable of Normandy. He was in his early sixties, a fiery little warrior who had campaigned under the Old King when the House of Anjou was the greatest power in Christendom. Eight years ago, during King John's last campaign, he had quarreled bitterly with Hubert, and as the ruler of a great Honor dating from the Conquest he was insulted by the preeminence of a simple Norfolk knight.

Oddly enough, with Falkes he got on very well; probably because Falkes never pretended to be a gentleman of ancient lineage. He owned a big, draughty, uncomfortable house on the Strand, between London and the Abbey of Westminster, and nearly every evening during October Margaret and her husband supped there, with a group of other discontented magnates. Margaret perceived that they were discussing some common plan, but she was not admitted to their confidence; mos of their talk was of French internal politics, intricate points of feudal law too tricky for her to follow.

Then came definite news that the new King of France had denounced the Treaty of Kingston, refusing to make peace with England. He would keep Normandy by force and at Easter, when the existing truce ran out, he would presumably attack Poitou and Gascony. Meanwhile England was ruled by an English politician with no interest in continental affairs, and everyone who claimed rich fiefs at present unjustly detained by the French must work for a change of government.

But there was worse to come. Hubert, safe in the remoteness of the March, had once more commenced his nibbling at the castles held by the old King's Men. Walter de Lacy and Ralph Musard were summoned to Gloucester, as Peter de Mauley had been summoned to Winchester, to consult in all friendship about the administration of their shrievalties. But once within the castle they were not suffered to depart until they had surrendered every royal fortress under their care. Both were English-born, and Lacy came of an old Marcher family, so there was not even the excuse that as foreigners they did not understand English law. They fell because they were loyal to the memory of King John and had governed as he would have governed; which, of course, made them disliked by their subjects, but should have commended them to an efficient Justiciar.

That was the last straw. One evening in November Margaret, who had gone to bed alone, was roused from her first sleep by the noise of Falkes rummaging in the chest at the foot of the bed; he seemed very angry and a little drunk, swearing continually under his breath.

"What is it, my lord?" she said sleepily. "There is nothing in that chest, except my jewels and my furs."

"Then where is that newfangled plate gauntlet you bought for me to wear on my right hand? It isn't with my mail. I ought to wear it tonight, since we shall be fighting on foot."

"Fighting? Who is the foe? And why haven't you summoned the band? Don't tell me you are going to murder someone. That is unknightly. If it must be done you should hire a rogue to do it for you."

"The foe is Hubert, of course, and he is too far away to

[223]

be murdered. With any luck there will be no real fighting. But if we have a scuffle it will be at very close quarters, and I want to wear that gauntlet on my sword-hand. It's all quite fair and aboveboard. Hubert has stolen Hereford and Gloucester from the faithful castellans of King John; so Count Ranulf has arranged to capture the Tower of London from Hubert in exchange. We have bribed the constable to let us in, but he wants a show of force to make it more convincing. At first light we shall surprise the main gate, on foot."

"Oh, Falkes, stop and think before you join this undertaking. Have you consulted Passelewe?" cried Margaret in dismay. "You are at the top of the tree. You have all to lose and nothing to gain. For God's sake don't give the Justiciar an opportunity to bring the Leopard banner against Bedford. What will become of Baldwin and the Honor of Redvers if your fiefs are escheated for rebellion?"

"All you think about is that little milksop and his fiefs. I have been insulted and oppressed by a jumped-up-tailed Englishman from nowhere, and I am going to repay him by taking the greatest castle in England from under his nose. Besides, there's no danger. Count Ranulf is in this up to the neck, and no one would dare to escheat Chester."

"But don't you see? Count Ranulf can do what he likes because of his noble descent. But you have powerful enemies. You must never put yourself outside the protection of the law."

"I don't understand English law and neither does anyone else; except possibly Hubert de Burgh, and he makes it up out of his head to suit his plans. This is a joint enterprise of all the noble magnates of the realm. It is a great compliment that they asked me to join them, and in their company I must be safe."

"Very well. You are a warrior by trade and you know what you are doing. But while you are gone I shall have our horses saddled."

Margaret saw clearly what Falkes could never understand, that a Norman mercenary would be judged by stricter standards than an English magnate. Merely to demonstrate his friendship with the noble Count Ranulf he was running his head into danger. But he was still her husband, and if he were outlawed she would share his fate. She put on all her best clothes and jewelery, ready for a sudden ride, and passed the hours until dawn in prayer.

In the murk of the foul November morning Falkes rode back to their uncomfortable lodging. He was in a very bad temper and nearly drew his sword on the sleepy groom who took his horse. She heard him storm up the shaky wooden stair, shouting for hot wine, before he flung himself on the bed, his greased mail staining the coverlet. After an outburst of really remarkable profanity, straight from the Brealte hay meadow, he at last explained the failure of the enterprise.

"That bloody constable wouldn't stay bribed, or else the go-between and kept the money for himself. Anyway, we found the drawbridge down and the outer gate open, as arranged. But when we entered we saw the bailey wall lined with crossbows. I wanted to go on all the same, and so did Peter de Mauley and Enguelard de Cigogne, and the other Norman veterans who can storm a castle against any garrison. But Count Ranulf listened to that half-wit Aumale, who can't see the difference between war and peace. He wanted the Tower, but he wouldn't fight for it. I suppose he was afraid of breaking the sacred laws of England! For ten minutes we stood in the gate, shield on neck and helms closed, looking very foolish with our swords in their scabbards. Then we went quietly away, as though we were travelers who had been directed to the wrong house by mistake. On the way back I asked Count Ranulf whether we are at war with the Justiciar, and he answered that he doesn't know! It depends on the line Hubert takes when he gets back from Gloucester! I've half a mind to ride for Bedford, display my banner, and show these islanders war as we wage it in Normandy. But the tail-wearing turncoats want to stay in London to meet the Little King, and I suppose I shall be safer if I stick by them. What a country!"

Margaret understood the situation perfectly. These influential magnates had demonstrated their opposition to Hubert, at the same time pointedly refraining from any breach of the peace. The incident would fetch the Little King back to London, where his natural counselors might explain their views to him in person; he would see that if he wanted their loyalty he must get rid of Hubert as soon as he came of age. It was in the tradition of the numerous armed demonstrations which had forced King John to concede the Charter, without a sword drawn, to rebels who continually avowed their loyalty. That was really a better way of settling disputes than the bloody fighting that came after. But Falkes was a Norman warrior, and when he put on mail he expected to kill or be killed. To him English half-measures seemed only feebleness.

Margaret had originally come to London intending to stay only long enough to enjoy the festivities in honor of the King of Jerusalem. Sir William de Brealte had been left in Bedford, and with him were not only little Baldwin, who should not be left to nurses and servants for months on end, but Robert Passelewe, the House of Brealte's only intelligent political adviser. Now it was already winter, and

[226]

it seemed that a scrambling inconclusive campaign was gradually getting under way without adequate preparation. There was none of the exhilaration, the sense of gambling for great rewards, that had bolstered their courage during the civil war. If Hubert de Burgh were hanged tomorrow the Brealtes would gain no more than they already held. Margaret felt uncomfortable, depressed, and bored, longing only to get back to her home.

But Falkes, though she thought he had been unnecessarily rash, had undoubtedly joined a powerful faction. On the 28th of November Hubert brought the Little King to London, and on the same day the opposition (who emphatically denied that they were rebels) retired northward to Waltham in Essex. The Count of Chester led two other great Counts, Gloucester and Aumale, a number of prominent magnates, Brian de Lisle, William de Cantelupe, John de Lacy, and the toughest of the Norman exiles, Philip Marc, Peter de Mauley and Falkes himself. It was a force which might have fought the Justiciar on level terms if they had made up their minds to fight vigorously. But they were all old King's Men from the days of King John, who shrank from open rebellion against his heir. When the Archbishop of Canterbury offered to mediate they jumped at the chance of negotiation; at Waltham they lived in all the discomfort of campaigning, without the excitement of active war.

At a pompous Parliament held at Clerkenwell the whole movement fizzled out, with a solemn declaration that the Little King was now of full age and entitled to dismiss his Justiciar if he so desired. The meetings continued for a full week, during which Margaret lodged in a verminous cottage near Epping. Ladies did not attend the discussion, so she missed even the distraction of the great

[227]

row between Peter des Roches and Hubert de Burgh, in which each blamed the other for the insolvency of the Exchequer and a quantity of most interesting dirty linen was washed in public. The Archbishop of Canterbury had his solution cut and dried; let every royal castellan surrender all his castles and give the new King a completely free hand. But it broke on the rocks of mistrust; Hubert would not be the first to surrender his castles, and no one else would move while he held the Tower. Presently Bishop Peter walked out in a rage; but the Archbishop ran after him and fixed up a truce to last until the Octave of Hilary, the 20th of January. As Margaret said crossly that evening, if a truce was all they wanted (though they denied that they had ever been at war) it might have been arranged from the comfort of her hall at Bedford.

On the 8th of December, while the opposition were preparing to ride home to gather their men for another bloodless demonstration, someone mentioned to Falkes, as a curiosity, that he had seen a writ sealed by the King *teste me ipso*. The Regency was ended, the reign of the Little King begun.

Falkes and Margaret were busy at Bedford arranging financial affairs after their long absence, when a messenger arrived from Count Ranulf with a most startling proposal. All the enemies of the Justiciar were invited to spend Christmas at Northampton castle; though the castle was held by Falkes as sheriff the Count had not consulted him beforehand, but then the revenues of Chester would provide the feast, and Count Ranulf was accustomed to getting his own way.

It would be a very striking display of disaffection; but it was not technically illegal, and they would be in no danger of outlawry. Two days later another messenger

[228]

arrived, whose letter made Passelewe roar with laughter at the ingenuity of the King's advisers. It was a summons to spend Christmas at the royal court, which on that date would be in the castle of Northampton, held for the King by his loyal servant and sheriff Falkes de Brealte.

"The best of it is that Count Ranulf has already killed every fat ox in Chester," Passelewe spluttered. "Now he must either dine with Hubert and the King, or improvise a Christmas feast in some other castle. These fainthearted English won't either wage war or live in peace. By the time all these demonstrations are over they will have cost Count Ranulf more than a real rebellion."

The Count prepared another feast in his own castle of Leicester. The Brealtes attended, but it was a makeshift affair; while only a day's ride away King Henry held court in greater splendor than had been seen since the days of William Rufus. In particular, more Bishops dined at his table than had ever assembled before, a reminder that the Church, indifferent to complaints from the old servants of King John, backed the faithful vassal of the Pope. On St. Stephen's Day these Bishops published a general excommunication of "all disturbers of the King, the realm, and the Church." This could only mean the Count of Chester and his followers, and after some fruitless and exasperated discussions the opposition agreed to visit the royal court. Falkes was not alone in wishing to face excommunication and civil war rather than give way; but the exponents of outright resistance were not strong enough to stand by themselves when the English magnates wavered.

On the 20th of December a great Parliament was held at Northampton to settle for all time the question of the royal castles. It met as publicly as possible, for a transfer of property needs many witnesses; even ladies were welcome, and Margaret attended with her husband.

The Little King presided, seated on a splendid throne; he was sixteen years old, but still childish in manner and obviously incapable of managing a stormy and bad-tempered meeting. That did not matter, for the real master of the assembled magnates of England was the Archbishop of Canterbury; not because he was more powerful than they, but because he had made up his mind and they had not. Stephen Langton was a practiced speaker, whose line was sweet reason and an appeal to public spirit. When he said that, with the new King of an age to rule, the time had come for every royal castle to be surrendered, and that if each castellan did his duty before that day's Parliament broke up everyone would be treated fairly, it was hard to gainsay him. He proposed a simple method of choosing new castellans for, of course, a castle could not be left without a commander; let each fortress be ruled by the Bishop in whose diocese it lay, until the King had leisure to command otherwise. The King might, if he chose, reappoint the old castellans; this surrender was merely an acknowledgment of his right to do as he wished with his own.

Then Hubert de Burgh stepped forward to render the castles he held as Justiciar, giving a glove or some other material object as seizin until he ran short of clothing and his three castles in Gwent must be represented by a single dagger. Count Ranulf came next, and when his turn came Falkes followed, giving up Oxford, Northampton and Hertford which he held at pleasure, though he kept Plympton as guardian of his stepson and Bedford which he claimed to hold in fee (though there was little evidence to back the claim, and the Chancery disputed it).

That was as far as they had planned to go. But the Archbishop did more. Instead of leaving the castles under their diocesan Bishops, he proceeded to appoint deputy-castellans. Falkes learned that he must hand over Oxford to Richard de Rivers, Northampton to Ralph de Trubleville, and Hertford to William de Eynsford, all native Englishmen and followers of Hubert. The opposition went home in dismay. They had genuinely handed over everything they held at the King's pleasure; Hubert had ostensibly done the same, but the Archbishop had appointed deputies who would obey the Justiciar only.

12: The Toils of the Law

ENGLAND WAS UNEASY. Now that Christmas was over great lords should be visiting their fiefs to arrange the spring sowing; but the weakened opposition was too nervous to disperse. The discontented felt safer if they could meet in the evening to rehearse their grievances. At another Parliament held in London, on the Octave of the Epiphany, 13th January 1224, the Archbishop demanded a reissue of the Charter, though the old King's Men maintained that it had been extorted by force in the first place and should be forgotten. The Archbishop had his way.

That evening the Brealte lodging was crowded. Count Ranulf, William Briwerr, John de Lacy and William de Cantelupe were there, important magnates with strong mesnies; there were also the Norman exiles, Philip Marc and Enguelard de Cigogne, the best soldiers in the land if someone would hire sergeants to follow them. All feared Hubert de Burgh, who could defend castles and fight at sea, but who had never led a victorious charge in the open field. To Falkes that seemed absurdly fainthearted, but Margaret knew better. In this degenerate age few knights would follow their lords against any foe; now that Hubert had the Law and the Church and the King on his side even Ranulf of Chester might find himself riding alone if he displayed his banner in open rebellion.

The visitors sat about aimlessly, complaining of the state of affairs. They knew how to fight, but that was all they knew; and as experienced warriors they would not initiate a struggle against an enemy who was obviously as strong as they.

Only Passelewe was bright and cheerful. He had been present at the Parliaments and conferences of Christmas-tide, a silent and irked spectator of military men making a hash of negotiations which he could have managed better; now he had a plan.

"Gentlemen," he said briskly, his forceful voice cutting into their muttered grumblings, "you all say you cannot overthrow the Justiciar because he is supported by King and Church. But is he really supported by the Church? Stephen Langton, the old rebel who invented that Charter, is not head of the Church. We should appeal to the long memory of Rome. What do they know at the Curia of Hubert de Burgh and the peculiar laws of England? But they will remember that King John, after certain temporary differences, proved himself a faithful vassal of the Holy Father. When the old King's Men complain that they are oppressed by new rulers of base birth the Pope will sympathize with their legitimate discontent. He may call his Archbishop to heel. At the worst he will commission a

[233]

Legate to inquire into the matter, and a Legate supersedes Canterbury. That will be a snub for the Archbishop even if the final verdict goes against us. Now I know my way about the Curia; a path that can be very expensive if you offer presents to the wrong Cardinals. Send me as your proctor, bearing credentials sealed by all the magnates of the realm. When the Pope hears that one man, Hubert, is the cause of all the discontent of England he may tell him to resign, or order the Little King to dismiss him, without inquiring further into the rights of the affair."

Since this was not a formal meeting, but a casual gathering of like-minded men, Margaret felt free to speak. She was fond of Passelewe and admired his intelligence; but it occurred to her that he might be seeking a graceful method of withdrawing from a lost cause. "It is a good idea to send a proctor to the Curia," she said, "bearing the complaint of the King's Men against the Justiciar. But it should be someone of higher rank, and, if Robert will forgive me, of better repute for a holy life."

That made everybody laugh, for Robert's adulteries were notorious. Yet she knew she was rash to advise her husband in the presence of his male colleagues; he might disagree without thinking, merely to assert his superiority. Her wifely duty was to sit back, knowing all, but powerless to influence events, watching Falkes gamble with her son's fiefs and perhaps even his life; she had been born female, and that was just another part of the Curse of Eve, a part often forgotten by theologians.

For a few minutes the magnates discussed the sending of a more impressive envoy to relate their grievances; the obvious choice was the Bishop of Winchester, the Archbishop's adversary among the clergy. But Peter des Roches, who had been listening in a corner, announced that he was unwilling to spend next summer in the heat of Rome, among Cardinals who would expect him to behave like a Bishop when at heart he was really a knight, and that he mistrusted the accuracy of his Latin. Passelewe wished to go; nobody else did. The conference took the easiest way and decided to commission him.

Margaret found living in London boring and expensive; there was no hunting and forage was sold for an absurd price. But Falkes was reluctant to leave, fearing that something important would happen when he was unable to consult his allies. The Brealtes avoided the King's court, fearing that Hubert might force an open quarrel; and there was nothing to do except sit by the fire and grumble at the January rain. After Passelewe had started on his long journey Falkes seemed to lose energy; and his allies were merely waiting for something to turn up.

What turned up, on the 18th of January, was a messenger wearing the badge of the Justiciar; with the King's signet as credential he delivered a writ depriving the lord Falkes de Brealte of the shrievalties of Bedford and Buckingham, Cambridge and Huntingdon. Falkes must either obey the writ or flee at once, to display his banner as rebel and outlaw. He visited Westminster to render the shrievalties by tender of a glove. Meanwhile Margaret packed their baggage and that evening they rode for Bedford.

It was important to get out of reach of royal messengers, whose writs must be answered without delay if they were received in London; but there was also real danger that in the absence of its lord Bedford castle might be seized. It was generally believed that the castle should go, with the county, to the new sheriff. In fact, the position was more complicated; until 1216, when King John escheated it for rebellion, it had been the fief of William de Beau-

[235]

champ; Falkes claimed that the King had granted it to him in fee, but there was no record of the grant; he really held it because everyone knew that he would die fighting before he yielded it. But if he were absent either Beauchamp, exercising the right secured to pardoned rebels by the Treaty of Kingston, or the new sheriff William de Patteshall, might bully brother William into admitting a strange garrison. The sooner the Brealtes were inside Bedford, with the portcullis down, the better.

Margaret was glad to see again that rather unsatisfactory infant, Count Baldwin of Devon. But life in the castle was uncomfortable. Falkes had always been unpopular with his subjects, as was natural with a strict sheriff; now it was known that he had fallen from favor, and the neighbors who hated him no longer feared him. John Marshal turned up once more with yet another writ about that confounded wood; Falkes shouted, in a crowded hall, that he would not forgo his rightful timber for thirty pairs of royal writs sealed by a boy whose throne had been won for him by the crossbows of Brealte; Marshal dared not distrain by force, but the story had lost nothing in the telling by the time it reached the King's court.

The Abbess of Elstow was polishing the sword of St. Paul, saying openly that her Apostle would soon be worthy to go armed; the burgesses of Bedford refused to provision the castle, threatening to bring suit before the new sheriff if the garrison plundered them by force; and the sergeants of the band, feeling themselves far from home among a hostile population, were either timidly weak or much too severe in their dealings with the town.

It seemed that the Justiciar was goading Falkes to hopeless rebellion. In February more writs arrived, commanding him to hand over the three Redvers castles, Carisbrooke, Christchurch, and Plympton. Now Falkes was out of reach of the court he might argue; he handed over Carisbrooke and Christchurch without demur, for they were remote places which brought in little revenue, and of no importance in a civil war. But Plympton was the head of the County of Devon; if he lost it he would lose his Third Penny. While Passelewe was in Rome he lacked skilled legal advice, but at least he knew, as every magnate knew, that the tactics for the defendant in any suit was to waste as much time as possible. He answered that he did not hold Plympton at the King's pleasure; it was the dower of his wife, and his by the Courtesy of England; furthermore, he had been enfeoffed by the Marshal in person, and the Justiciar, who was of lesser rank, could not resume what had been granted from such an exalted source.

All through Lent the long-range argument continued. The Little King wrote to point out that he might resume any fief granted by a Regent acting in his name, ordering Falkes to come to court and deliver seizin in person. Falkes, in reply, sent a copy of the Marshal's charter. At Easter the dispute was still unsettled. But on Easter Day, the 14th of April, the truce with France expired, and he was confident that the Little King would not quarrel with the best captain of crossbows in Christendom at the outset of a great foreign war.

Then came news that plunged the house of Brealte in affrighted gloom. The knight-service of England was directed to assemble on the 16th of June for an invasion of France; but they were ordered to meet at Northampton, miles from the south coast but very handy for an attack on Bedford. The Little King was willing to lose Poitou while he destroyed his father's faithful captain. At the same time Falkes was cited to answer in the Bedford sheriff's court

[237]

for an alleged murder committed in the year 1216; he could not recall the circumstances of the case, but the killing had been done in time of war, when the Leopard banner was displayed and ordinary process of law suspended. Indignantly he decided to ignore the summons. Eventually the court would outlaw him but, of course, the King must issue a free pardon; otherwise Hubert himself ought to stand trial for the deaths of any Frenchmen killed at the siege of Dover.

When his first rage had calmed Falkes changed his mind and discussed the affair quite cheerfully. To Margaret he declared: "The Little King needs money for the defense of Poitou and he stoops to any means to raise it. So did his father, and I don't complain. But I wish he had asked me for a free gift. He would have had it if it is to be spent on fighting King Louis for the liberation of Normandy. Now he will compel me to pay an amercement; but pay I shall. Let us regard it as only another example of the natural lack of courtesy which you would expect in a Justiciar from Norfolk."

Margaret was relieved; if it was only a question of money she knew that insolvent governments (and governments were always insolvent) frequently adopted unedifying positions.

Then it was announced that the King's Justices would visit Dunstable at Whitsun to hear the Eyre; both the Brealte brothers, Falkes and William, were summoned to answer charges of novel disseizin. William blustered at large about defiance and rebellion; but Falkes regarded it as only another move in the campaign to raise money.

"The judges will remember me as the victor of Lincoln and the chief prop of the Little King's rule," he said weightily to his assembled family and advisers, sitting in council after dinner. "If these claimants had waited another ten years my services might then be forgotten. This is land escheated from rebels which I occupied in the course of my duties as sheriff. I have possession and that is the important thing. But my title looks pretty thin. It will be much more firmly founded when the Judges had decided in my favor at the Eyre."

"Pardoned rebels were promised their land. That was agreed by the old Marshal," Margaret objected.

"The old Marshal craved peace. But the terms of that treaty can't really be carried out. What about land escheated by King John before the war began? It's all hopelessly vague, like any other agreement drafted by a chivalrous knight wishing to be friends with all the world. Besides, Louis has not carried out his part of the bargain; he still detains Normandy from its rightful heir. The whole thing is invalid and I shall say as much to the Judges. But I wish I had Passelewe here to put it into legal language."

Falkes took the matter seriously enough to attend the hearing in person, instead of sending a proctor. But it did not worry him. The gathering of the knight-service of England at Northampton was much more disturbing, for the place of assembly could only have been chosen as a threat to Bedford. But he himself had been summoned, as was his due; that gave him an excuse to mobilize and rearm the band, and to provision the castle; this last was only prudent, for such a numerous gathering must cause a local shortage of supplies.

On the Monday after Pentecost Falkes and his brother set off for the Assize. They wore their most splendid cottes, and carried no swords to impress the Justices with their peaceful habits. But they were accompanied by a strong escort to remind the world that the House of Brealte

[239]

could defend itself if attacked. Margaret was apprehensive. Without Passelewe to calm him there was no telling how Falkes would behave if he lost his temper, and he was taking the whole affair so lightly that he was sure to lose his temper if it turned out to be serious after all.

But that evening when the brothers returned Falkes was grim and silent, though William was almost hysterical with fury. "Hey, Margaret," the latter shouted as he swung down from his horse, "do you know who is trying the charges against us? Henry de Braybroc! To set such a traitor to judge loyal King's Men is open denial of justice. We ought to have hanged him from the door of the Assize hall, and then led the true knights of the Angevin cause to the hanging of Hubert de Burgh. But your Falkes wouldn't move, though our escort was stronger than theirs."

"It is in fact shameful," said her husband more calmly. "Perhaps you don't remember Braybroc. While we fought at Lincoln he was holding Mountsorel for Louis. He was a rebel out and out, though they say he is a gallant knight. But he isn't even trained as a lawyer, so they can't pretend they are overlooking the past conduct of an indispensable expert. He will never give us justice. All the same, we must submit patiently and then appeal against his findings. All the world knows he is prejudiced against me, and when my appeal comes before the Council, Count Ranulf and the other King's Men must take my part."

"But suppose they don't wait for the appeal?" asked Margaret. "They may escheat all our land the moment judgment is given. Then what shall we live on and what will become of my son? Can they escheat his County for the wrongdoing of his guardian and stepfather?"

"Even if they order me to leave Bedford I shall go quietly," answered Falkes. "They may escheat the Honor

[240]

of Redvers, because to harm me they may do anything. It would be unlawful, but that won't worry the Archbishop and his jackal the Justiciar. Yet time is on my side, so long as I remain loyal. The Little King will be compelled to defend Poitou. The army is summoned to meet here because they feared I might resist. When I don't they will beg me to lead my crossbows against King Louis. Meanwhile, you and little Baldwin will live comfortably as guests of Count Ranulf or Bishop Peter, and when eventually these cases come before the Council my friends will see justice done. I don't blame William for threatening to fight, but there's no need for that just yet. During the next week, while the cases are heard, we shall have to swallow some nasty public insults. Luckily I am not chivalrous, and I have taken some pretty foul abuse from old King John. In the end we shall be vindicated after Braybroc, on the bench, has made such a fool of himself that he will never be employed again. All we need is patience."

This was not the Falkes of the old days. He had never followed the punctilio of chivalry, but he had been quick to resent insult. He must be more worried than he would admit; for his one idea was that if he broke the peace he would be ruined. The most important thing was to soothe William before he did anything rash; Margaret made some trite remark about patience, and led the way to an excellent supper.

For the rest of the week she was alone in the daytime while her husband and his brother attended the Assize. She had plenty of time to consider her future, but it was not an exercise in which she was practiced. All her life she had submitted to Fate, first marrying young Baldwin because her father ordered it, then taking Falkes because such was the King's will. On the whole it had worked out for the best. She was one of the greatest ladies in England, mistress of a strong castle, enjoying all the comforts she could desire. Men had given these things to her, and the way to keep them was to do what men, in particular her husband, ordered. That was an impeccable position, enjoined by the Church, by the Law, and by public opinion. An obedient wife could not put herself in the wrong.

On the 17th of June, the Monday after the Octave of Trinity, the judgments in no less than sixteen suits of novel disseizin against Falkes and several against William de Brealte were to be delivered together, and it was imperative that the brothers be present; though the knight-service of England had been summoned for the 16th, and they would be in danger of another prosecution for neglecting the summons. The solution they decided on was to take the whole band of Brealte to Dunstable, then ride to Northampton as soon as the Assize finished. Margaret was left in the nearly empty castle; though Falkes had arranged that she should accompany him overseas when the army marched and the servants were already packing her baggage.

At midday a sheriff's messenger shouted across the moat that he bore an urgent message for the castellan. In normal times William de Brealte was castellan of Bedford and Falkes had made no other appointment; but Margaret gladly came forward to receive the packet through the grating of the portcullis. She enjoyed acting as castellan, considering it her chief reward for what was really an unsuitable and disparaging marriage. But when the writ had been read to her she recalled that Passelewe had often advised her to ignore messengers who sought the castellan. It might be better to pretend that the castle had been left without a commander. For in legal proceedings it was half the battle to delay the receipt of hostile documents.

What she heard was a writ of outlawry. Falkes had not appeared to answer that ridiculous charge of homicide, for the killing of a rebel during the civil war; he should have been summoned again, once a month for at least three months, but his foes had jumped at the opportunity to put him beyond the protection of the law. The judgment would be reversed, of course, as soon as the Council heard of it; but meanwhile the House of Brealte was exposed to considerable danger, which she had made worse by accepting the writ. They could not plead that the outlawry was clandestine and that they were ignorant of their legal position.

She could do nothing except inform the meagre garrison, close all posterns, and await her husband's return. Margaret tried to console herself with the reminder that she now commanded a great castle in wartime, which had been the dream of her girlhood; but she had never expected it to come like this, suddenly, and with most of the garrison absent.

Her first thought was to put little Baldwin in the top story of the keep, telling him not to go near the windows, where a stray arrow might come in; she spent the rest of the afternoon sitting just inside the portcullis, ready to lower the drawbridge quickly when the band returned from Dunstable.

She sat there for a long time, her mind filled with gloomy thoughts. Many powerful men hated Falkes, ecclesiastics and well-born magnates of old-fashioned views; that was inevitable when a tough soldier rose from captain of crossbows to be one of the greatest lords in the realm. But in the past if he had been hated he had also been feared.

[243]

Now his foes wanted him to fight, because they were certain that they could beat him. It was a new situation. Margaret had married a man of low birth, accepting the disparagement because he was powerful; if he lost his power there would be nothing to recommend him. She toyed with the idea of taking little Baldwin to seek refuge with the Nevills in the far north. She was now in command of the castle and the gate would be opened for her without demur. But Falkes would probably catch her before she had ridden twenty miles, and then she might be shut up in a dungeon for life. He would be within his rights if he imprisoned her; in the face of God she had consented to take him for better or worse. Anyway, she could not make up her mind at such short notice. And, of course, he might overcome all his enemies. Then, one day, she would sail with him to Outremer, as the rich and respected wife of one of the greatest men in England. It was too soon to desert him, and indeed the time might never come; for the present she was tied to his fortunes and must do what she could to help him. She walked once more around the outer wall to encourage the sentries.

At sunset a few horsemen galloped up to the gate. The drawbridge was lowered in record time, as soon as the sentry recognized the half-moons of Brealte on his lord's shield. Neither the main band nor William de Brealte were with him. Of course, Margaret told herself, they would have ridden straight to the muster at Northampton; Falkes had just dropped in to give her news of the law suits and instructions for the future. She curtsied as he dismounted, and remembered to present him with the key which really unlocked the gate.

Falkes was unarmed, still wearing the fine cotte he had put on to impress the Justices with his peaceful ways. But his dusty face was as drawn and haggard as on the eve of Lincoln. She handed him the sheriff's writ, murmuring something about the need to get the outlawry removed at once. He brushed it aside.

"We have more to worry about than a sheriff's outlawry," he gasped in weariness. "Oh dear, I must be growing old. Once I could gallop with King John, and now this little journey has exhausted me. Well, my fine lady, I have work for you. You must hold this castle against all comers. William may be here in a day or two, but you can count on the whole knight-service of England to arrive before tomorrow's sunset. While the walls stand and the sergeants will obey your orders you must keep them out. Do you understand?" He glared at her fiercely. "You are my wife, my partner whom I trust. You can betray me. If you do the Little King will reward you and I shall never be in a position to punish you. My fortune lies in your hands. I can only remind you that I have been a good husband, and that the repute of fitzGerold and Redvers is now in your keeping. Here is your chance to be much more than a noble lady. You can be a heroine, as was Nicolaa de la Haye when she held the walls of Lincoln."

"Oh, my lord," said Margaret, a warm gush of noble sentiment flooding through her, "I am the Lady of Brealte, I shall hold your castle against all the powers of this world, myself drawing the sword if need be. But for God's sake tell me why this has happened. Where is your brother, where are your men, why have you engaged in open war against the whole knight-service of England?"

"Because my enemies have forced me to it," Falkes answered with a snarl. "War they want, and I shall show them what war can be. Louis marches against Poitou, Llywellyn is stirring, Chester is discontented. Before harvest England will be in flames, if a harvest remains to be reaped at all. They have compelled me to draw the sword. By God's toenails I shall handle the sword as only a Norman can handle it. Sixteen suits of novel disseizin given against me at one sitting; and just to make everything complete they raked up three suits against William. Henry de Braybroc, the pardoned traitor, mocked me from the bench as 'a foreign disturber of the peace.' Oh well, his punishment came quickly. But this part must be kept secret. Come with me into the hall."

They huddled close on the dais of the empty hall. There was no reason why they should not sit, but a sense of urgency kept Falkes standing as he muttered in undertones.

"After the judgments we all left Dunstable to join the muster at Northampton. Presently Braybroc overtook us and mocked us once again. Poor William could not endure his sneers. With the flat of his sword he knocked the scoundrel off his horse. You know the kind of sergeant they pick for a judge's escort nowadays; his rascals ran away, while his wife galloped off screaming. I wish I could hear what she is telling the Little King at this very minute. I bet she says her husband went down fighting after unhorsing a dozen knights. Anyway, William has captured the King's own Justice in Eyre, and that's an assault on little Henry's dignity for which there can be no forgiveness. I don't know what I am to do. I must get in touch with my friends and find out whether they will follow my banner in open war. They must at least make peace for me if they are afraid to fight in my cause. I have told William to keep his eminent captive hidden in the forest; then I can truthfully tell the King's envoys I don't know where he is. Braybroc will not be harmed, but I must be in a position where it is out of my power to release him. Shut up here I can do nothing.

[246]

Tonight I shall take sanctuary in St. Paul's church, where the King's envoys can find me. Tomorrow I ride north for Chester or Anglesey, whichever seems more promising. Then William will come here to take charge of the defense. Do you understand? You hold this castle without thought of surrender until you hand over to William. Then you will stay here until you hear from me. Now I want the best horse in the stable and all the gold and silver he can carry. Oh, and a flask of wine and a lump of bacon; it's cold and comfortless hanging on to the altar while the King's knights debate whether to break sanctuary by seizing me. I don't think they will dare to do it, for little Henry fears the Pope. But if they do, and you know for a fact that I am a prisoner, disregard any commands I give you and make the best terms you can for little Baldwin. Once I am in the King's hands I shall hang, anyway, so don't yield Bedford to save me. I think that's all. I wish I had Passelewe to advise me. But once I get to Chester, or north Wales, or anywhere else where the King's writ does not run, I can negotiate at leisure. Your stores should last for a year, and when William arrives you will have my band, the Band of Brealte, the best crossbows in the world. Your defense will give me time to gather allies. By September at the latest you will hear from me. All you have to do is sit quiet in the strongest castle in England, with your husband's banner displayed; and when the trouvères sing the War of Bedford you will be famous."

Margaret understood that Falkes was not quite sure of her fidelity. He was praising her as he heartened doubtful troops before battle. It did not put into her mind the idea of deserting him, because that idea had been nagging at her all day. Now she dismissed it, deciding to serve him faithfully; he had given her a splendid role in what must

[247]

inevitably be a stirring story; and he would not be present himself to steal her glory. She could manage William, and with him in command she would be the real castellan of Bedford. She would win fame while she was young enough to enjoy it, and ever after she would be pointed at as the Heroine of Bedford. When Falkes rode off, a furtive and rather frightened figure, with every man's hand against him until he reached the altar he had once unroofed, she looked after him with a stirring of affection; if it had at that moment been necessary to rescue him she would have jumped on the nearest destrier.

13: Downfall

ABOUT SUNSET on the evening of the 14th of August Margaret was standing over the straw pallet on which little Baldwin tossed and whimpered; she was applying wet cloths to his forehead in the hope of reducing his fever. But even when he was well he could not sleep, for he was unused to the din of the crowded keep, packed with more than a hundred restless men and women. She hoped he would soon lie quiet while she got her supper; the thought that existence would be much easier if he died and left her without all this nursing peeped into her mind to be dismissed with a shudder.

The stench was enough to keep a child awake, she told herself angrily. They had plenty of water from the well in the basement of the keep; but there was no more fuel, and washing clothes in cold water seemed a waste of time; many knights and sergeants had remained fully armed since the last assault, and everyone had worn the same shirt for six weeks. The sun beat down on the flat roof above them, and the narrow windows were shuttered to keep out random arrows; the air of the crowded room tasted thick and revolting. Her son would never sleep naturally; but he was nearly eight years old, and he ought to exercise the self-control that befitted his birth.

"Count Baldwin of Devon," she whispered urgently, "you are the chief of fitzGerold and Redvers, born to the sword; you must learn to lie quiet through the noise of war. Be still while I eat my supper and consult with Sir William. Lie still like a gallant knight."

The fevered child smiled up at his mother; he even clenched his teeth to stop their chattering; she saw that he was fully conscious and determined to be brave for as long as he could. After laying a fresh cloth on his forehead she walked gently to the main doorway.

The keep of Bedford castle was more than a hundred years old, a thick-walled rectangle of rubble built in the style of the Conqueror. It comprised three storys; just one large room on each floor with the stair huddled away in a corner turret. For greater safety the single door to the outside world pierced the first story; now it opened on nothing, for the wooden ramp leading to the ground had been destroyed by the garrison when they fled in haste to this last refuge. The door remained, a stout piece of oak planking; but a perrier-stone had broken it from its hinges, and now it was kept in place by improvised wooden bars. Round its edge crept a few beams of sunlight; these, and similar gleams from the window shutters, emphasized the gloom and made the crowded room feel all the more stifling; but the garrison watched them greedily. Soon they would disappear and the dark boredom of another night must be endured.

Sir William de Brealte was seated on the only bench (the rest of the furniture had been burned to heat pitch as they repelled the last assault). He wore full mail, sword and helm lying on his lap, so that only his face and hands were visible. From his person came a revolting stench, partly the dirt of a body long unwashed, partly the reek of the rancid grease which protected his armor from rust. From unnaturally bright eyes he strained to watch the door; but he was obviously very sleepy, very tired, and very sorry for himself.

When Margaret approached he did not rise, though his legs twitched slightly in a subconscious effort at courtesy. She noticed the movement and was gratified. "Keep your seat, Sir William," she said kindly. "I shall sit here on the floor. I wear no mail and it is easy for me to rise."

"Thank you, my lady," he replied in a weary monotone. "I don't think they will attack again before dark, but we get little warning now they are lodged so close. I sometimes wish they would charge again and give us a chance to fight. If we took some more prisoners it might discourage them."

"You should rest, sir, and let another knight take your place. You are our best swordsman, and your strength protects us all."

"No, my lady. It is through my fault that we are in this fix, when we should still be guarding the outer bailey. I must hold this door which, because of my negligence, is our last defense."

"You reproach yourself unduly," said Margaret, with a sigh. She compelled herself to speak with polite formality; if she blamed him that would destroy the last flickers of courage which burned low in this exhausted and incompetent, but fundamentally brave, knight. "Against such a battering even my lord could have done nothing. No one foresaw that the Little King would consume all the resources of his realm to capture one castle; and I did not believe such engines existed in the world. At the last assault you conducted yourself gallantly, and it is thanks to your prowess that we have these prisoners, who may be so useful if we have to seek terms. May I rest here beside you? My son gives me little rest in the night."

She sank down, closing her eyes. It was a blessed relief to hand over responsibility for a few moments, even into the incompetent hands of William de Brealte. For there was no doubt about it; the strong castle which Falkes, an experienced judge, had considered capable of holding out for a year, was tottering to its fall after only eight weeks principally because of its commander's errors of judgment.

The new siege engines had been a surprise because the trebuchet, which lobbed great stones by the use of counterweights, was a new invention. No one could have prevented the breaching of the bailey walls by such powerful instruments. But Falkes, or any other castellan who understood the engineering side of defense, would have erected palisades behind the breaches; instead of meeting the attackers sword in hand on the crest and retreating when valour could no longer compensate for lack of numbers. In a fortnight they had lost the outer bailey, which could have been held for six months if they had worked properly with spade and axe.

But the crowning disaster had been the loss of the inner bailey, which contained their stores. In the first place the stores and horses should have been sheltered in the basement of the keep; the forage and fresh provisions had only been stacked against the wall of the inner bailey because the men who brought them in were too idle to carry them farther than the stable. Later William had delayed to move them, hoping to impress Henry de Braybroc, shackled in the dungeon, with the courtesy of his jailers; it would seem unchivalrous to make him share his prison with restless destriers and kegs of decaying butter. When the royal army escaladed the inner bailey without waiting for a breach they had fired the straw and the defenders must retire to the keep or stifle in the smoke. As the besiegers followed William had turned to bay, cutting off a dozen of the King's knights in the doorway of the keep; two died of their wounds, but the defenders now held eleven valuable captives. That was something to bargain with if it came to surrender.

William, in person, had captured these men, and that must be counted to his credit; but it was his fault they had been driven into the keep, which was uncomfortable, unhealthy, and unprovided with fuel or fresh food. If the garrison were compelled to yield William would be entirely to blame. The thought was a comfort to Margaret.

She knew that the men and women around her, in the inescapable close quarters of this last refuge, were very near despair. If she herself had been consulted she would have advised immediate surrender before sickness attacked them all, as it had already attacked her son; sickness that was the inevitable result of heat by day and cold by night, dirt, and a diet of salt beef and biscuit; all caused by William's stupidity in allowing them to be shut in without fuel. But the Band of Brealte was not yet ready for surrender. They feared that the Little King might refuse quarter.

Eight weeks ago everyone had been full of hope. It was right for Falkes to escape and thus preserve his freedom of

[253]

action. The knights in the castle knew the political situation; that the Count of Chester was a friend, and the Prince of Wales eager to help anyone who made trouble for the King of England. The castle could hold out for a year, and during the autumn their lord would gather allies; in any case, now that the truce with France had run out little Henry was urgently needed in Poitou. They had been sure that time was on their side.

But they had received only two messages from Falkes, and both told nothing but bad news. The letters had been shot into the castle tied to arrow shafts, and it was easy to guess who had arranged their delivery; for among the besiegers were crossbowmen wearing the Lion of Chester on their surcoats, smart soldiers who shot very accurately and yet never wounded a defender. The first letter announced that Llywellyn would not intervene; he dared not risk his light-footed infantry in anything so certain to bring on a pitched battle as the relief of a castle in the heart of England. That was only reasonable, since Welsh javelin-men could not face mailed knights.

The second letter was a greater disappointment. It told that Count Ranulf had withdrawn from the siege with most of his followers; but he refused to wage open war on the King, even to bring down his enemy Hubert de Burgh. He offered to use his influence to get quarter for Falkes and his men after they had yielded, and the fact that he promised such an elementary service as though it were a great concession proved the extreme danger of their position.

For a month there had been no more news. Then only two nights ago a trumpet had blown for a parley, and a herald standing below the door sought an interview with the castellan. But William had rightly refused to meet him, for nothing saps the resolution of a besieged garrison so much as the knowledge that negotiations have begun. The herald, refused admittance, read from a document at the top of his voice; his message announced that Falkes had come in to negotiate under safe conduct; he then read what purported to be a message from Falkes himself, sent through the Bishop of Coventry who had met him on behalf of the King; this advised the garrison to make what terms they could, for their lord could no longer help them. Of course the whole thing might be a lie; Hubert was capable of any dirty trick. The herald had been willing to hand over the document, but that might only prove that it had been forged with care. It could not be genuine; Falkes was not the man to despair so easily. Since Margaret would be in a fix if it were true she made up her mind that it must be false, and did her best to forget its existence.

But though the last attack had been beaten back with heavy loss (for the Band of Brealte were skilled warriors who fought to kill, more than a match for chivalrous gentlemen accustomed to fencing with blunt weapons in the tournament), there was no doubt that soon an assault might carry the keep. The mercenaries did right to worry, since in a sack they would be killed to the last man. But a noble lady would be spared, and so would a child on his sickbed; Margaret might regard the situation with detachment.

She was aware of a stirring in the crowd, and opened her eyes. It was only supper being distributed, but that was one of the two moderately pleasant events of the day (the other was dinner). She rose to take her share from the amazingly sluttish and stinking kitchen wench, unwashed for six weeks. Even the wooden platter stank for lack of scrubbing; that might be remedied with cold water, and

Margaret made a mental note to see it done; on it lay a greasy lump of salt beef and a square of twice-baked bread as hard as marble. She nibbled at the beef, whose rancid fat did not quite turn her stomach; but the square of biscuit she plunged into a bucket of water, hoping that long soaking would make it soft enough for little Baldwin to swallow. She experienced a queer longing for lettuce or fresh butter, food she seldom ate when it was available; veterans said besieged garrisons often experienced these odd cravings; but vegetables were notoriously unhealthy, and could do no good to her sick child. What he needed was plenty of beef to keep up his strength; yet there was no point in offering it to him if he vomited it at once.

William belched loudly and Margaret, looking up in some anger at this breach of courtesy, saw that he had fallen asleep as he sat on guard. With his boyish mouth open and his haggard eyes closed he looked rather engaging in an innocent way; she felt a pang of motherly concern. Poor William! He was a slack engineer and an incompetent commander; but he fought with great energy and courage whenever he had a chance to use his sword; and he was desperately in earnest, never resting in his anxiety to guard the fortress which had been entrusted to his care. He would willingly die for his adored elder brother; and, in fact, he was likely to do so. There was no getting away from it; Falkes was beaten and the House of Brealte destroyed. Her most sensible course would be to change sides, if only she could find an opportunity to change sides without loss of honor. If they sued for a truce the Little King would demand hostages; she would offer herself and then seek the advice of the Archbishop of Canterbury. What a pity that she had not already begun to sue for an annulment! It would be hard to convince even the most friendly church court that her marriage to Falkes had never received her free consent.

Meanwhile William was the prop on which all depended. She must make him eat; if he fell ill a subordinate would take command, some desperate ruffian who thought only of dying while his blood was hot and his sword wet. The only chivalrous gentleman in Bedford, the only knight who would remember to look after a lady when the end came, was William.

"Leave the door, sir," she called, shaking him. "You have still eleven knights besides the sick. Let one of them relieve you while you sup. And when you are at leisure I wish to ask you a favor."

William struggled to his feet, motioning another knight to take his place, and limped stiffly to a corner of the crowded hall. There he squatted on the floor, Margaret squatting beside him. Castles were always crowded, and the lower orders knew they were forbidden to eavesdrop when their lords talked privately.

"It's about my son," she began. "He can't eat salt beef straight from the cask, and for his health I must cook him a hot meal. In this emergency could we sacrifice the door of the dungeon? It's thick, seasoned oak, enough to make one good fire. We might heat water after cooking and some of us could wash. Our prisoners are shackled, and if we tie them to the wall they cannot escape."

"I never thought of that," William answered slowly. "The door of the dungeon will certainly give us one fire. The danger is that if our men see the prisoners constantly they may cut their throats. That would be most unchivalrous. Perhaps I can find a reliable sergeant to guard them. But this is too early to burn our last fuel. Autumn is

[257]

coming and we shall endure the frost better with the promise of a blaze at Christmas."

"You don't think, do you, that Bedford will be holding out when Christmas comes?" gasped Margaret in astonishment. "We have nothing between us and the foe save one broken door. In a week at the longest we must seek terms."

"My brother said we could hold for a year. We have food and water, and my mail is sound. If you talk publicly of surrender, madam, I shall put you also in the dungeon. There must be no weakening. This castle is held for Brealte. We cannot yield without the permission of its lord."

"As you wish, Sir William. You are in command. But your reply to the King's first summons was ill advised. Your lord has sworn allegiance even though you have not, and that binds you."

"Not by the old custom of Normandy. I hold for Falkes de Brealte, acknowledging no other superior."

"Yes," Margaret said wearily. "A great many chivalrous gentlemen will agree with you, but it was a mistake to say it in public. To an Englishman it recalls the days of King Stephen. The Bishops, in particular, dread a return of that time of anarchy."

"It was the right attitude. Posterity will remember that William de Brealte was a well-spoken knight, who delivered his defiance with spirit."

Margaret did not answer. She saw at last that William had no hope of survival; he was resigned to death and thought only of ending his life bravely.

She, herself, was not especially afraid of death. She had been brought up to think of it every time she said her prayers, and she knew that whether it came tomorrow or in forty years' time was of no real importance; what mattered was the condition of her soul when she left the world. Unfortunately, that condition could hardly be worse than it was at present. At the beginning of the siege the defiant garrison had been excommunicated, as rebels everywhere where automatically excommunicated nowadays; the Archbishop of Canterbury had pronounced sentence in person, standing in full vestments on the rim of the moat. The chaplain, who was devoted to Falkes, continued to say daily Mass; but there could be no doubt that if death came now it would find Margaret in mortal sin, filled with rage, anger, and disloyalty to her husband; and lacking an unsuspended priest to absolve her. She must find some way of escape; and, of course, little Baldwin, who was in no way to blame, must be saved also.

She was planning how to reopen the subject of surrender, perhaps when William had eaten and his temper had improved, when she was called back to the present by a sudden change in his demeanor. He dropped his wooden spoon and sniffed the air like a dog.

"Madam," he whispered excitedly, "did you tell anyone else about burning the door of the dungeon? If not, someone has thought of it by himself. Can you smell smoke?"

Margaret pushed away her stinking beef, sniffing gently. Through the familiar reek of unwashed bodies stole a faint odor of woodsmoke; not the scent of green twigs which meant that some enterprising spirit had snatched from the moat a handful of brush to heat his supper, though brave and greedy men sometimes risked an arrow for that purpose. This was dry seasoned wood, burning fiercely.

[259]

"That is dry fuel, certainly. Could it be the cooking fires of the enemy?"

"Not cooking fires. We should smell the meat. But the fire may be one kindled by the enemy, and in that case our defense is ended."

Neither dared to utter the dreaded word "mine," lest they be overheard. But it did not need speaking, so plain was it in their thoughts. "Have you set men to listen for the sound of picks?" Margaret breathed in a low whisper; and saw from Sir William's stricken face that he had forgotten to order that elementary precaution.

A thrilling pulsation now ran through the vaulted stone floor; the whole room felt it at once and a murmur of anguish arose from the crowd. Then, with a creak, the floor shifted and settled. The stair turret gaped in a long zigzag crack, and a cloud of gray smoke seeped from it.

The women scampered quickly but gently to the far end of the room; but the veterans, also treading gently, went each to his little bundle of valuables stacked by the wall. For all in the castle knew that the fighting was over. The King's miners, brought at great expense from Cornwall and the Forest of Dean, had tunneled beneath the corner of the keep; they had propped the completed passage with seasoned timber, and when all was finished they had heaped the chamber at the end with dry straw and left a candle burning; as the props were burned through the collapse of the tunnel brought down the foundations of the tower. Against a finished mine there was no defense, though a more skillful commander would have been aware of it in the making, and either sallied to destroy the workings or countermined to win the tunnel from below. Now there was nothing to be done; the garrison must surrender at discretion before they were killed in the downfall of the whole structure.

William de Brealte looked oddly relieved. Margaret perceived that he was actually glad that the defense was finished and his responsibility ended. He would probably be hanged, but he need do no more; what came next would be done to him.

"Gentlemen," he announced in a firm voice, "this castle is untenable and we must seek the King's mercy. I shall unbar the door, but it would be unwise to walk straight into the ranks of our enemies. For the present we shall stay here, since there seems no danger of a further collapse. We shall send out our prisoners to remind the King that we, in our turn, showed mercy. That gives us an opportunity to appeal to our friends in the royal army. Think of any comrades or cousins who may be there, and implore their help. Henry de Braybroc is an honorable knight, and if he promises to deliever a message he will keep his word."

In a few minutes the captives, filthy, hungry, and haggard, stood by the door, moving their legs clumsily in the delicious absence of fetters. Braybroc agreed to tell the King that the Band of Brealte sought mercy, though he refused to deliver messages to individuals. When the envoys scrambled down through the open door Margaret joined them, carrying little Baldwin. The child was very weak, but his fever had left him; he could walk, though he hardly knew what he was doing.

The women of the garrison followed Margaret when they saw that Sir William permitted her to leave. But no warrior attempted to desert; the Band of Brealte stuck together to the last.

[261]

14 : Desertion

IT WAS nearly dark when Margaret dropped the last few feet to the inner bailey and sniffed moving air. It was foul air, for a large army had been encamped by the castle for eight weeks, but after long confinement in the stinking keep it smelled delicious. Little Baldwin straightened himself with a smile and said he felt better already.

Margaret was hugging to herself the anticipation of a bath, clean clothes, and hot food; she was a lady of rank seeking mercy, and in all the romances such unfortunate females were kindly treated. But the sergeants gathered below the open door wore the badge of the Archbishop, and they evidently had no more chivalry than their lord. All the women, ladies and kitchen wenches alike, were surrounded by lowered spearpoints and marched, with no consideration for their fright and exhaustion, to a stone warehouse in the town. There they were locked in a large room by guards who would not speak to them. A servant brought salt beef and water, exactly the fare they had endured through the siege. Then they were left to themselves, no better off than they had been for the last six weeks.

Presently a priest put his head around the door and addressed them coldly. "Women, you are excommunicate. Tonight think of your sins, and tomorrow, after penance, you may hope for absolution." He withdrew, pretending not to hear the clamor of questions. They were in the hands of the Church, which nowadays reckoned rebellion as a very deadly sin.

Margaret requisitioned cloaks to cover little Baldwin, exercising the last flickers of her authority as Lady of Brealte. Among the prisoners were other children, some of them smaller and more helpless, and tending them took the minds of their elders off the grim prospect of the morrow. Margaret's thoughts were busy. Falkes was popular with the warriors of the Little King's Council, and if their advice was heeded nothing very drastic would be done to him; he would lose his land, but his reputation as a captain of mercenaries would win him employment in any other kingdom. She would be wise to stick to him. Besides, it was the honorable course. All trouvères admired fidelity in a wife, though they did not expect it from a husband; she would be remembered as the unlucky Lady of Brealte, who was faithful to her lord in good times and bad.

But if the ascendancy had remained with the chivalrous magnates of the Council, old comrades of Falkes from the days of the civil war, she would not now be cowering on a stone floor without even straw to sleep on. They would have given her a good supper and listened to her account of the Great Siege of Bedford with the eagerness every soldier shows for a first-hand story of battle from the enemy's point of view. The Archbishop of Canterbury, and presumably that low-born Hubert de Burgh, must be in control of the Little King's actions. She took it for granted that some adviser was in control, for the Little King, even at the age of sixteen, notoriously had no will of his own.

The Church thought in cut-and-dried categories. For every sin there was an appropriate penalty, and the sinner could not expect forgiveness until the penalty had been exacted. The penalty for rebellion was death, and Stephen Langton would see it inflicted. She also might be sentenced to hanging. That would, in fact, mean life-imprisonment; no lady had been executed since the death of Matilda de Braoze, an atrocity that had shocked even the tough supporters of King John. But in law she would be dead; all her property would be taken from her, she would never wear silk or jewels; and she would never again see her son.

If the Church was strict it was because Bishops administered a law they had not made. Since a clerk could show no sympathy for a gallant knight driven to rebellion by unjust persecution, her best chance of safety was to find some point of law that justified her. Suppose she claimed that she had never willingly been Falkes's wife? If she stuck to her story the judges must accept it. Thank God poor, silly William had been in command of Bedford throughout the siege. Once she had been angry that Falkes never thought of making his wife castellan, but now she was grateful that she could plead duress. Let brother William pay the penalty for his crimes; he was to blame for the whole thing, for if he had noticed the mine earlier the castle would not have fallen. Falkes had insulted her, a fitzGerold and widow of Redvers, by putting her under the

[264]

orders of a landless exile. There was her justification. The most chivalrous trouvère would see that she acted only out of a delicate sense of honor.

If she raised the plea of annulment she must leave Falkes. That would make a gap in her life. For more than seven years he had been her master, not always present but always to be reckoned with. And that first winter all the forays against the suburbs of London, and even that odd experience at St. Albans, had seemed strangely enjoyable; Falkes was a good man to have at your side when you felt cold and tired and hungry, with your over-driven horse stumbling at every rut on the road. But then, if she had not married him (though truly she had never married him), she would never have been cold and tired and hungry. She would have sat out the war in some warm castle, no one daring to offend the powerful Lady of Plympton. What had she, the daughter of a staid chamberlain, to do with these devil-may-care Norman exiles who lived by the sword? Great magnates might like Falkes, but they did not regard him as an equal. When the pinch came Count Ranulf was neutral, and even Llywellyn of Wales would not offer him an open alliance. Hubert de Burgh had never trusted him, and Hubert's pomposity embodied all the respectable feeling of the English-born landholders. Falkes was a wicked man. She was right to desert him. In fact, it was her duty to do so, lest her son lose his inheritance in the general crash of the fortunes of Brealte. She was a woman who could never act with only her own welfare in view; there was always some man she must serve. But that man need not be Falkes, who was not truly her husband; it was time to put little Baldwin first.

Most of her companions slept soundly. Their future was black in the extreme, but this was the first night for eight weeks in which they had not been in danger of death from a stray perrier-stone; safety made up for the lack of bedding. But Margaret remained awake until dawn, planning the speech she would make to her accusers, and by a natural transition recalling every detail of her life with Falkes.

She remembered it with pleasure, for he had been a stimulating companion. To watch him heartening sulky troops, or persuading tired men to march to the end, made you think better of the whole sinful human race. He was brave and loyal, and fundamentally honorable, in spite of the sneers of the well-born. In his company she had never been bored.

But she had never considered him really as a fellow human being; all those fantastic Norman warriors of King John's mesnie had been so strange to her, so outside the experience of her guarded childhood, that she could see them only as some strange but interesting kind of animal. Falkes had come into her life and illumined it. Now he was gone, because prudence demanded that she leave him. She would miss him, but she could only imagine her own feelings. It was impossible to conceive of Falkes himself suffering loneliness or betrayal, because it was impossible to see him as anything but a clever and busy captain of crossbows, looking after his castles or commanding his men. In her mind he had no private life, no personal feelings.

At dawn sergeants roused the captives. They brought no breakfast, but this was a good omen; if the excommunication was to be lifted they would probably receive the Sacrament after. The women were not even permitted to wash, a hardship which was also a help; their best hope was

[266]

to appeal to the Little King's mercy, and it was prudent to look as dishevelled and miserable as possible.

They were led through the streets to the market hall, a building of no great dignity but the largest covered space in the town. The few burgesses showed little interest in the procession; what mattered was the punishment inflicted on the captured warriors, and the women would be hanged or set free as an afterthought, probably at the whim of a subordinate. They were not important enough to be stared at, when determined shoving might win a place to see the trial of their men. Margaret understood that for her own safety she must break away from this cluster of irrelevant victims as soon as she had the chance.

They were all herded into the back of the hall. A dense crowd stood in front, but at the far end the judges could be seen on a dais. The Little King, wearing his crown and full regalia, sat in the center of the bench; on his left sat the Justiciar and a handful of lay magnates, and on his right nearly a dozen Bishops. The laymen furtively munched bread dipped in wine, for the court had been summoned hurriedly before they could breakfast; but the Bishops, in copes and mitres, ate nothing; this was the 15th of August, the great Feast of the Assumption, and as soon as mundane business had been disposed of they would hurry off to sing the Mass of the feast. All were silent, and the whole bench looked grim and ill at ease.

After ten minutes of silent waiting, which the women found very lowering to their spirits, the King's sergeants cleared a space before the dais and the male accused were brought in. There were nearly a hundred of them, barelegged in their shirts, hungry and dirty and exhausted, many bandaged over recent wounds. So haggard were they that the spectators stirred in pity; as siegecraft the defense

[267]

had been incompetent, but these men had fought very gallantly in the breach against overwhelming numbers. Only the judges gazed unmoved, until the King seemed ready to open proceedings.

With an impatient gesture the Archbishop of Canterbury silenced him. Even when little Henry was in full agreement with his Council no one wanted to hear his opinion. This was the boy for whom Falkes and the gallant Marshal and Peter des Roches had risked death at Lincoln, but all their courage had been in vain; they had set him on the throne of his forefathers, but he would never govern his inheritance.

The Archbishop rose, glaring around to enforce silence. "The King of England in full parliament is about to pass sentence on rebels," he declaimed in the clear tone of a preacher, "but first it would be well to safeguard the due rights of the Church. No clerk may be sentenced by a temporal court. Do any of these excommunicate wretches plead clergy?"

The chaplain of the garrison hobbled forward; there was a festering sword-cut on his leg and he could hardly stand. In silence two clerks of the Archbishop's house-hold led him off to lifelong imprisonment.

Then all the Bishops rose together, preparing to descend from the dais. The only door was behind the spectators, and they moved slowly, to give time for the King to intervene. Little Henry was obviously abashed by this concerted desertion; though the Bishops must have planned their withdrawal beforehand they had not bothered to warn their lord. He whispered to Hubert de Burgh, his left-hand neighbor. Hubert answered in a declamatory tone. This was a public demonstration and it was necessary that the world should understand it.

[268]

"By the same sacred laws which preserved that chaplain from your just vengeance, my lord," said the Justiciar, in his carrying politician's voice, "clerks are forbidden to take part in a judgment of blood. It is your plain duty to condemn these rascals to the gallows. Therefore these holy men will withdraw to sing their Masses."

The boy seemed taken aback; Margaret understood it was one thing to swear vengeance against men who held a wall in defiance, impersonal helms and shields from which came arrows and javelines; and another to condemn brave warriors whose silent dejection roused every instinct of his chivalry. The King might yet have shown mercy. In fact, he was hesitating, perhaps because what he had expected to be a long and impressive trial seemed already finished, when the Bishop of Bath turned and spoke loudly, as much to the onlookers as to the King.

"Remember, my lord," he said with controlled bitterness, "if you had hanged the garrison of Bytham these men would not have dared to hold their castle against you."

"And you would not have lost Poitou to King Louis while the knight-service of England quelled a treacherous revolt, if Falkes had proved loyal. My lord, you might now be encamped before the walls of Paris." That was Hubert, still goading his young leader to vengeance.

But, of course, no son of King John would genuinely feel merciful, Margaret reflected. William had known the risk he was facing and run it willingly for love of his brother. The rest were only mercenaries, and no honest man cared what fate befell a man who fought for pay.

That was the way of the world, which she could not alter.

The King signed to his sergeants, who began to hustle the culprits out of the hall.

Count Ranulf rose from his place. "My lord," he said formally, "all these men lie under the ban of excommunication. As their temporal lord you may dispose of their bodies, but surely as a Christian you will not heedlessly condemn their souls to Hell? Let them be absolved and reconciled. If that is done decently and reverently it will take a few hours. Suppose we adjourn until after dinner and then discuss further the fit punishment of traitors."

The Little King hesitated. Hubert had told him to order the hanging, and it was what he wished to do; now Count Ranulf hinted that he should show mercy; as usual, after hearing conflicting advice he could not make up his mind.

"I am a Christian King," he said reluctantly, "and it is my duty to save the souls of my subjects. Let the traitors be absolved before they die. I go now to hear my Mass. Then I shall dine and the Council will meet again after dinner."

"What shall I do with their women?" asked the knight in charge of the escort. He spoke casually. He was not really interested; all that worried him was that while others dined he might still be stuck with a crowd of grubby captives.

"Have them absolved also," answered Hubert, without even bothering to make a pretence of consulting the King. "Then fetch them back this afternoon, when we meet again. Falkes himself should be here by then, and it will be good for him if he witnesses the payment for his treason."

(So it was all true, everything the herald had shouted below the keep. Here was the end of a hero, in the prosaic modern world. The victor of Lincoln, the great captain of crossbows, rode off alone from his threatened castle to beg help from his friends; and when they would not help him he tamely surrendered to judgment.)

Margaret wondered whether this was the time to appeal against her marriage; but the Archbishop had already left, and it was useless to raise a point of ecclesiastical law before a bench of laymen. For a few hours longer she must endure confinement among traitors; then she would make clear her position and be dismissed until her cause had been judged by Rome. Besides, she wanted to see Falkes once more, probably for the last time. How would he look now that his fortunes were in the dust? Much of his charm had been based on self-confidence, and without it he might appear so abject that any lingering regret she still felt would be killed.

She went quietly with the other women. They were guarded outside a church until Mass was finished, then brought in one at a time for absolution and Communion, and at last given bread and wine when they had been reunited to the Church Militant. The absolution had been entirely formal; the priest did not bother to inquire about their sins; it was enough that they had been put to the ban by the Archbishop of the province, and now admitted their error. It was a very good thing to enjoy again the protection of the Church, but breakfast was really more important.

As they were led back to the market hall they passed through the public square. Margaret was in the midst of the group, leading Baldwin by the hand, and at first she could not see why the women in front were wailing. When she saw she hastily covered her son's eyes with her skirt.

In the square stood a long wooden gallows. From one side a row of bodies already dangled. She recognized William de Brealte by his shirt, though the purple face and protruding tongue might have been anyone's. While she watched the ladder was moved a few paces and another sergeant mounted it to be pushed off. A line of bound men awaited death, some kneeling and begging the few onlookers for their prayers; but most, as befitted professional mercenaries whose trade was courage, held themselves erect and chatted with their guards. This was the end of them, the Band of Brealte, the best soldiers in Christendom; they were dying very decently and she need not feel shame that for some years, against her will, she had lived among them.

It was not until the little column was once more on the move that she understood the treacherous cunning and spite by which these deaths had been encompassed. Count Ranulf and his friends would never have agreed to the hanging of a whole garrison for the venial crime of open rebellion; that would be a bad precedent if ever they themselves meditated revolt. After condemning the prisoners the court had adjourned, but the lay magnates expected that when it met again they would have another opportunity to plead for clemency; they lingered over dinner, ignorant that a dozen gallant knights and more than eighty good sergeants were suffering ignominious death. Yet their consent had technically been secured; they could not protest when faced with the accomplished fact.

As the shaken women entered the hall they were overtaken by the Archbishop of Canterbury, accompanied by the Bishops of Lincoln, Chichester, and Bath, and a splendid train of clerks. Had these holy men been gloating over the executions? That was a disgusting thought. But Margaret decided to spread the story. Whether true or false it would be believed by the malicious, and Stephen Langton deserved any harm she could do to him. As for William de Brealte and his companions, she had already forgotten them. William had been a gallant, though silly, knight, and it seemed wasteful that he should meet such an end; but unwanted mercenaries were hanged every year, in all the lands of Christendom.

The women were again made to stand at the back of the hall; they had been on their feet since dawn and drooped with fatigue; little Baldwin crouched at his mother's feet in a sobbing heap. If the Council wished these criminals to display a convincing penitence they had brought them into a suitable frame of mind.

At last the dais filled. Count Ranulf and most of the laymen were obviously furious. In fact, the Count of Chester reproached his lord in a shout, intended to be overheard.

"A wise King shows mercy, lest one day he may need it. Your father was a brave leader who could hold his own against his vassals. You, King Henry, are not. I think it very likely that one day you will be in the power of your enemies. Perhaps you will receive the mercy you did not grant, but I hope you will always remember this Feastday of the Assumption. Now I shall leave Bedford. In these disturbed times my place is on the March. You understand that I cannot bring my mesnie to Poitou. But perhaps you will not cross the sea after all, for Poitou has been lost while you battered Bedford."

As he strode from the hall Margaret reflected that if only he had made this stand earlier nearly a hundred lives would have been saved. It proved that loyalty was the only safe course, for friends would not give help until too late. Once she had shaken herself free from the lost cause of her husband she would be completely loyal.

The Little King glanced nervously from the Archbishop to the Justiciar. They smiled encouragement and the boy shrugged his shoulders to demonstrate his indifference to the anger of Chester. Then he spoke up, in his voice the shy resolution of an adolescent taking the initiative among older men.

"If Falkes the traitor is here let him stand before us for sentence. Oh, are those the wives of the dead rebels? We shall deal with them before we pass to more important matters. Let them abjure my realm. Naturally their lands and chattels are forfeit."

This was Margaret's very last chance to speak; already she had delayed too long. Thrusting herself forward, she fell on her knees to begin her formal appeal. Little Baldwin stood beside her while she emphasized his innocence and his right to the County of Devon, together with her own lack of consent to that forced marriage of eight years ago. Like any great lady whose father had presided in his own court, she knew the legal jargon in all its copious repetition, and once begun she found words without thinking.

As she spoke she was aware of a stir in the crowd behind her. Falkes had entered, but she must look twice to be sure that it was he. As befitted an excommunicate seeking absolution, he wore only a shirt; his hair and beard hung matted and dirty; his shoulders stooped; he groped as he walked, for his eyes were blinded with tears. He had just passed below the dangling bodies of his brother and his veteran companions, and as he tottered to his own judgment every line of his body expressed the hopeless, resigned misery of an old beggar at a church door. His red eyes lifted to glance at his wife, and his mouth twitched in a wavering attempt at a smile of sympathy. Then Margaret turned once more to the dais, squaring her shoulders. Stephen Langton held her fate in his hands, and she must make it clear to him that she had done with Falkes and all he stood for. That was not difficult, for the silly old man now showed no trace of the strenuous soldier who had taken her by force, long ago. Falkes, the true Falkes, was dead of grief and disappointment; that thing walking about in his shirt had never been the lover and friend of Margaret fitzGerold.

Now the Archbishop spoke, without reference to the Little King who followed his orders so obediently. "Madam, I am disposed to entertain your appeal. But first a day must be fixed and witnesses heard; perhaps this recreant who claims to be your husband will dare to appoint a proctor to oppose you, and then we must listen to his case. Meanwhile you are under my protection. You need fear nothing."

The Justiciar interposed, also without consulting his lord. "The Count of Devon, a minor, lacks a legal guardian. He shall be in the wardship of the Count of Warenne. Madam, tell him to come here."

Margaret had not understood that an appeal would mean separation from her only child. But it was too late to argue. Little Baldwin stepped forward to leave her protection for ever.

Then the King pronounced judgment on Falkes; he was glad to do some talking of his own, instead of listening to instructions from his advisers. It seemed at first that the chief rebel would be hanged beside his supporters, but Peter des Roches, who had hitherto remained silent, as though hiding behind the other Bishops, interrupted to say that if a Crusader and an old King's Man who had helped to win the Battle of Lincoln was to be killed before his eyes, he would leave immediately to join Count Ranulf and some other friends of his on the March. The Little King flinched at the threat. Falkes was condemned to forfeit all he possessed and to abjure the realm as soon as his excommunication had been removed in a public ceremony in London. Meanwhile he would remain in the custody of the Bishop of Coventry, who had arranged his surrender. He was led out between two sergeants. Margaret never spoke to him again.

As an afterthought the Justiciar announced that Henry de Braybroc was the best man to supervise the complete destruction of Bedford castle. There was an interruption as the Abbess of Elstow, pushing forward among the spectators, marshalled a procession to restore to her image of St. Paul the sword with which he had at last taken vengeance. Margaret understood that very soon the town of Bedford would contain no reminder of the rule of Falkes de Brealte, who had once been "mightier than the King." It was now an old story. When the court rose she walked over to leave in the train of the Archbishop.

It was all coming out right at last. She was free, and soon she would be restored as co-heir of fitzGerold, though never again would she be Lady of Redvers. Her next task was to make friends with her new companions. She set her face in an ingratiating smile.

This was very odd. The ladies of the Canterbury household made way for her, but she seemed inaudible when she spoke to them. Surely they did not disapprove of her conduct? She had never taken a lover; always her first thought had been the welfare of her son; she had ordered her life as commanded by the gentleman in charge of her, for ladies do not understand politics. As a daughter she had obeyed her father's command to marry young Baldwin de Redvers; then she had faithfully served her father-in-law. Widowed, she had done as the King commanded. She had ridden with her second husband on campaign, and cleverly preserved him when he was threatened by the wrath of St.

Alban. The Marshal himself had praised her courage and devotion during the crisis of Lincoln. Now she was still doing what she had been told to do, by men entitled to her obedience; namely, the Archbishop who was her Metropolitan, and the Justiciar who was the King's chief minister. She could explain everything; though perhaps it would show weakness to volunteer explanations, as though her conduct called for them. . . .

Ten days later Margaret witnessed the absolution of Falkes from his excommunication. She heard him rated in a long and abusive sermon before dismissal to lifelong banishment. He looked as he had looked at Bedford, old and broken and spiritless; he was obviously unfit to be the husband of a lady who needed a competent guardian. She felt no regret; the sooner she was quit of him the better. But then the tiresome rebel delayed her project by appealing to the Pope. As they left St. Paul's the Archbishop informed her, with genuine regret, that nothing could be settled until Rome had given the judgment of God's Vicar.

That same evening she supped in the Archbishop's hall at Harrow. Her status was undefined, so she was not offended at the very low place they gave her; she was seated between a bad-mannered deacon, evidently a scholar of low birth beginning his legal career, and an undistinguished knight. Her companions ate in silence, until the knight leaned rudely across her and spoke to the clerk as though she were not there.

"I'm glad the old rascal escaped with life and limb. I was at Lincoln, on the other side, of course. I saw him cross lances with the Count of Perche. He had guts, the old routier, to ride at a French knight trained for the joust. After he was knocked over his men rescued him, and that's more than hired mercenaries will do for most leaders. He was loyal to his lord, and though I fought against him from loyalty to my own lord, the Archbishop, I wish his good service had been better remembered."

"The Curia has a very long memory," said the sub-deacon wisely. "I shouldn't be surprised if his appeal succeeds. Then we shall have to live with him here in England. I'm glad I never crossed his path. On me he has no reason to seek vengeance."

"Have you heard that when he left Dover five of his old bachelors followed him from sheer devotion? Of course, he can't pay them, and they had refused good offers from the Justiciar. How many knights would follow Hubert at their own charges, if he was sent into penniless exile?"

"Loyalty is a virtue," the clerk agreed. "There's not much of it in this fallen world, and when we encounter it we should honor it. Most Christians, even if well-born, are too quick to desert the fallen."

Margaret rose from the board and hurried to the bower where the ladies would take refuge when the drinking got under way. She had been hungry when she sat down, but now the smell of food nauseated her. The bower was cold and dark, and there was nothing for her to do there. She felt lonely. But she must get used to that; she was going to feel very lonely in the future.

Epilogue

ON Michaelmas Day, 1252, the Franciscan Friary of London was in some confusion. This was a great feast, and the Office in choir needed the voices of all the brethren; but the lady Margaret, grand-mother of the young Count of Devon, lay dying; she had not a friend in the world, and a friar's first duty is to befriend the friendless. After a short discussion the brothers decided to visit her deathbed in a body, even though it meant that the Office was cut short. Most of them were foreigners, but an English novice explained that if the charity of St. Francis failed she would die alone.

"Poor lady," he told them, "she sinned greatly, but in this world she has been greatly punished; we may hope that her past sufferings will lighten her burden in the next. She deserted her lord, Falkes de Brealte, when that faithful servant of the Pope incurred the displeasure of the then Justiciar of England. I don't suppose you have heard of

[279]

Hubert de Burgh. He died ten years ago, and I regret to say he left a great bequest to the Dominicans. He was foremost among King John's evil counselors, the actual murderer of Count Arthur. He enjoyed great power until the magnates compelled our foolish King to imprison him. He ruined this lady's husband and she could not face poverty. She claimed, falsely, before the Curia itself, that she had never consented to the marriage. She lost her case, naturally, when the facts were published, and meanwhile all her noble friends had turned against her. Her son by her first husband, the Count of Devon, was removed from her care. He proved a cowardly knight, I suppose on account of his bad upbringing; and he died young. The present Count is her grandson, but even he is ashamed of her. He refuses to visit her sickbed. Unless we go she will die alone."

"I suppose she is, in fact, a widow," said the sacristan, "not merely separated from her husband? It makes a difference to the trimming of the bier when she is carried to burial."

"Oh yes. Falkes died long ago, on his way back to England after winning his appeal in Rome. They say Hubert de Burgh had him poisoned, but then they say so many evil things about that Hubert. This is a very wicked realm and its magnates are notoriously faithless. Perhaps Margaret was no more faithless than the rest. She always claimed that she had only done as she was told. Yet somehow her self-seeking caught the imagination of the world. Since Falkes died she has been shunned like a leper. Dear me, that was twenty-eight years ago. How time flies."

"Her sin against her marriage vows was grave," answered the sacristan, "but twenty-eight years of earthly penance outweighs many sins. Let us do what we can to ease her passing. She was a most unhappy lady."

[280]